Jane W Bruner

Free Prisoners

A story of California life

Jane W Bruner

Free Prisoners
A story of California life

ISBN/EAN: 9783744748568

Printed in Europe, USA, Canada, Australia, Japan

Cover: Foto ©Andreas Hilbeck / pixelio.de

More available books at **www.hansebooks.com**

FREE PRISONERS.

A Story of California Life.

BY

JANE W. BRUNER.

"We have all to be laid upon an altar; we have all, as it were, to be subjected to the action of fire."

PHILADELPHIA:
CLAXTON, REMSEN & HAFFELFINGER,
624, 626 & 628 MARKET STREET.
1877.

Selhelmer & Moore, Printers,
501 Chestnut Street.

TO HER

DOWNINGTOWN FRIENDS

OF 1873,

𝔗𝔥𝔦𝔰 𝔙𝔬𝔩𝔲𝔪𝔢 𝔦𝔰 𝔄𝔣𝔣𝔢𝔠𝔱𝔦𝔬𝔫𝔞𝔱𝔢𝔩𝔶 𝔍𝔫𝔰𝔠𝔯𝔦𝔟𝔢𝔡

BY THE AUTHOR.

CONTENTS.

FREE PRISONERS.

CHAPTER I.

THE EXCHANGE.

IN the suburbs of New Orleans was a stately mansion, from which two tiny coffins, covered with rarest flowers, were borne silently and reverently to be laid in our mother earth. Following, were two hearts almost broken by the loss of the sweet spirits that had filled them for a little season, and left them dreary and void at their flight.

Over the way was a vine-covered cottage, very humble, but ever so cheery, where a young mother bent anxiously and lovingly over her two cherubs, lest they, too, might take wings and fly away.

Fever was sweeping the purest and sweetest from mothers' hearts and breasts. Every hour struck a death-knell. Pestilence was everywhere in the heated, poisonous atmosphere. It seemed as if the great Creator had need of very precious jewels in his heavenly mansion, for the harvester was merciless.

The rich man's children died and were buried; the poor young mother's lived.

For weeks after, the street before the stately house was covered with straw, lest the rattling of vehicles would disturb the anguished mother, who lay at the verge of death, calling continually, in her delirium, for Mrs. Neal, the young mother opposite, who, she fancied, could bring back her lost babes.

Though Mrs. Neal and her aged mother had but a short time previously moved into the neighborhood, and lived in great retirement, the children had brought the young mothers together.

Mr. Warren, anxious to gratify every wish expressed by his wife, called at the cottage to tell Mrs. Neal of his wife's oft-repeated request, and asked her to come to the sufferer.

Mrs. Neal went at once, and by one of those unaccountable electrical influences we all experience at times, Mrs. Warren seemed soothed by her presence. As she took no interest in any one else, and her mind was clouded much of the time, the physician expressed to Mrs. Neal the hope that, through the strange attachment for her, his patient might be saved.

Unconscious self-immolation was Mrs. Neal's greatest charm. Her life belonged to those who needed her. She at once took her post at Mrs. Warren's bedside, leaving her little ones, quite recovered, to her mother's care.

As time passed, Mrs. Warren slowly but surely recovered; but nothing could rouse her from the dreadful apathy into which she had fallen. Mrs. Neal became the one great necessity of her existence. As soon as her morning duties were over, she was by her side until the day was far advanced, when she would return home, put her little ones sweetly to sleep, and often, when Mr. Warren was obliged to be absent, would spend an hour or two with his wife in the evening.

Three months had passed. It was a dark, gusty night. The wind howled and whistled as it swept through the windows and doors. Mrs. Neal was sitting by Mrs. Warren's couch reading aloud, when she was suddenly interrupted by her asking:

"If God is kind and merciful, why did He take my children and leave yours, Agnes Neal?"

Mrs. Neal dropped her book, and regarded her friend attentively. There was something ominous in the wild black eyes and pale face before her. The question was so foreign to all their thoughts and conversation, so strange, that she shuddered; but it was for the safety of Mrs. Warren's mind.

The wind whistled in wild and desperate shrieks; windows rattled and doors slammed in every direction; servants were hastening to close the house before the coming storm.

Mrs. Warren's acute nerves seemed to have been touched by some electric spark, indefinite and incomprehensible, that prompted that strange question, for at that time, in the garden, at the rear of the cottage, which communicated with the back street, while the winds were wailing through the vines and trees, a man, closely muffled in a large dark cloak and soft hat slouched over his face, stepped from behind a cluster of bushes and went stealthily to the window. He smiled with grim satisfaction at the aged grandmother, who sat alone rocking and reading. The place seemed perfectly familiar to him. He passed to an open window, the rooms all being on one floor, where he could see, by the dim light, the crib with the sleeping babes. He regarded the heavens an instant, then his watch, and with an oath muttered, "This storm may bring her back too soon," and hurriedly left, as he had entered, by the back gate.

In half an hour he came again, surveying the place as before, and finding nothing changed, he quietly entered Mrs. Neal's chamber, where the children slept; placed a handkerchief saturated with a powerful anæsthetic a few seconds to their nostrils; then took them in his arms and softly stole away through the garden to the back street, where a carriage was in waiting.

Not a word was spoken between him and the occupant, a woman, who handed him two children in return. He hastened back to the deserted chamber, laid the little strangelings in the crib where Mrs. Neal's darlings had been so sweetly sleeping, turned out the light, dropped a note on the floor, and as he left the room, stopped on the threshold and, looking back, with clenched fist in menace, hissed between his teeth:

"Agnes Neal, you have lost your children, but you still have *his*. Hug them for *his* sake. You would not love a poor man, and the rich one would not love you. You have had your choice, and I have my revenge."

The wretch hastened from the house to the carriage, and, without even glancing toward the occupants, mounted the box, and drove off.

Hearing a noise, the grandmother entered her daughter's room, but seeing no light, hesitated an instant, when a sharp gust of wind blew in at the open door, and she said, impatiently, "How careless Agnes has been, to leave the door open. The wind has blown out the light." Then closing the windows and bolting the door, the old lady returned to her reading.

The wretch was right. Agnes Neal would not leave her mother and children alone when a raging storm was imminent. Mrs. Warren's strange question hastened her return. All interest in their reading was thereby broken off; so she bade her friend affectionately good-night, and went to her mother's side, where she sat while the storm raged without. Gradually the wind subsided; the rain poured in torrents. Then came the dripping from the eaves and vines. All nature sent forth a strange sobbing. The moon peeped through the drifting clouds, and a balmy atmosphere, purified by an autumn storm, filled the earth.

"Good-night, mother, dear," said Mrs. Neal, and kissing her mother fondly, she left her for the night. On entering her room, she opened the window that the moonlight might stream in, and looking out over the earth, a sweet smile lighted her bright young face as she said half aloud :

"How lovely the earth is after a storm. She seems so grateful for the refreshing rain. How thankful I should be that my storm is over, and my heart at rest again. Oh, Richard, if you had come back, and found your cherubs gone."

She went intuitively, with deep feeling, to the crib and kissed each child. Then, while she knelt by their side, and offered up such a prayer as only a mother can offer for the safety of her little ones, a fiendish face peered in through the open window, drinking in that mockery of peace with infinite satisfaction.

CHAPTER II.

AFTER MANY YEARS.

IT was a wonderful era — '49 in California — a new Golconda was announced to the world. Plenty of gold for everybody! Gold! The lever of the world — the mainspring of this mundane sphere, that is said to be governed by laws of gravitation. The beautiful, dazzling, bewitching gold — that builds up cities and destroys them ; raises men and lowers them ; kindles love to leave it ashes — the severest tempter of manhood and womanhood, in its acceptance and appropriation,— a glittering thing more fatal than the scintillations from the serpent-charmer's eyes — a magnet that draws from principalities and hovels, from homes and brothels, from pulpits and

2.* B

prisons. It is the one thing that strikes a reverberating cord in every human breast.

"Gold in the far-off West," was the cry, and a human tide went westward, from all parts of the earth, all nations and tongues. Gentlemen of broken fortunes; villains whose only fortunes had been dishonor; young wives and mothers, and women whose lives began anew, for better or for worse. It was a concourse of humanity as intricate as a Roman mosaic; yet the one object of pursuit made all men equal — patrician and plebeian labored side by side in one common brotherhood; gentlemen did menial labor, and menials were as gentlemen.

There was no law of society other than Nature makes, when she creates nobility and infamy — two currents that forever run side by side, yet never assimilate. This state of society could only last for a little season, for humanity's streams, like rivulets from the mountains, soon find their centre of gravitation, and form classes and sects.

On this inflowing tide came George Gray, with his young wife and two small children. Mr. Gray was a young man, the only heir to a large estate in New York, but was possessed with a longing for adventure and quiet enterprise that would make an estate for himself.

His wife, although from the South, had been sent at the early age of twelve, when her mother died, to be educated under the care of an aunt residing in New York. There she met George Gray, who was their neighbor's son. The two families were intimate friends; so the younger members became constant companions.

Nellie French was a fine musician, and George Gray played the violin with more than ordinary ability; so from their love of music arose almost imperceptibly a friendship which ripened into a pure and lasting affection. And not until the time approached for their separation, did they in the least realize how essential each was to the happiness of the other.

Nellie's eighteenth birthday was near at hand, when she was to return to her Southern home, where, from her beauty and accomplishments, she was to become a bright star in a brilliant constellation of fashionable society. Nothing was talked of but her departure, and George first thought how much he would miss her, then how much he loved her. He was not long in making his sentiments known, and they were betrothed. Nellie's aunt, Mrs. Van Winkle, not only gave her hearty approval, but declared it had been her most earnest wish.

Nellie felt sad at parting from her aunt, who had been to her as a mother. And George, too; it was hard for her to leave her old friend and new lover, but all bitterness was effaced by her fond father's tender welcome. As he held her at arm's length, regarding her attentively, he said, with a shade of sadness in his voice: "My little girl has grown to be the likeness of her mother, when I courted her twenty-five years ago."

For two months Nellie's visit was a perfect ovation. General French always kept open house, and when it became known his accomplished daughter had returned, and she was pretty, too, there was no end to visitors and invitations. Nellie had one brother, Walter, six years her senior, who was always her ready escort, and the General, being very social, usually accompanied them.

One morning the General's trusted servant entered the breakfast-room very excitedly, where Walter and Nellie were awaiting their father. He whispered something to Walter, who immediately left the room with him. As it lacked a few minutes of breakfast hour, Nellie thought nothing strange of the occurrence, but picked up the paper Walter had laid down and began reading.   After a while she heard confused conversations, mysterious whispers.   The groom dashed down the avenue on her father's fleetest horse ; servants ran hither and thither, and she joined in the general tumult.   After repeated inquiries, she learned from an old negro that the General was very sick. She ran to her father's apartments, and there found Walter and the attendants rubbing and working over his apparently lifeless form.   The family physician soon arrived, but shook his head, as he said all efforts at resuscitation were useless — their father was dead.   He had long been suffering from a disease of the heart, and had been perfectly aware of the uncertainty of his life.

General French had lived in princely style, and was supposed to be wealthy.   As it often occurs in such cases, at his death his affairs were found to be hopelessly entangled.   After the sale of all his possessions, and the payment of mortgages and other indebtednesses, little remained.

A letter full of sympathy and love, from Mrs. Van Winkle, welcoming Nellie back to her heart and home, and one from George sympathizing in her grief, but happy to have her return so speedily, provided for her well and tenderly.

There was little choice for Walter.   As a poor young man, he could no longer mingle with the revellers of fashion, and his first impulse was to leave the place where the lightness of his heart seemed to have gone out like a meteor.   He was fine-looking, with prominent, but regular features ; tall, stately, and formal in his address to strangers.   His hair was almost black. His eyes were deep and fathomless, when softened by affection, but fierce and burning when fired by anger.

He was engaged to be married to a charming creature of fashion and wealth, but could not marry her then — perhaps never.   He told her so in his straightforward way, but with a shade of pride and coldness in his manner, which some sensitive natures cannot avoid when humbled or wounded.

Belle Burton was proud, talented, and rich, and, although not a beauty, had many admirers. She haughtily released her lover, and when the door closed and he was gone, she thought, "Go, if you choose; there are many who would be proud of Belle Burton for a wife."

Then there came a little feeling of remorse. She might have been wrong, considering Walter's changed circumstances. She knew he had loved her dearly, and, hard as it was to admit, she also had loved Walter better than any one else. There was no human eye to see the weakness, so, unrestrainedly, the tears of real regret coursed down her cheeks. She would gladly have called him back and told him she would do her part in the labor of their life, but it was too late — he had gone.

A servant entering with the card of Major Wall, a dashing officer, brought back her old pride; and as she chatted gayly an hour later, seemed to have forgotten there was anything in life for her to regret.

Walter left quietly with his sister for New York, without a single adieu, except to the faithful old servants; one of whom, a negress of thirty-five years of age, Nellie's nurse in childhood, accompanied them. He remained in New York until George and Nellie were married, then left to swell the band of California pioneers.

CHAPTER III.

CALIFORNIA IN '49.

ON arriving in California, Walter's party, lured into the Sierra Nevada Mountains by the fabulous reports of wealth, decided upon Grass Valley as their temporary home. This was in '49 a beautiful valley, nestling between high hills, through which a mountain stream went leisurely on its way, singing to the wild flowers that decorated its borders, like a weary spirit after a toilsome day chanting its lullaby as it sank to rest. As if it had gained new force and vigor by this gentle interlude, one would scarcely recognize this peaceful, murmuring stream a few miles distant, in the foaming, dashing waters that madly plunged over rocks and precipices. Grass Valley was so called from its luxuriant growth of grass, which, in its emerald beauty, would have done honor to old Erin. The surrounding hills and mountains were covered with lofty pine-trees, with thick undergrowth of balsam, manzanita, and chaparral, beneath which clustered fragrant pinks, delicate roses, and myriads of exquisite flowers, that would have graced a princely estate; yet there, in the wilderness, they bloomed unplucked and unappreciated, and only the great Giver of blessings knew for what strange purpose. The giant grizzly bear passed them by grumly. The lions and the wild cats heeded them not, and the bushes, in whose branches nestled quail, doves, and beautiful singing-birds, only paid them obeisance when bowed by the weight of their fair occupants. The patrician pines sighed and wailed over a scene so enchanting, lonely, and wild; but the arrival of the pioneers changed all this—the emerald sward covered glittering gold, and the murmuring water nestled in its bosom precious treasures, that caused its peace to be disturbed and its crystal purity to be converted into a muddy stream. The wild flowers ceased to grow upon its borders, for the busy hand of man transformed the fairy land into a scene of confusion and desolation, and the wavering pines moaned a pitiful dirge over the havoc done the enchanting Grass Valley.

Four years later, George and Nellie came to make their home in this mountain town, with their two little children and the faithful Sofie.

Walter had a nice little cottage in readiness for their reception, but it was a comical little home in comparison with the luxurious one they had left in New York. The furniture of this pioneer home was principally of mountain manufacture — unpainted pine. There was a lack of many domestic comforts, which was amply supplied after Nellie's unpacking process.

One might have fancied that the magic wand of an enchantress had been waved over the plain little home, to make it inviting and cosy. The table had a snowy cover and was furnished with choice books. In one corner stood a cottage piano, near by lay a violin. A crimson and gold-striped cloth covered the dining-table, for this snug little place served as parlor, dining-room, and family sitting-room.

Servants were not to be had, so Nellie assumed the care of the children, while Sofie was installed as cook and general house-maid.

"What can a New York gentleman know of the hard, wild life of a California pioneer?" was a question Walter asked himself with considerable trepidation, as he welcomed George to his mountain home. He found him a faithful, industrious young man, who had seen only the sunny side of life, but cheerfully accepted discomforts. He aided him in business, and in return felt a fatherly sort of care and interest in his new friend and brother, from his greater experience of life and its trials.

They were strangely different. George, rather fair, was tender and delicate, almost to effeminacy, and was perfectly happy with his wife and babies. He soon came to regard Walter as a shield between him and the perplexities of life. As for the world at large, he seemed to care as little for it as he knew of it. On the other hand, Walter had seen all phases and forms of humanity — from the experience of a youth passed under the indulgent care of a mother, who idolized him, to that of early manhood, as the flattered, petted idol of aristocratic society, and afterwards hurled at one blow from this pedestal of fortune to poverty. He had no profession; why should he have? Was he not the heir to a large estate? His education had been such as to fit him for society, to control his slaves, to entertain and fill his father's place as the son of General French should, when the haughty, but hospitable General would be laid in the family vault.

This polished Southern gentleman found himself almost helpless, at first, in the vocation of a California pioneer; but he had a stout, brave heart, always ready to try; and the rapidity with which he learned from that stern teacher necessity, astonished even himself.

CHAPTER IV.

THE BROKEN LINK OF LOVE.

YEARS passed with little change in the happy, monotonous life of the inmates of the cottage. The mill still stamped with its steady beat the crystal quartz. The bed of the little stream at the foot of the hill was almost dry, and the muddy water dashed furiously along in sluice-boxes which the miners had constructed in their placer-diggings. The surrounding hills had lost many waving pines, but neat cottages marked their places. Here and there were piles of yellow earth dug up by ambitious miners in search of gold. Afar off came the dull sound from distant mills. Heavily loaded teams went slowly clambering over the uneven roads, with precious burdens, from mines to mills. It was a busy place, and many fortunes were dug out of those once beautiful green hills, with their forest of waving pines.

One evening, Walter returned from the post-office with a package of letters from *home*, as the Eastern States were generally designated. These letters came every fortnight, and many unsuccessful miners were comforted and encouraged by the precious burdens the steamers bore to the Western shore every two weeks.

He handed one to Nellie, saying:

"Read this, Nellie; it is from Belle Burton. You remember her, do you not?"

"Yes, perfectly," answered Nellie; reading the letter.

"She and I were brought up something like you and George," resumed Walter; "were engaged when very young, and were to have been married when she became twenty. She says,

3

'after years of fruitless effort,' she has in a most unaccountable manner discovered my whereabouts, and gives me a characteristic feminine lecture, as you will see.''

"I do not blame her," said Nellie, returning the letter. "If you have broken your promise, her displeasure is pardonable."

"You do not understand the case, little sister. I have done nothing of the kind. Our engagement was broken off by mutual consent; and I supposed she had married some dashing fellow long before this."

"It seems she has neither forgotten you nor your engagement, and alludes, in a lady-like manner, to her estate being at your command. As she has taken the trouble to find out where you are, and has written you the first letter after your neglect, I think the least you can do is to renew your old friendship. And who knows? you may eventually marry her. She must love you, or she would not have written you that letter; besides, she is rich."

Nellie spoke thoughtlessly, for riches had no weight in her honest decision.

Walter's face flushed, as he asked, bitterly:

"Do you think I would marry her for her money?"

"I do you no such injustice, dear Walter. But when you loved a young lady from childhood, and were engaged to her for years, I do not think a fortune in her possession should be any obstacle, especially when your position was equal, if not superior, to hers at the time of your engagement. I am sure no one would accuse you of marrying for money under such circumstances. Besides, you are not poor."

"You have a wonderful facility for arguing away all difficulties, Nellie; but I doubt if we would even be congenial friends now. Our lives for years past have necessarily been so different, that I do not feel there is any tie to bind me to the fancies of my youth."

"Surely, the words of betrothal that bound your young life to that of Belle Burton are a tie that should not be lightly cast off. It is a matter of honor. She has been waiting for years, hoping for your return, and still you did not come. Go at once, Walter," pleaded Nellie, "to your patient Belle. Tell her she need pine no longer for her truant lover, but rest her heart in your keeping. Bring her out to our mountain home, and we will all be sweet, good friends together."

"Do not waste your sentiment, little sister; the case in hand is not worth it. I assure you, Belle would find this rough life little to her taste. You do not understand that the charming, witty Belle, with her cold conceit, has fooled with her admirers until she has unwittingly flirted herself into the unredeemable realm of old maids, and thinks a cast-off lover in a wilderness better than none at all. With regard to her fruitless efforts to find me, she knew perfectly well, by sending a few lines to Aunt Harriet Van Winkle, she could get my address. I am not so easily caught, my dear, even by an expert angler. You will have your model brother on your hands now, henceforth, and forevermore. I am a confirmed old bachelor. The disease has become chronic — first, from necessity; second, from habit, and third, and lastly, from inclination."

"Nonsense! Walter. I despise old bachelors. They are such selfish, unfeeling mortals. But you will, at least, write Belle a nice letter?"

"Yes, Nellie, I will write her, and say anything you like. For instance, if my business prospers, I may pay a visit East within the next quarter of a century, and if she can love such a sunburnt heathen as I have become — who knows? — my tender, susceptible, yielding heart may succumb to the infatuations and tender outbursts of an old maid's first passion."

"You cynical old bachelor! You do not deserve to have a wife!" said Nellie, sharply. "There you sit, making sport of your old sweetheart, without the least conscience. Do not let me see you again before dinner. You are getting worse and worse every day. Even my patience is becoming exhausted."

"I never saw you so provoked with me before, Nellie," said Walter, coaxingly. "I suppose I am a crusty fellow; but never mind, I will try to be better in future. You are the only sincere admirer I ever had, and I could not lose your sweet, unselfish affection. I will do anything you may command, to make amends for my unfeeling remarks toward that young lady of uncertain age, but get married, and that — well, I vow I never will have the courage to attempt to go in double team."

"No, you prefer tandem, with your sweetheart behind," and Nellie smiled in spite of her anger.

"You deserve a kiss for that, Nell. Good-by till dinner."

Walter passed down the well-beaten path to the mill, and thought, "What a treasure that Nellie is. I believe she would be contented under a tent, with bread-and-water diet, if every one about her was comfortable. She never seems to think of herself at all, but is continually looking after the happiness and pleasure of others. If all women had such dispositions, and were willing to make the sacrifices she does, we would have a very different world, perhaps a happier one."

CHAPTER V.

A DOMESTIC AFFINITY.

IT was the habit of the family to congregate on the portico after dinner and have a general review of the day's doings.

There were no places of entertainment, and few congenial per- sons in that mountain village, so they were greatly dependent upon one another for amusement, and the most trifling incidents of the day were of importance. To watch the sunset was the closing duty of each day, and they never wearied of the grand and varied freaks of nature's artist among the pine-covered Sierras, that vie in warmth and coloring with those of tropical regions.

"There is smoke from the chimney in the new addition of Captain Wetherell's house. I wonder if it is finished," asked Walter, carelessly, as he laid aside the paper he had been reading.

"Oh, yes; I forgot to tell you," answered Nellie. "Mrs. Williams was here this afternoon with her sewing, and she told me ever so much news."

"She can tell you news, if any one can," said Walter. "If she has none on hand, she is a good manufacturer."

"I am sorry you do not like her," said Nellie. "I think she is a very good woman, although she does know everything that is taking place in this little town. She told me Captain Wetherell's house was completely finished, and he expects his wife and daughter next week. And she told me, too, that the Captain and his wife had not lived together for a number of years. That is, dear, they live in the same house; but — well, they do live together in the eyes of the world."

3 *

"I understand exactly," laughed Walter. "You mean they live together in the eyes of the world, but they do not see it in the same light."

"Walter, you are getting in the habit of using California slang phrases to such an extent that I fear you will be very rough by the time you go home to marry Belle."

"Never mind about my getting married, Nellie," said Walter, a little sarcastically. "What were the rest of to-day's revelations? It cannot be possible that was all Mrs. Williams had to tell."

"Oh, no," she said. "You know the Captain has not spoken to his son Ben for nearly two years. Of course, I told her I knew nothing about it. Then she informed me Ben was such a wild, dissipated fellow, that his father was obliged to ignore his existence entirely, and never even permit him to come home. The poor old gentleman's heart is almost broken with grief, through that misguided son. He asked the members of the church, with tears in his eyes, to pray for him, last prayer-meeting."

"Did she not say it was because the old Captain was so busy making love to that French girl from Limerick, who is keeping house for him, that his son was in the way, and he shipped him? Was not that the story, Nell?" asked Walter.

"No, indeed. I was trying to tell you what she did say, but you shock me by insinuating such things of the Captain. He is the most pious and best old gentleman I have met in this country. He makes beautiful prayers, and was the means of getting our church built."

"Did he have the contract to build it? if so, that accounts for his piety."

"Oh, Walter, you are getting so wicked. You make sport of everything that is pious, lately."

"No, Nellie; you misunderstand me. For sincerely good and pious people, I have great respect, but not for the sort to which your friend the Captain belongs."

"I wish you knew him as he really is. I fear you are prejudiced."

George had gone into the house, as it grew dark, and was rocking the two children, one on each knee, telling them a fairy tale. The lamps had not yet been lighted, and from a side window Captain Wetherell's house was distinctly to be seen, only a short distance off. George called Walter and Nellie to come in and witness some private theatricals, and added: "The play is a romance of real life."

They immediately obeyed the summons, wondering what George could possibly mean.

"Look out there," said he, pointing to the open window.

"Ah, Nell," laughed Walter, "there is your pious old saint at his devotions. To what form of religion does that style of worship belong?"

Nellie made no reply, but looked in blank amazement. There sat her ideal of goodness and piety with his housemaid on his knee, and they were sporting like young lovers. He would kiss her freckled face, with the *nez retroussé*, and she would pull his whiskers in return. A very tender embrace, and the Captain left his accommodating housemaid, took up his gold-headed cane, and went out into the street as serene and saintly as ever.

"Homer says:

'So lovers to their fair one, fondly blind,
E'en on their ugliness with transport gaze,'"

quoted Walter, jocosely, and turning to Nellie, asked:

"What of your pious friend now, Nell? I suppose he is on his way to prayer-meeting, is he not?"

"I am sorry to admit it, but this is the evening for prayer-meeting."

"He is one of your pillars, is he not?" asked George.

"Yes," said Nellie; "but I am so shocked. I wish I had not witnessed the little drama, as you called that disgusting scene a few moments ago."

"Oh, that was only a domestic affinity," laughed George. "There are worse things in the world."

"Do you think Mrs. Williams was right, when she said the son was so bad the father could not get along with him; or was I right when I said he interfered with the old reprobate's love-making with his servant?" asked Walter.

"Let us admit that each might have faults," said Nellie, in her conciliatory way. "Mrs. Williams told me the Captain wrote his son a note, a few days ago, asking him to come home, and he would receive him with open arms, and forgive him all the past. The son replied, he had committed no offence, and consequently required no forgiveness; but if his father would endeavor to be honorable and upright in future, he would forgive *him* the past. I thought that a very impudent message from a son to a father."

"I do not think he meant it as insolence," said Walter, earnestly. "To tell you the truth, Nellie, I cannot cultivate any interest in the country gossip. The Captain must have unburdened his heart to Mrs. Williams, or she would not have been so familiar with his grievances; and I assure you, when a person can give his troubles to the village to take care of, they have ceased to oppress the original owner. True sorrow never goes abroad, but bides at home. As for young Wetherell, I have known him for three years, and never heard a word against him. He and his father disagree because he knows the old gentleman's real character, and is not sparing in his criticism of his conduct. As I said before, the old Captain will not be interfered with, and yet he wants to make himself out a saint. So he turns his son away from home, goes about telling all the world how bad he is, puts on a long face of injured innocence, and asks the pious brethren to pray for his misguided son. The pious sympathize deeply with the grief-stricken parent, and pray for the lost son, while the father hugs the housemaid. Young Wetherell is an imp of Satan, and yet the son of one of God's chosen disciples. How can you solve that enigma?"

"Do not try, Nellie. It is a miracle," interposed George.

"You must not become sacrilegious, too, George," said Nellie, earnestly; and turning to Walter, "what does young Wetherell do for a living?"

"He and two other young men own a mine a few miles from here. He is ambitious and industrious, and doing well, I believe. It is a wonder to me he is even honest, with such a father."

"I am sorry we have such neighbors," said Nellie; "but Mrs. Williams told me that Linda, the daughter, is an unusually fine girl. Her sister attended school with her a long time in New York State, and considers her in every way very superior, besides being beautiful."

"There will be a chance for you, Walter," suggested George.

"No, I thank you," replied Walter, scornfully. "That stock will never do for me. Why, the mother is a regular termagant, and with such parentage, what may not the daughter be?"

"Ah, yes, Walter; but the ways of the heart, like the workings of Providence, are inscrutable," added Nellie.

C

CHAPTER VI.

THE DISCARDED LOVER.

"She tells thee where to love and where to hate."—*Juvenal.*

IT was a charming spring morning when the "Ocean Queen" sailed out of New York harbor, crowded with passengers for California, among whom were Mrs. Captain Wetherell and her daughter, Linda. The mother was a cold, stately woman, apparently about forty years of age, with jetty black hair and eyes, and a firm, hard mouth.

The daughter had brown hair and large hazel eyes, which sometimes looked black, but they were soft and true. Her complexion was fresh and rosy, her mouth pretty and expressive, unlike the mother's, for it lacked the iron bars that seemed to shut out all human sympathy from her soul. There was a girlish elegance and grace about everything she did that made her perfectly charming, and withal such a forgetfulness of self, as she waited upon her mother, bathed her sick neighbor's aching head, and amused the little girls whose mothers were sea-sick, that, unconsciously, she made herself generally useful and universally admired and beloved.

Everything was wonderful to her, because it was new. She was looking at life with the first glow of pleasure, and saw only the sunshine, and did not dream that storms might be gathering in the distance that would break over her young head.

When they arrived at Aspinwall, she was greatly amused by the natives, who, like swarms of bees, went buzzing about quite as primitive in dress as Adam and Eve when they wore but fig-leaves. The little children running around looked like diminutive bronze statues, in their blessed ignorance neither desiring nor needing more to clothe them than the sunburnt skin their great Creator gave them.

As they crossed the beautiful Isthmus of Panama, where Nature runs riot in her exuberance of spirit; where the luxuriant vegetation weaves into the wilderness a perfect bower of wild beauty — with the stately palms, cocoanuts, bananas, tree-ferns, and majestic rubber trees decorated with orchids and other parasites, with their drooping stems knotted here and there with air roots, the bush ropes hanging from them in graceful festoons, intermingled with running plants, decorated with variegated green leaves, and serjania and bignonia voluptuously interlaced and entangled — she almost imagined, while gazing into those fantastic bowers, that she was looking into an enchanted abode of fairies, so light and airy was the picture. But when she thought of the creeping reptiles, venomous insects, and wild beasts that had their abode there, the fairy scene became a labyrinth so dense and heavy, that the very atmosphere seemed infected, and she longed to be gliding over the Pacific, whose waters were so calm that it seemed useless for the steamer to be puffing and blowing and making such hard work of skimming the glassy surface.

Among the passengers was a Mr. Warren, an old acquaintance of Mrs. Wetherell, a widower, who had an adopted daughter, about Linda's age, at school in Boston, of whom he frequently talked to Linda, telling her how much she reminded him of his own open-hearted girl Alice.

Mrs. Wetherell was pleased to have his attentions during the monotonous voyage, and Linda accepted them as kindness from an elderly gentleman. Before the voyage was ended his manner changed, and instead of fatherly attentions they became unmistakably the smiles, simperings, and contortions of an old fool trying to play the youthful lover.

Linda did not notice his altered manner — in fact, she thought little of Mr. Warren at best — only it was pleasant to have a gentleman to accompany her upon deck to admire the glorious sunsets and see the moon rise, and in the morning to count the nautilus, as they floated by with their mimic sails, and watch the schools of porpoise as they sported and tossed in the fathomless deep.

Steadily the ship went on; land was in sight; on the morrow they would sail through the Golden Gate and enter the picturesque bay of San Francisco. It was moonlight, and Linda wished to pass the last evening of her sea voyage on deck. Mrs. Wetherell complained of indisposition, and requested Mr. Warren to accompany her.

They sat some time in silence watching the moonshine playing upon the phosphorescent waves. Linda was the first to break the stillness.

"Mr. Warren, you promised long ago to tell me the history of your adopted daughter, which you said was very strange. As this is our last evening together, may I claim the fulfilment of your promise?"

"With pleasure, Miss Linda. Your slightest wish is a command; but it is long since I have even thought of it, and the whole event was so completely enveloped in mystery, that it may prove less interesting than you expect. However, your womanly curiosity shall be gratified.

"About sixteen years ago, we lived in New Orleans. My wife was a very domestic woman, devoutly fond of her home and family. We had three darling bright children — two boys and one girl. That summer the scarlet fever raged like a fiend of fury among the little folks. The brightest and loveliest dropped off by dozens. Ours were all swept away within a week. My wife, never very robust, was so overcome by the blow that she lay for weeks hovering between life and death. Near us lived the widow of a clergyman and her daughter, who had two children. These children were among the few who had the fever and recovered. Hearing of our misfortunes and my wife's illness, the young mother left her little ones with her mother, and spent days by my wife's bedside. She became devotedly attached to her, and the good young woman was ever ready to minister to her comforts. One night, she went home quite late from our house, and retired as usual, with her children in their crib by her side. The next morning, when she awoke, she found them changed. They were smaller, and did not know her. She, poor soul, thought her eyesight and reason were leaving her, and called to her mother, who was equally at a loss; for without doubt the young mother's children were gone and two strange ones left in their place.

"The bereaved mother was almost crazed, and in fact the entire neighborhood was greatly excited over the event, for it was so singular, and apparently uncalled for, that no one could comprehend it. When my wife asked for her friend, I told her of her affliction, hoping that others' sorrows might draw her from her own. It acted like a charm. She forgot herself entirely in the endeavor to console her friend.

"The boy's resemblance to the lost one was so remarkable, the mother clung to him madly; but she positively refused to have anything to do with the girl; so my wife took her. That is all I know of my lovely, nameless, adopted daughter."

"How mysterious!" said Linda, musingly. "Was nothing done to discover the truth?"

"Yes, everything that was in their power; and I entered into the search with all my heart, but not the slightest clue could

4

ever be found. We moved North soon after, and I have never heard of them since."

"How exceedingly strange and sad it must be, to live in this world and not know one's own parents," and Linda sat silently thinking a long time, then, in her girlish way, exclaimed:

"How delightful to think we will be in San Francisco to-morrow. I am so glad!"

"And I am so sorry," said Mr. Warren, languidly.

"Sorry? How can you be sorry? I have enjoyed our voyage exceedingly, but am heartily glad we are so near our destination."

"There is something strangely fascinating to me about the tropical regions," continued Mr. Warren, "where the posts put into the ground for fences send forth young branches and form beautiful hedges. There Nature is so lavish with her products, that man is exempt from the command, ' By the sweat of thy brow shalt thou earn thy bread.' She furnishes her people with fruits according to the seasons, and a few posts, with palm leaves for roofs, suffice for houses for the poorer ones. No clothes are required in childhood, and few when they are grown. Speculative controversies are useless, as existence is a certainty and death a settled fact; but, of course, always a great ways off, in the impenetrable mists of futurity."

"It is a wise dispensation, for it surely would not be very gratifying to those poor natives to. contemplate the immediate approach of death, when they know their remains will be deposited in one of the double rows of vaults surrounding the open square of their burying-ground, of two or three acres, and finally burned as rubbish. You should have gone with us there, Mr. Warren. It is horribly interesting. When all the vaults are full, the thin layer of mortar is broken open that shuts the oldest reposer in his narrow cell, and coffin and contents are hurled into one of the small open squares left in each corner for that purpose. When these are full, the whole mass is removed and burned. In some places the mortar covering was broken, and we could see the decomposing corpse in the open coffin. It was not such a disgusting sight as one might imagine, for decomposition there is generally a mere drying process, that leaves the corpse as inoffensive to sense and sight as an Egyptian mummy. Some are honored above the rest, by having their skulls placed upon the top of the vaults, to grin dismally down upon those who enter there, in mockery of their bright dreams of life. There is nothing in the centre of this square but rank weeds, so suggestive of reptiles it makes me shudder to think of it. I am sure Longfellow would never have called that loathsome place, with its *débris* of human bones and broken coffins, God's-acre."

"That is rather too sacred a title for such a mouldering place as you have described," answered Mr. Warren; "but I think you regard it with too much feeling. You forget the church dignitaries and high officials are buried with great honors in the churches, and only the common people are interred in that potter's field."

"True, Mr. Warren. But the common people are the masses; very few receive church honors."

"Still," persisted Mr. Warren, "for a semi-barbarous race, I do not find that burial system so disgusting. In the world-famed 'Père-la-Chaise' of Paris, in the potter's field, there is a deep trench ever open, where daily the coffins are packed in, with only a thin layer of earth between, and every five years these trenches are dug over for new occupants, and the old ones are exhumed and burned."

"Thank Heaven," exclaimed Linda, "in the free country where we are going, there is ample room for the dead to repose until called by the great Voice on high. With all the attractions of Panama and Acapulco, with their beautiful and varied foliage, I am glad they are so far behind us, and to-morrow I will meet my dear father and brother Ben once more. I cannot understand why you are not glad our journey is so near ended."

"Because I will have to leave you, Linda," sighed the enamored old widower.

"Oh, is that the only reason?" laughed Linda.

"Surely, that is sufficient cause," and Mr. Warren's manner became very earnest. "Linda, you are as lovely in mind and disposition as you are in form and face. I love you; forgive me for telling you so; but I cannot control the passion that fills my heart and soul, and occupies every corner of my brain. I may seem too old to woo one so young and fair as you," for he noticed a strange expression about Linda's mouth that strongly indicated disgust. "I may seem rather old," he continued, "but I can offer you an honest, faithful heart, and it would grieve me to have a mind so pure and bright and mature as yours thrown away on some unappreciative person. I am wealthy and can provide for you lavishly. In a few years my adopted daughter will be with us, and you will find her a charming companion. Every wish of your heart shall be gratified, if possible, before your sweet lips have time to give utterance to them. Although you regard me now in the light of a friend and protector, or, as you jokingly said last night, of a father, I feel sure the time will speedily come when, from my untiring efforts to please, you will learn to love me. Linda, darling, will you be the wife of one who loves you better than life?"

He attempted to take her hand, but Linda drew back.

"Mr. Warren, you shock me!" and her pale face showed she was either shocked or angry. "I have one father, sir, and until he dies do not wish to engage another. I bid you good-night, sir.''

Before Mr. Warren had time to appreciate fully what had transpired, his beautiful Linda was safely down stairs in the state-room with her mother.

'' Mother, what do you think? That old imbecile, Mr. Warren, asked me to marry him,'' burst forth Linda, as she rushed into her mother's state-room quite out of breath.

''Well,'' asked the mother, coolly, ''what was your answer?''

'' My answer!'' Linda was as much surprised at her mother's manner and tone of voice as she had. been at Mr. Warren's. ''I told him I had one father, and until he died did not wish to engage another,'' answered the excited girl.

'' Linda!'' said Mrs. Wetherell, sharply, ''I am sorry you spoke in that manner to such an estimable gentleman as Mr. Warren. I was in hopes you would be flattered by such an opportunity, and accept his offer.''

Linda sat down and buried her face in her hands, as Mrs. Wetherell continued:

'' Mr. Warren is wealthy, and, as you have been frequently told, your father is only in moderate circumstances. You are a handsome and accomplished girl, and surely do not intend to throw yourself away on some poor, good-for-nothing fellow, for the fancy of love. Girls at your age are apt to dream of love and lovers, but when you get older, you will find them only in name and in novels. A woman does well who marries a man of position, and has power to command. Money gives that power, and nothing else can. Mr. Warren may be a little too far advanced in years to suit your present fancy, but I gave his proposition my most hearty approval. When he conversed with me on the subject, I bade him make his own proposals to you, thinking, with your good sense in other matters, you would

4*

feel that our family affairs required you to marry one who could well support you. I will see Mr. Warren, and bid him be patient until you have had time to reflect. You were taken too much by surprise; but he need not be in the least discouraged, for I intend you shall marry him. Do you hear, wilful girl? You are to marry Mr. Warren. I have not raised you, and educated you, to be thus opposed by your girlish whims. You have no right to any opinion on the subject, and I grant you none."

Linda raised her proud head, and her flashing eyes, like burning stars in that dimly-lighted room, proved that the daughter could be as firm as the stately woman, her mother. Coldly, but respectfully, she answered:

"For what you have done, I thank you with all my heart, and through my whole life hope to prove my gratitude. I have always endeavored to be an obedient daughter, and it is my most earnest wish to continue so; but I know of no law of God or man that compels me to yield all my hopes of happiness, in fact, sacrifice my whole life, to a heartless requirement of a selfish mother, to prove me a faithful child."

"How dare you speak thus to me?" shrieked the exasperated woman. "Am I not your mother? Do you not owe your life to me? Have I, then, not a right to command it?"

"Have you a right to kill me?" asked Linda, calmly.

"No, silly child; neither have I the desire," answered Mrs. Wetherell, in a more subdued tone.

"Tell me, mother, do you think the only death is when the heart-throbs cease? No! There are worse deaths, a thousand times worse — living deaths. I would rather you would pierce my heart, and let my life-blood ebb away, than compel me to marry that old simpering fool, for in either case you would be guilty of murder. I will never change. I despise him; he is

abhorrent to me. I am seventeen, he is forty-six. It is a pity ,
grandfather is dead, for he was rich.''

"Cease your insolent mockery, girl," cried the angry
mother, taking her by the shoulder and turning her pale face
to the light. The cold, selfish woman was livid with rage, and
her eyes were as black as the eyes of a demon of darkness, as
she said, fiercely: "I will go and find Mr. Warren, and tell
him you will marry him when he wishes it, that you have so
promised me. If you deny my words or oppose me further, I
will curse the hour that gave you birth, and every hour of your
life. I will crush you to the very earth until you will be glad
to comply with my command. You shall feel the depth of my
hatred. You do not know me, girl. We have lived pleasantly
thus far, because we have seldom been together, and when we
were, nothing transpired to disturb our peace. Now, when I
command, and you disobey, you shall have a glimpse underneath my cold exterior. You shall be introduced to *your
mother*. Listen, and I will tell you my history at your age, and
since then the pages are no fairer.''

CHAPTER VII.

REVEALING THE GRAVE OF MURDERED LOVE.

I WAS a child, as you know, but ten years old when my
mother died. She was a gentle, amiable creature. My
father followed her two years later. He was a severe, stern,
heartless man. It was said his neglect and indifference killed
my mother.

"After the death of my father, I was sent to live with a

cousin of my mother's, who had an only son, Henry. He and I grew up like brother and sister. We went to the same school, played together, in short, were seldom apart.

"I loved my gentle, new mother and merry brother. I was free and light-hearted, knowing nothing of the ills of life. My mother, as I always called Mrs. Graham, was a widow in moderate circumstances. She never had a daughter, and I believe loved me as deeply as if I had been her own. When I was sixteen, Henry was twenty, and we were engaged to be married.

"About a year after our engagement, an army officer in the place came to see me frequently, and paid me quite marked attention. I encouraged him for amusement, not that there was one thought in my heart false to my plighted lover. One day Henry came home unexpectedly, and found us sitting side by side in the arbor, reading from one book. He knew his mother was absent, and all the jealous anger he had previously so well concealed burst forth. He ordered Captain McDonald to leave at once, and bade me retire to the house. I asked the Captain to remain, and quietly told Henry, although I was burning with rage, his company could better be dispensed with; I was not in the habit of being ordered by any one, and he could consider his right, if he ever had any, forfeited. Still, I went into the house, and left the young men together. All I ever knew of what passed between them was from a note I found under my door the next morning, in which Henry told me he had challenged Captain McDonald, and expected to be killed. Life had become a burden to him since I ceased to love him and renounced our engagement. At seven he said he would be a corpse, and bade me be kind to his mother. I flew out of the house like one mad. At seven he said. It still lacked a few minutes of that time. I might yet save him; but where were they to be found, those murderers? I started to the hillside, but turned back. I thought of the woods, but they were two miles away. I met a small boy, and asked him, excitedly, 'Have you seen Henry Graham this morning?' 'Yes, ma'am,' he answered, 'I saw him going down toward the creek, a little while ago, with a gentleman.'

"Toward the creek! I never thought to ask what part of the creek, but rushed on. The wind and my running disarranged my hair. My dress caught in the bushes, and left great pieces behind, and yet I sped on. Just as I was emerging from a thicket into open space, I heard the report of a pistol. I almost fell, for it seemed to strike my heart. Not seemed — it did! and left it paralyzed.

"I saw Henry stagger, and sprang forward to catch him in my arms. 'Great God! I am too late,' I screamed. 'Yes,' said Henry, 'I am killed.' 'And by me,' I cried. 'No, Laura, not by you,' he answered, in his kind, old way. On my knees, with his dear head pillowed on my breast, I begged in my agony for Heaven's sake to be forgiven.

"'Dearest, I have nothing to forgive. I only loved you too selfishly, too well.' As he spoke, every instant with more difficulty, he added: 'I have but a moment longer, darling. Tell the news gently to mother. I fear it will break her heart. Be a good daughter to her, and try to be happy. God be merciful — to — me — good-by.' His head fell back, his hands released their hold on mine. He was dead! Did you hear me, girl? I said he was dead! dead!"

Mrs. Wetherell fell back in her chair, trembling and sobbing violently. Linda hastened to her side to comfort her; but the paroxysm was past, and she was herself again, only a little paler. She pushed Linda away, saying harshly:

"Sit down; that is only half the story. There I sat, with

my murdered lover, until aroused by his friend, who had stood
by and witnessed the deed.   I was to break the news gently to
his mother, so he told me ; and I went home to do his bidding.

"Mother was arranging his room and singing, or rather chanting, an old hymn.   'What ails you, child?' she asked, coming
toward me.   I must have looked startling, with my dishevelled
hair and torn dress all stained with blood — my livid face and
staring eyes, for I seemed to see death all around me.   'What
can be the matter, child?' repeated mother.   I think I lost
my senses for the moment, or the devil took possession of me,
for I screamed out, 'I have killed your son, my affianced
husband!'

"The grief-stricken mother fell to the floor.   The fall aroused
me.   I stooped to pick her up, but she was senseless.   I heard
footsteps ; I knew they were bringing the lifeless form of my
darling.   I shed not one tear, only directed them to the room
which his mother had just arranged so carefully for his reception.   I sent for a physician, and had mother well cared for ;
but she lay in a perfect stupor all that day and the next.   Then
she gradually awakened to consciousness, but she was paralyzed.

"Friends were very kind, and did all they possibly could ; but
what I endured those days and nights no human being could
ever imagine.   I never closed my eyes in sleep until after the
funeral.   I wandered to the chamber of death, and there tried
to think, to feel grief, but it was useless.   I was paralyzed, too,
but not like mother ; my heart was dead.   I went to mother,
and when she would turn her eyes upon me, — those tender,
loving eyes, — I felt as if they were two coals of livid fire upon
my heart and brain ; that was all I could feel.   I wanted to die,
but did not know how.   If I could only have become unconscious, and awakened to new sensibilities.   If I had been very
ill, and gradually recovered, I might have been something like

my old self. Being full of health, the blow that stunned me left me semi-conscious. There was nothing to soften me, not a human being to whom I could unburden my heart and expect sympathy in return, and every sensibility in my nature seemed gradually, but surely, to be consumed. I was a murderess that the law could not reach, and my life a wreck.

"One short month passed, and mother died, too. There in the still old churchyard they lay, the two precious ones I had loved so well, killed by my rash conduct. I was alone in the world, without a friend or relation. Seventeen years old — beautiful and accomplished, and the author of two murders. Girl! Do you hear? I had committed two murders at your age!"

Again the strange woman gasped as if for breath, and fell back on her chair exhausted.

Linda arose to aid her, but was again repulsed by the wave of her hand. The poor child, not less excited than the mother, sat staring vacantly at the pallid face before her.

In a few moments, Mrs. Wetherell continued: "I had a monument erected over the two graves. I remained there in that graveyard every day, until I felt sure I had buried every feeling of human sympathy and human love in those two graves. My heart was dead. I buried it there with those I loved — trampled upon the clay, and covered it with sward, and until this day has the moss-covered tomb never been disturbed.

"My kind, adopted mother, in fact, the only one I ever knew, had a sister married to a poor mechanic, who lived some distance from us. I wrote her immediately after Henry's death, and she came to attend her sister during her illness. From the goodness of her heart, she resigned all claim upon the Graham estate, which had become quite valuable, because I had been engaged and was shortly to have been married to

Henry. That I peremptorily refused, renouncing all claim, in short, had none, and told the good woman it was rightfully and justly hers. Then she came with her husband and four little children to live in my old home. I did not know where to go, or what to do, but fancied some strange place would suit me best. So I started, leaving the old home and the two graves behind; but I had two ghosts with me, and they have been with me ever since.

"Being unaccustomed to travelling, I asked for the captain of the steamboat on which I had taken passage, and told him I was alone, that I had lost my adopted mother and brother suddenly, and, with limited means, wished to visit a Southern city for a while, as everything had become hateful to me in my old home. He was very kind, and told me he knew of a place which would exactly suit me in the city where his boat stopped, the home of a widowed friend of his, whose slender means compelled her to take a few boarders, and he thought she would be a nice, kind person to advise with in regard to any future plans. The place proved all the captain had represented. He called to see me every time he came to the city, which was twice a week, and appeared greatly interested in me. My landlady told me he was wealthy and good-hearted, but a very immoral man.

"My monotonous life soon became wearisome; I yearned for a change of any kind. My limited means compelled me to live economically, and that did not suit me. I longed for excitement, the only thing I felt that could drown my unhappy past. I knew I was attractive, and determined to marry the captain, for whom I had not even a feeling of gratitude, as I considered his kindness entirely selfish, because I was handsome, and my lonely position made his attentions a novelty for the time.

"It was not difficult work flattering him into love-making, and in less than six months we were married. It was arranged that I should continue living in the same place, and my husband would be there two days in the week. I was no sooner married than I threw aside my amiable submission, moved to the first hotel in the city, and, knowing the Captain's wealth, furnished myself with an equipage and attendance accordingly. Finding all opposition useless, he let me have my own way, and I led a gay and merry life. Soon after, the Captain purchased an elegant home, but our princely magnificence was short-lived, for he failed a few years after, and went to India, where he remained ten years. We have lived in the same house since, but I have never been a wife to him, and never will be. He and I know the reason, which is sufficient. I despise the old idiot, and he fears me.

"Now you know *part* of my life. You will never love me, but you will fear me. Once more, you must marry Mr. Warren, because I command you. I go in search of him, to give your answer."

She closed the state-room door, and was gone.

Linda sat like one stupefied ; then, from the depths of her heart, she cried in bitter anguish : "Merciful God, and are the sins of the parents to be visited upon the children?" As if waiting for an answer, she sat silently gazing before her, then instinctively fell upon her knees, and poured out her first heart sorrow to Him who is ever ready and willing to hear those who call upon His name.

Miss Adams, the principal of the school where Linda had been educated, was a good Christian woman, who tried to inculcate moral and religious principles in the young minds committed to her care, besides making them accomplished young ladies. She was a good judge of human nature, and from the manner in which Mrs. Wetherell placed her daughter in school,

5   D

leaving her there for months without visiting her, when, by three hours' travel she could have been with her, made Miss Adams think she was an unloving woman, and, true to the religion she professed, she took the lonely Linda to her heart.

Linda loved her preceptress, and was deeply grateful when troubles came, for to her she owed much of the strong, womanly character she possessed, and years after, when far away from her protecting care and motherly advice, she realized what a watchful friend she had been during the many years passed under her guidance.

Half an hour passed, and Linda still knelt with her face in her hands, occasionally sobbing aloud from the bitterness of her sorrow-laden heart. Then she rose and retired to her narrow berth over her mother's.

"How everything has changed," she said, half aloud. "This morning, the steamer seemed gliding along without any effort, breathing like a child; to-night, the moon is hid, the billows roll, and the ship works as if under a heavy burden. So my heart was all sunshine this morning, but now my sun is eclipsed. My heart beat lightly this morning; to-night it throbs and wells up as if it would overflow."

The moon came peeping in at the half-open window, leaving a silvery pathway over the trackless ocean, and a ray of light in Linda's aching heart, that brightened the sweet young face, and left it full of hope, as she asked herself, with childish disdain: "Why should I despair? That is God's handiwork, and so am I. He guards that with its myriads of creatures and its fathomless depths, and so He will me. That is vast and sublimely grand, and so am I, for am not I made in the likeness of God himself? One storm does not annihilate old ocean, but makes it all the mightier and grander; and so shall the storms that overshadow my heart leave it all the more patient and good. Old ocean, you are a queer old personage to compare with a maiden of seventeen."

She heard her mother bidding Mr. Warren good-night, in her pleasantest tone. The door opened and Mrs. Wetherell swept in, filling the entire state-room with her august presence. Through the partly drawn curtain Linda regarded her face as she disrobed for the night. Not once did she even glance toward the berth where her daughter lay. Her eyes had a strange, wild expression, and her face was very pale. She did not kneel to ask God's blessing during that last night out on the sea; so Linda involuntarily offered up a childish petition for her.

CHAPTER VIII.

THROUGH THE GOLDEN GATE TO THE MOUNTAIN HOME.

IT was noon when the "Sonora" fired her gun as she passed through the Golden Gate. The bleak, barren, sand hills of San Francisco were anything but inviting, and the weight at Linda's heart made everything appear terribly dismal.

She expected her father and brother to meet them, but neither was there. Instead, a stranger handed Mrs. Wetherell a letter from the Captain, stating it was impossible for him to leave home, but his friend being in San Francisco on business, would kindly pay them any necessary attention. Mrs. Wetherell thanked him politely, but declined any assistance, as Mr. Warren was going with them as far as Sacramento, and would gladly attend to their wants.

It was two o'clock in the afternoon when they landed, and having no object in remaining in San Francisco, they took the steamer for Sacramento at four, and were soon on their way up the picturesque stream of that name. They arrived at Sacramento during the night, and at six o'clock the next morning took the stage for Grass Valley, leaving Mr. Warren behind, much to Linda's delight.

It was six o'clock in the evening when they arrived at their destination, after having been driven rapidly for twelve hours, by a reckless driver of four rearing, plunging mustangs, over hills and down dales, over rocks and ruts, that almost sent their heads through the top of the stage.

Mrs. Wetherell did not speak one word to Linda during the entire day. While Mr. Warren was still with them her manner was unchanged, but after leaving him, one might have taken them for strangers. Linda would not force any conversation upon her mother when she met with no response, and Mrs. Wetherell took that unwomanly way of showing her displeasure towards her daughter.

The stage took them to the door of their vine-covered cottage, where the Captain was waiting to receive them. He took Linda in his arms and kissed her affectionately, but he only shook hands with his wife.

There was a pleasant-faced housemaid, who had a steaming supper in readiness; but the brother, Ben, was not there.

"Father, where is Ben?" asked Linda.

"He stepped out a short time ago, my dear," answered the Captain; "perhaps he went to the stage-office, thinking you might stop there."

The door opened, and Ben made his appearance. Linda ran to meet and embrace him.

"Dear Linda, I am so glad to see you once more," he said, and went to welcome his mother. She offered him her cheek, which he kissed, and going back to Linda, stood with his arm about her waist, regarding her with affectionate admiration. They were a handsome couple, that brother and sister, for Ben, in his commanding, manly way, was quite as handsome as Linda.

"You quite surprise me, Linda. You have grown so handsome," said he, earnestly.

"Happiness is always a great beautifier," laughed Linda. "But I think I can safely return your compliment."

"Owing, undoubtedly, to the same magic power."

"None of your raillery to begin with, Ben. I remember well what a tease you used to be."

"I have changed since then, Linda. In fact, I am so completely reformed, I have lost the art of tormenting."

"For which I offer up thanks," said Linda, with feigned seriousness.

They passed the entire evening together, talking of the changes that had taken place since their separation, of the old pleasures in the years gone by, and asked and answered innumerable questions interesting only to themselves.

"I am very fortunate in having you to escort me around this wild country, Ben," said Linda.

"I am sorry to disappoint you, but I am working very industriously now, and will have little time to come down here."

"Where do you work, and what do you do?" asked Linda, eagerly.

"I am mining, not very far from here, with two splendid young fellows."

"Then I am disappointed, indeed. I thought, of course, you would be at home with me at least every evening."

"That will be impossible. I can only be with you on Sundays, and perhaps not every Sunday. Besides, I would not stay at home, if I was in town all the time."

5 *

" Pray, why not ? "

" For reasons that are better left unexplained," said Ben, bitterly.

" As you like, dear," answered Linda, who never forced a question upon any one. " I often wondered you never wrote me what your business was, and father only mentioned occasionally that you were well."

Ben laughed a hard sort of laugh.

" He actually took the trouble to report occasionally that I was well, did he? I wonder how he obtained his valuable information."

" I was speaking of father," said Linda, in astonishment. " You could not have understood me."

" I understood perfectly," and Ben compressed his lips firmly an instant. " But that is a topic I should have avoided, for my feelings towards him make me say bitter things. For over two years I have not spoken to him nor entered this house."

" You really cannot mean what you say, Ben? "

" Every word, Linda. But I did not mean to tell you such things to-night," added he, regretfully.

" Before you came in, I asked father where you were," continued Linda, " and he told me you had just stepped out. Perhaps you had gone to the stage-office, thinking we might have stopped there."

" Here is a note I received from him yesterday. It will explain."

Linda took the note and read :

MY DEAR SON : — Your mother and sister are expected to arrive in Grass Valley to-morrow evening. Perhaps I have been a little severe with you. Although I have scarcely seen you for the past two years, I invite you home to meet them, and hope all differences between us will never be again thought of, much less mentioned.

Your forgiving father,

RICHARD WETHERELL.

"What could you have done to displease father so?" asked Linda, with tears in her eyes.

"It is one of those inexplicable things better left unanswered, Linda. Differences and disagreements usually arise from a want of mutual understanding, but sometimes from too good an understanding. Even with those immediately connected, friendship is a curious thing, and fragile as an exotic. Respect and confidence are its vital organs. When they become diseased, the shadowy thing vanishes, as if swept by the four winds of heaven, and can no more be brought to life than the ashes of the dead."

"Then I am to infer that you and father have had a misunderstanding?"

"Au contraire, ma chère, we have had an understanding—a much more fatal thing in its result."

"I hope it is all a mistake. It would grieve me to have you and father at variance, for mother and I had a very unpleasant scene the last night out at sea, which has caused a coldness between us."

"I am sorry to hear that. What was the matter, little one?"

"As you have already said, Ben, we must not speak of unpleasant things to-night. Besides, it was nothing of much consequence, now that it is over," answered Linda, blushing deeply.

"We will not resurrect it then," said Ben, noticing her confusion. "We will speak only of pleasant things the first evening we have been together for five years: it seems ten to me, Linda, I have missed you so much. Try to be patient, and endure as cheerfully as possible the unpleasant life you may have to lead here, and I hope, before many months, to be able to take you to a home of my own."

"That would be delightful. Do you know, I think I would make a very efficient housekeeper for you, Ben."

Ben smiled rather incredulously at Linda's remark, as he bade her affectionately good-night.

CHAPTER IX.

A FAIRY IN THE SIERRAS.

IT was one of those sweet, balmy days when spring is being lost in summer. Nellie and the children had wandered far away from home over the hills. The little ones were running about gathering wild flowers, while Nellie sat in the shade of a great cluster of manzanitas, reading. Her attention was attracted by a sweet voice saying:

"Where did you come from, little folks? Are you not lost upon these great mountains?"

"Oh, no, ma'am," answered Nellie's bright boy, Hugh. "We came from home, and we know the way back."

"Do you, indeed? Then you are wiser than I am." Taking Daisy up in her arms, Linda Wetherell, for it was none other, said:

"I think you are a little fairy, and have no home."

"Do you really think she is a fairy?" asked Hugh, very honestly.

"I almost believe so," said Linda, amused at his earnestness, "because she is such a tiny creature to be running about here alone."

"We are not alone. There is our mamma."

Hugh pointed to where his mother sat, and ran to her side with the mysterious whisper, "Mamma, here is somebody we do not know, and she is such a pretty lady."

Being thus introduced by her little son, Nellie immediately rose to meet Linda with her habitual affability.

"I thought my little ones and I were the only wanderers over these hills. It is a pleasant surprise to meet with company."

"Thank you," replied Linda, warmly. "I am a stranger here. We only arrived a short time ago, and, from the appearance of the place, I did not think there was an agreeable human being in it. It is a happy surprise to meet some one with whom I can converse. I am home-sick, though I have no other home to yearn for. I never was so utterly unhappy in my life."

"I am sorry to hear such expressions from one so young," said Nellie, sympathetically. "I admit this is not a very inviting place, but you will soon become accustomed to it, and like it better. I have been here several years, and am quite attached to it."

"But were you not very unhappy when you first arrived?"

"No, I never was unhappy, for my husband and children were with me, and where they are I could not be unhappy. Besides, my brother was here to welcome us, which made it much pleasanter than it otherwise would have been, for we felt satisfied to live any place where he was."

"I am old enough to be more philosophical," said Linda, with a sigh; "but look at that cluster of little houses, and those barren hills. The heart of the place has been dug out by miners, and it is an unshapely mass of red earth, with nothing left of the pretty stream but mud puddles here and there."

"True, the miners have done great damage to the beauty of the place, but great wealth has been found ; and, after all, we are only staying here until we feel able to live in a pleasanter place."

"I would rather be a beggar in New York than a millionaire in California," exclaimed Linda, desperately.

"It is to be hoped you will soon have cause to change your unfavorable opinion," and Nellie's sweet persuasive powers were strained to the utmost to lay the foundation for the fulfilment of her wish, as they strolled down the hillside, chatting merrily. When they arrived at Nellie's home, they parted like old acquaintances, with promises to meet the following day.

"So that is the daughter of that old hypocrite, Captain Wetherell," thought Nellie, as she stood a moment looking after Linda. "Her brother is a wild fellow, her mother a termagant, so Walter says; and, notwithstanding those connections, she is just as sweet as she can be."

"I was just thinking of going in search of you runaways," said George, as he met them at the door. "You must have enjoyed your walk, for I saw you when you were starting out over two hours ago."

"We did, my dear," answered Nellie, as she sat down by her husband's side. . "We met Miss Wetherell, who was also wandering over the hills. She is very lonesome here, poor thing."

"Is she a Venus or a Sphinx? a demon or an angel?" asked Walter.

"I think she is an angel," answered Nellie, decidedly.

"Of course you do. My little sister thinks this world is populated with angels, but I am afraid this one will soon shed her wings."

"Walter, you should see her before you judge."

"I am not at all anxious. If her society affords you pleasure, I am content. For my part, I am not desirous of cultivating my acquaintance with that family."

CHAPTER X.

ON-FLOWING TIDES OF DESTINY.

"A form more fair, a voice more sweet,
Ne'er hath it been my lot to meet."

THE next day, according to promise, Linda wandered for hours with Nellie and the children over the hills, gathering the choice wild flowers, and went home laden with their pretty treasures. As Nellie insisted upon her remaining to tea, she left word at home where she could be found, and returned delighted to be a visitor in that cosy, homelike cottage.

She possessed a special gift for charming children. When with them, she seemed almost a child herself, so merry was her laughter, so true her hazel eyes, and so heartily did she enter into all their youthful pleasures.

Sitting on a stool with Fairy, as she insisted upon calling Daisy, on her lap, Hugh kneeling on the floor by her side, leaning with both arms upon her knee, she was telling them a wonderful fairy tale about "Hop o' my thumb."

When Walter came up unheard, seeing the little group so deeply interested in their story, he quietly sat down upon the veranda until it was ended. He felt sure the pretty narrator was Miss Wetherell, and would have been quite inclined to think with Nellie that she was almost an angel, had she been the daughter of any one else than Captain Wetherell. She had a pleasing, musical voice, and as she finished the story, she kissed each little one sweetly, and, to Hugh's .entreaties for another, said :

"No more stories to-day, dear. You might get tired of listening. The next time I come I will tell you another. Let us go ôutside, now, and see if we cannot find something there to interest us."

Hugh caught sight of his uncle, and ran to him with out-stretched arms, saying : "Oh, Uncle Walter.. You should have come a little sooner, and heard the lovely story."   .

Nellie immediately came and introduced her new friend to her brother, and they sat talking, as strangers naturally do, of everything in general and nothing in particular, until George came, when supper was announced.

Walter was determined to dislike Miss Wetherell, but when he felt inclined to be sarcastic or disagreeable, a single glance of her soft, brown eyes would compel him not only to speak very respectfully, but kindly.

They were leaving the table, when Walter said :

"I almost forgot to tell you about the stage robbery last night."

"Stage robbery!" exclaimed Linda. "Oh, this barbarous country !"

"Was it near here?" asked Nellie.

"About nine miles from here, just this side of Indian Springs. One of the passengers was so frightened, he let himself down from the top of the stage and walked back. He says it was one of the boldest robberies ever perpetrated. There were eight men in the stage and two on top with the driver. The horses were going along at a lively trot, when suddenly a lighted torch was thrown in front of them. It demoralized the little mus-

tangs so completely, that it was impossible to proceed. The
leaders threw themselves back on the wheel-horses, which, in
their desperate efforts to get away, became worse entangled.
Of course, that all happened like a flash. Simultaneously, four
masked men came out of the bushes and demanded Wells &
Fargo's treasury box."

"They did not get it, did they?" asked Nellie, impatiently.

"Yes, they did. The driver and the passengers were taken
so completely off their guard, they were wholly unprepared;
whereas, the four men each held two pistols ready for use.
The driver felt not only his own life, but that of his passengers
were at stake; so he was really compelled to surrender.

"The man who gave the report said he let himself down
from the top of the stage while the box was being delivered.
He was in the chaparral when the robbers passed within three
feet of him. He saw them break the box open, and heard their
discussions about dividing the spoil. He says he can identify
every one, for he saw them distinctly by the light of their lan-
terns, with their masks off."

"I hope he can and will. Such desperadoes should be
brought to justice," said Nellie, energetically.

"It is scarcely probable they will be caught," answered George.
"The country is so thinly populated, they can wander about
for months and avoid detection, if they have had the fore-
thought to provide provisions."

"They will not be likely to do that," said Walter. "In all
probability they will come directly into town, and show they
are flush by betting heavily at a gambling-table, and in that
way betray themselves."

"If robberies will occur, and robbers will get caught, it is
surely no fault of mine," said Nellie. "So long as you and
6

Walter are honest and good, why should I grieve over others' bad husbands and brothers?"

Walter looked inquiringly at this new development in Nellie's usually sympathetic soul, as he exclaimed:

"What a philosophical little woman you are getting to be, Nell! I have no doubt they cause enough hearts to ache without yours to swell the number."

They were all anxious to hear the latest news, so Walter and George walked up town to hear if there were any further developments, and if any of the robbers had come to grief.

CHAPTER XI.

UNDER-CURRENTS.

MONTHS had passed since Linda's arrival in Grass Valley, during which time her mother had left her entirely to her own resources, scarcely noting her existence, except on the reception of letters from Mr. Warren, and once during a visit from that gentleman she assumed her motherly interest.

The Captain appeared very fond of her, but was always occupied, and spent very little time at home.

Soon after the arrival of his family, he purchased an interest in a mill above Nevada, about seven miles from Grass Valley; and as it did not prove a success under the management of his partner, he went there himself to superintend it, and seldom visited home oftener than once a month.

One evening, after a peaceful, happy day spent at the cottage, Linda went home, and, unobserved, retired to her own room. Hearing her father's voice, she started to meet him, when she

was arrested by her mother saying in an unusually loud manner:
" What is your object in remaining in Nevada all the time,
Captain Wetherell?"

" I do not remain in Nevada, madam." replied the Captain,
coolly. " I am overseeing my mill, three miles from there."

" Do you intend remaining there?"

" Yes, so long as it is necessary."

" Then, why did you insist upon my coming out here, to
mope my time away. My society is surely no pleasure to you."

" Well, I cannot say that it is absolutely disagreeable, seven
miles distant."

" What do you mean by that?" demanded Mrs. Wetherell,
curtly.

" Simply, that distance lends enchantment even to your
amiability and loveliness," said the Captain, bluntly.

" I never could understand your stupid efforts at witticisms."

" I know you were always rather dull, my dear."

" That will do, Captain Wetherell. Once again, I want to
know what your object could have been in bringing me out
here. You know I would have been much more pleasantly situ-
ated East."

" Yes, I know you would."

" It is surely no pleasure to have me with you," continued
Mrs. Wetherell, in a more subdued tone.

" I should say not," and the Captain's serene, almost smiling countenance, exasperated Mrs. Wetherell much more than
anger would have done.

" Then," exclaimed she, excitedly, " what in the name of
Heaven did you bring me here for?'

" Do not call upon places so remote, my dear, and so utterly
unattainable by you, and I will tell you."

From the Captain's complacent manner, one might have

thought he was making a few pious remarks at a church meeting, as he continued :

"I brought you here to make you as miserable as possible, my fair old dame. You are piqued because there are other ladies here quite as handsome as you were fifteen or twenty years ago. Then gentlemen, in all probability, prefer the handsome daughter to the old mother. I bid you good-evening, my sweet creature," and he stalked past her and out of the house.

Seeing Linda, and not dreaming she had overheard his conversation, he embraced her, and imprinted a kiss upon her forehead.

"Why, my dear, have you returned? I feared I was not going to see my little girl this visit. Go in, dear, and stay with your mamma. This dull place is tiresome for her. You know she has always been accustomed to gayety, and I am compelled to be absent so much." He kissed her again and was gone.

Linda, in her amazement, could not answer one word. She sat long in the twilight, thinking what a strange world had been revealed to her during the few previous months. How the pathway of spring flowers she had so lightly trodden was suddenly transformed into a precipitous, rocky cliff, rising higher and higher as her weary feet essayed to climb. The poor child, the beautiful girl, felt like a wreck tossed upon a boundless sea without rudder or compass.

CHAPTER XII.

THE OLD LOVE AND THE NEW.

" She listened, while a sweet surprise
Looked from her long-lashed hazel eyes."

THE next morning the sun rose gloriously; the air was bracing and fresh, as it went sighing through the lofty pines that filled it with their aromatic perfume.

Linda took a long walk, and returned by the cottage, where she found Nellie busy as usual.

"A bad penny always returns," she said, with her sweetest smile, as Nellie greeted her. "I am sure, if some busy goddess were to take upon herself the arduous task of transforming me into my normal condition, I would develop into nothing more nor less than that valueless appendage to your household gods, for, wander where I will, I naturally gravitate here."

"It is because you are always welcome, Linda; not that there is any simile between you and the old proverb."

"You are very generous and kind with your friendship, Mrs. Gray, for idlers, like me, often levy heavy taxes upon their friends by robbing them of their valuable time in frivolous visits."

"Seriously, Linda, you have no idea what a comfort you are to me. I have not the leisure, had I the inclination, to visit among my neighbors, and your unceremonious visits are a real source of happiness to me."

"It is very sweet of you to say so," and Linda wound her arm about her friend. "As beggars seek their daily bread from door to door, I come to you for happiness. You live in

6 *   E

such sweet harmony in your little cottage, and in my own home I find no congeniality.

"There was an old widower on board the steamer, when we were coming out here from New York, who wished me to marry him," and her eyes flashed at the mere mention of those disagreeable scenes of the past. "Mother said he was rich, and she wished me to marry him on that account; although she knew my only feeling for him was profound contempt. It was the first time I ever disobeyed my mother; but I could not comply with her request, and positively refused. Since then she has only spoken to me when compelled, and from her manner, I live in daily dread of renewed trouble. In fact, she insists upon enforcing her determination."

"You poor, dear child." Nellie's sympathizing heart was touched. She drew Linda's head upon her shoulder, and stroking the soft brown hair, said, in her sweet, gentle way:

"I cannot advise you to do anything contrary to your parents' wishes, but I think it equally sinful to marry a man for gain whom you cannot love."

"Thank you for those reassuring words, Mrs. Gray," and Linda's soft hazel eyes were moist with unshed tears. "I know it is not right to disobey, yet I am equally sure it would in this case be wrong to obey. Of the two evils, I choose the lesser, and bear the ills myself, rather than force them upon another, who is surely deceived. I can never marry him. Never! no matter what the result might be. It is possible I cannot live with mother, but in that case I will go to Ben. Poor fellow, he has no one to care for him but me."

"You shall never be in want of a home, Linda, for you have endeared yourself to us all by your sweetness and intelligence. Sometimes, dear," and Nellie drew her closer to her, "I tremble for Belle Burton when I see Walter looking so fondly at you. Do you remember I told you once of their having been engaged to be married, and how it was broken off, and about her writing to him after so many years?"

"I remember," said Linda, softly.

"I do not believe he loves her at all," continued Nellie. "Not exactly that, either. I am sure he loved her once, and if they were to meet again under favorable circumstances, he might be as fond of her as ever. I think she expects him to return and marry her."

Little did Nellie think what sharp pain she inflicted upon her listener with every word she uttered.

Linda simply answered, "I hope they will be happy." There was a slight quiver about her mouth as she uttered those words, but Nellie did not notice it, and soon after left her to attend to some duties in an adjoining room.

Although the morning had been unusually fine, there had been indications of rain for several days. Before noon, the heavens became clouded, the wind blew fiercely, and great raindrops fell — the first of the rainy season.

Linda sat by the window watching the drops as they fell faster and faster, until they came down in torrents. It seemed as if the flood-gates of heaven were opened wide to pour down upon the earth, all at once, what the dry summer had so long been thirsting for.

It was one of those days that are dark and dreary, that naturally make one feel forlorn, and Nellie's conversation added bitter drops to the wretched rain. Linda felt as if it was raining in her heart, too, it seemed so chilled, and from its very depths she cried:

"Why was I ever brought here to love those deep black eyes, that seem to read my every thought, and make my life-blood bound and burn in my veins? What torture to hear of his marrying another. Thrice blessed Belle! Can ye take him from me, ye fates, and leave me in desolation, as seared and barren as the scorching wastes of Sahara?

"Dante, I could tell you of another hell. At eighteen I have found it. What could be more exquisite torture on earth, or in the infernal, than to smile and seem indifferent when you hear how the only one you love on earth loves another, and she is to become his wife?"

There were footsteps on the walk; a manly form came towards the house. What of the rain in Linda's heart? After the shower the sunshine, and one smile from Walter French, as Linda opened the door for him, dissipated every cloud from her stormy heart. Women are tender plants. They only grow in sunshine; shadows deform the heart, as every sorrow embitters a joy.

"Is this not an unusual hour for you to come home?" asked Linda.

"It is rather early; but I am at leisure, and would much prefer being with you than remaining alone at the office?"

"But how did you know you would find me?"

"I submitted myself to the gods, and they brought me to my goddess. If I could only say with Julius Cæsar, after his victory over Pharnaces, 'Veni, vidi, vici,' my happiness would be complete. So far as I can I will quote the noble victor. I came, I saw, and when may I add conquered, Linda?"

"When you have married Belle Burton. You know the old song says:

> 'It's good to be merry and wise,
>   It's good to be honest and true,
> It's good to be off wi' the old love,
>   Before you be on wi' the new.'"

Although Walter's searching gaze never left her face, he read there only what he had already seen. Her eyes were frank and truthful, her voice soft and musical, her cheeks crimson. If a little more so than usual, his remarks had been a little freer than ordinary, and Linda was a modest maiden.

"I will never marry Belle Burton," said Walter, firmly. "Nellie has been talking nonsense to you. She is so fond of me, she says and thinks whatever she fancies would give me the greatest pleasure, — and it would be useless to restrain her so long as she is happy in her womanly arrangements. I foolishly showed her a letter from Belle, over a year ago, and that resurrected the old, dead topic. I answered the letter, and told Belle, if my business would permit, I would pay a visit East a year from that time; that I wanted to see my old home in the South, and would be pleased to meet her. That was the extent of our renewal of friendship. There was nothing whatever said of marriage. . I have received two or three friendly letters from her since. The last one is still unanswered. I could not conveniently leave my business when the year had passed, and now do not wish to.

"If you had not grown so dear to me, Linda, I might have gone, and perhaps — What is the use of talking such stuff! I never would have married Belle Burton. What has a boy's fancy at twenty to do with a man's love at thirty? There is a pair of brown eyes I do love, and would like to make the owner my wife. Could you love a rough miner like me, Linda?"

He took both her small hands in his, and with a look of inexpressible tenderness seemed to penetrate her very heart.

"I will not love any one whom I have no right to love," said she, softly. "So long as Belle Burton is awaiting your return, I shall not be the cause of her disappointment."

"You love me, then?" asked Walter, passionately.

"Yes," she answered, scarcely above a whisper, "as the noblest, best friend I ever had," and despite her great effort at self-command, her voice was tremulous and strange.

"But I cannot be only a friend to you, Linda. I must be more," and Walter's soft black eyes pleaded more eloquently than words.

"Come here, Linda," called Nellie from the kitchen; "I will give you your first lesson in cooking, which I have promised so long. Sofie, poor soul, has such a headache that she was obliged to lie down."

Linda went instantly, to avoid further conversation on a subject that pained while it pleased. She would gladly have given her whole, loving heart to that noble, good man, if it had not been for Belle Burton. Fortunate Belle, to hold him in such thraldom. Fortunate Linda, to know he loved her. Such thoughts went constantly flashing through her brain, and the first lesson in cooking proved a sad failure.

Nellie asked her how she had done certain things, after having taken great pains to instruct her. She stammered woefully, and finally said:

"I really have forgotten. You will have to show me again, I am such a dull scholar."

Nellie's merriment over Linda's stupidity brought Walter to the kitchen. He seemed also greatly amused at her incapacity for cooking, much to Nellie's surprise, for he was a great admirer of fine housewifery. But Nellie could not dream of the distracting elements in Linda's brain that would not be overcome by mashed potatoes or macaroni.

CHAPTER XIII.

ROBBERY.

THE peace of the village had been undisturbed for a long time by acts of violence. Crime seemed on the decrease.

Still, an occasional outrage was added to the long list. The last, though insignificant in itself, was so bold in its perpetration that it caused the wildest excitement. No citizen could feel safe a mile from the town, if such things were permitted to go unpunished.

When Mr. Gray came home, he repeated the circumstance as it had been told by the excited teamster on his arrival in Grass Valley.

The man had been robbed, in Rattlesnake Cañon, of five hundred dollars and his watch. He said a young man, with a shot-gun and a hunting-coat thrown over his shoulders, with the most perfect nonchalance, and without any effort at disguise, came out of the bushes, and pointing the gun at him, demanded his money and watch. Being unarmed, and thus menaced, he surrendered them ; and the young fellow walked off as coolly as if nothing had happened.

"It was the audacity of the thing," continued Mr. Gray, "as much as the loss, that exasperated the ire of the teamster ; and he swears he will remain in the neighborhood until he finds the thief."

"It is no wonder the poor fellow is furious," said Linda, indignantly. "But who could be so unprincipled as to rob a poor, hard-working teamster ?"

"So unprincipled ?" asked George. "Why, some of those fellows would rob their mothers."

"By the way, has that other stage-robber ever been caught?" asked Nellie.

"No, I believe not," answered George. "One, as you know, turned State's evidence, and two were arrested on his statement. The other has escaped all search."

"I do hope the teamster will find the man who robbed him," said Linda, thoughtlessly, as we all often hope for things we do not want when they come. And George took up the refrain quite naturally, saying:

"I hope so. He should be made an example, for the safety of others."

"I pity the examples," said the kind-hearted Nellie.

"They are unworthy your sympathy," chimed in Walter, as if suddenly awakened from a dream. "If men will commit outrages and violences, they must be punished, to stop their own bad career, and intimidate those who would follow in their footsteps. Laws are the result of civilization, and are for the protection of mankind. Without them, we would soon return to the feudal times, when might made right, and power was law."

"Do you believe in capital punishment?" asked Linda.

"No. I do not think any man should die to enforce laws. There are other punishments — imprisonment for life, or banishment from home and friends — more terrible to sensitive natures; yet they have then a hope of something, however remote or indefinite."

"I quite agree with you," said Linda. "Still, as Mr. Gray remarked, there must be examples for the benefit of the world at large. Even Renan admitted Christ was the only perfect man that ever lived, yet He was crucified."

"You blood-thirsty little woman," said George, in astonishment. "Would you have all offenders, even though they were as guiltless as your Saviour, punished to the extreme?"

"I do not believe a guiltless man suffers as much from pun-ishment as one who is guilty, for he has no prickings of con-science to add to the bodily suffering," interposed Nellie.

"I should think the prickings of conscience would very effectually deaden the bodily agony," argued Linda. "To be ignominiously punished for what one has never done, must be fearful; but to meet with punishment for a perpetrated crime must bring with it a sense of just retribution that would make it more endurable."

"You talk as earnestly as if you really were experienced in crime, Miss Linda," said Walter, amused at her earnestness.

"I think we are," she answered, decidedly. "It would be impossible to live long here and not know something of crime. We are unlike the women of old countries, who read of crimes in the newspapers, with doubt as to the veracity of three-fourths of the story. We are brought in closer contact with it. We know the victims of crime, and men who have escaped the vigi-lance of the law, although their lives are chapter after chapter of blood and violence. Crime is to us no romance — thrilling in narrative, but a matter of oblivion in a week. We have in it the real tragedies of life. How can we be otherwise than conversant with it?"

"It is true, pioneer women of all countries see the darkest side of life. Every new colony is the rendezvous of bandits and outlaws — those who flee from punishment, and those whose punishments have been followed by crimes *ad infinitum*; but they fight and murder until the desperadoes are killed off, and the peaceful and industrious make thriving countries of their new homes," replied Walter. "Take the penal colo-nies of England, for example. Felons, whose deeds did not warrant capital punishment, were exported, because the govern-ment could not be burdened with their support. The desper-

7

ate exhausted themselves, but three-fourths settled down to industry and honesty. Although the original blood of rebellion boils over occasionally, and ends in deeds of crime, those colonies are as respectable in deportment and government as any new colonies. Look at our own California, with its aristocratic landed natives. Most of their forefathers were criminals driven from Mexico. In the fertile valleys of California they found no resources for crime. Instead, there was ample reward for light labor, and they became honest men. Their families know nothing of the stained past, and history will forget it."

"You are right, Walter," said Nellie. "It is the first lesson we learn from sacred history. Adam and Eve were cast from heaven for breaking the Divine laws. God did not hang them to the tree from which they ate the forbidden fruit, but sent them from His presence. If this beautiful earth was first inhabited by outcasts, even from Paradise, why should not the deserted islands in the remotest seas, teeming with vegetable life and lavish with nature's stores, be brought into use as homes for the wretched, steeped in crime, in our own land."

"Mrs. Gray speaks of outcasts from heaven, and we are always taught to prepare for heaven, yet how do we know there is such a place?" asked Linda.

"We do not know," answered Walter, "but it has come to us as an undying tradition from those who have been there. Adam and Eve must have fallen from some perfect condition of happiness, and told their children, and, with all the terror of their fearful fall, taught the result of sin, and made heaven and hell from their own lives. It is generally supposed that this world of ours was in a state of chaos not many thousand years ago; but even so, it must have been, as it now is, a small world in the firmament, performing its revolutions in harmony with the infinitude of worlds. What is in the many greater worlds about us, we cannot tell. Astronomical calculations make them uninhabitable from excessive heat or cold; but we cannot imagine the conditions of nature that might fit beings for their habitation.

" It evidently became necessary to people and bring into use our world, and, the story is, by those unworthy of Paradise; and they left their traditions, which became history, as every nation in the wide world has done since. History speaks to us so much in metaphor, every brain must be its own interpreter, according to its understanding. For instance, the old superstition of walking with God and talking to Him, is entirely figurative. God's voice speaks to us, as it did to the ancients, in every breath of nature, but mostly through man, nature's noblest work. Nature is God's direct work, His very breath, and so perfect, so reliable, that we believe in her. If the labor is so absolute, so munificent, why not bow to the Laborer? Why not? We must. We are mere spokes in the great wheel of life, and must turn with every revolution. And it is a most unpleasant fact, that we are of so little importance, in the great machinery of life, that we can be dispensed with, and leave no vacuum.

" Every life history finds a parallel in ancient tradition ; for instance, we are all like the wandering Israelites, with a cloud of uncertainty ever before us, patiently plodding on, searching and prying into the veiled future for a single glimpse of heaven and happiness, and after all dying with the misty veil never lifted. This life is a training-school for something higher: it is a warfare with shadows. Nothing is real, because nothing is sure. We are serving an apprenticeship for something, because nature wastes nothing."

" But nature is sometimes defective," suggested George.

" Never without a cause," answered Walter, emphatically.

"We are too apt to combine the artificial with the natural, and attribute the defects to nature. We cut down forests, and future generations will abuse nature for her deserts. Nature is revengeful and exacting; when we abuse her, she cries back."

"Don't stop, Walter. I am just getting interested," said Nellie.

"You would make a first-class preacher to start a new school," suggested George.

"All right; when I get too lazy to work for a living I will go to preaching," answered Walter.

It was late when Walter took Linda home through the mud and the rain. Fortunately, the distance was short, for there was no spare room at the cottage. As he bade her good-night, he said, earnestly: "Think over what I asked you to-day, Linda, and tell me soon, for I shall be anxious."

"My good friend, when you can prove to me that Belle Burton has wholly released you, and is not awaiting your return to marry her, you can ask me the question of to-day over again. Good-night."

A slight pressure of the little hand, and the door closed between Walter and his angel.

"Nellie was right," he soliloquized. "The first time she saw her she said she was an angel. Women have much quicker perceptions than men. They comprehend by intuition what men stop to consider and prove. I believe I have been a fool all these years, and am just getting sensible. It may be exactly the reverse, for I am in love, *et cela, on dit*, always makes a fool of a man. I certainly would never go, for practical philosophy, to a man in love.

"What of the night-winds moaning through the tall trees and the pelting rain? They go on, notwithstanding my heart is as light as noonday, and the black heavens, to my fancy, are illuminated by two bright, burning stars. Ah, Linda, your beautiful brown eyes, so soft and bright, yet so firm and true, are radiant jewels in my heart. I believe I am a fool! I wonder if every man makes such a simpleton of himself when he is in love. It is very pleasant idiocy, Walter, my boy. I guess you are willing to be a fool of that sort all your life. She wants proofs from Belle. I will write to-night, and to-morrow's mail will meet the steamer. But, no. I would write too earnestly. I once knew a woman to swear to what she saw through an adobe wall three feet thick. And as for men's hearts, why, their contents can be delivered printed at a moment's notice. If Belle Burton should mistrust that I loved a pretty girl with brown eyes, she would swear we were engaged before we were born. I will wait until I can write a quiet, friendly letter, and tell her. I have given up all idea of going East, and hope soon to hear of her marriage with some splendid fellow ; that I shall positively remain an old bachelor, for the most veritable Hebe alive could not inspire me with the tender passion. If I should say that, she would surely think I was in love. Oh, woman! woman! you are as variable as the kaleidoscope. When one fancies he has a right square, honest view of your character, you present an entirely different picture. I can no more comprehend you than the infinity of the universe ; but, like all Christians, suppose the best way is to shut my eyes to facts, and take my chances.''

7 *

CHAPTER XIV.

A MODERN AGRIPPINA.

THE next day Linda did not visit the cottage as usual, but busied herself quietly at home. Toward evening, Nellie came to inquire if she was ill, or anything unusual had happened. She gave a plausible reason for absenting herself, and when Nellie invited her and Ben to dine with them the next day, she made all manner of excuses, which were readily explained away; and it was finally arranged, if Ben had no other engagement, they would accept, although Linda felt great delicacy in going, as formerly, where she was sure to meet Walter.

Before Ben's arrival the next morning, Mrs. Wetherell entered Linda's room with an open letter in her hand.

"Here is a letter from Mr. Warren, Linda. He will be here to-morrow or next day. You know I have promised you should marry him on your eighteenth birthday, three months from to-day. He is coming to make arrangements concerning your future home in Sacramento. It is my command that you receive him in a manner befitting my daughter and the Major's future wife. He has been appointed major on the Governor's staff, and you must respect his title."

"It is useless wasting words, mother. I can only tell you once more, I will never marry Mr. Warren."

"I suppose you want to marry that poor fellow, Walter French," said Mrs. Wetherell, sarcastically. "He is a good-looking man, and in all probability will give his wife enough to eat, and live after the manner of the Grays, in demi-poverty, — love in a cottage style."

"Yes. If I can ever be the wife of a man fond and true as George Gray, and have a home full of contentment and happiness as his, simple though it be, I will be happy as a queen."

"Of course, you picture Walter French lord of this humble paradise of yours," said Mrs. Wetherell, bitterly.

"I picture a man I could love, and no amount of gold could replace to me the want of affection in a home," answered Linda, earnestly.

"Go on, wilful girl; love Walter French; adore him if you choose; you shall never marry him. I told you long ago my will is of iron. Would that I were another Agrippina, that I might convert my son into another Nero, and my daughter, a second self—anything whereby I could see those who oppose me writhe in mortal anguish. Girl, I am a fiend when enraged. Turn pale, and tremble, too! I am to be feared. I want money. I came to this miserable country for money, and will sacrifice you for gold. I must have it, by fair means or by foul. I am wretched! wretched! I must have money to make me free to go —"

"To the devil!" interrupted Ben. "I have overheard every word of this conversation. You said well — you are a fiend, woman! You may find another in your son, if you provoke him too much. You shall never compel Linda to marry that old fool."

"Dear Ben, do not talk so," pleaded Linda.

"I am sorry our mother compelled me to use such language in your presence," said Ben, bitterly. "But she outraged all claims of maternity. You need not marry that old Warren, Linda. I will put him over the Styx first."

"There will be no need of bloodshed. I will never marry him," said Linda, decidedly.

"I will leave you, amiable children, to discuss your obedient inclinations." Mrs. Wetherell left the room trembling with rage, her face was livid as she gasped for breath. She had so long given way to her passionate temper when anything extraordinary happened to enrage her, she almost went into spasms.

"Poor Linda!" said Ben, as they were left alone; "I am sorry for you in this home. It is a perfect mystery to me that a mother and daughter can be such perfect contrasts in disposition and feelings. How do you manage to live with her?"

"Oh, very well. Mother says little to me. She lets me do just as I choose, so I pass most of my time with Mrs. Gray. I am always happy there."

"I am inclined to think the attraction is not altogether Mrs. Gray," said Ben, jokingly. "How is it, my sweet sister?"

"I confess I love them all, they are such good people."

"We all like contrasts, and I know of no more striking one than that family and ours," said Ben.

"True. I wish we were more like them. I would even be contented, if you and I could be together more."

"You shall have me all day to-morrow. I have made arrangements with the boys to do without me one day, in order to fulfil the promise made long ago to take you over the mountains; but then you must not expect me next Sunday."

"I shall be so delighted to have you with me all day to-morrow. We will not borrow trouble about next Sunday; but you know that disagreeable old Mr. Warren is coming here to remain a week. What will I do without you all that time?"

"You need not be in the least concerned about his coming. A note will reach me in a short time; and if you should be in need of friends before I could get to you, go to the Grays. They will be happy in serving you."

"Let me live with you, Ben. Can I not be of some service to you?" asked Linda, like a coaxing child.

"You go with me?" Ben laughed heartily at the idea. "You could not live in a log cabin, Linda. A delicately reared New York boarding-school Miss housekeeper for her brother, in a log cabin with two rooms! That would be a pretty picture to send back to your friends."

"You do not know what I can do until you try me. I could endure a great many hardships to be with you," said Linda, modestly.

"You do not know what hardships are," said Ben, kindly. "Besides, if you knew what a bad, rough fellow I am, you would not be so fond of me."

"Yes, I would love you just the same. If you are rough and bad, as you say, you need some one all the more to love and care for you."

"I wish we had never been parted, Linda. I would not have become such a rough miner as I am now, and perhaps been more capable of taking care of you as you deserve and need."

"It is not too late, Ben. Divine laws supply all our necessities."

"Do not begin preaching, or I will leave," said Ben, good-naturedly.

"You naughty boy, you need preaching to every day."

"Well, we will postpone it for the present, and make arrangements for to-morrow. I am wholly at your command, and the day shall be spent according to your dictation."

"Then let us go over the mountains on horseback," decided Linda, at once.

"That will suit me splendidly. But I must leave you now, and go up town on some business, and will meet you in a little while at Mr. Gray's. Until then, good-by."

F

CHAPTER XV.

GRAND PATHWAYS TO A CELL.

" Die Lüfte weh'n so schaurig,
    Wir ziehen dahin so traurig,
    Nach ungewissem Ziel."

THOSE who have never ridden among the Sierra Nevada
Mountains can form but a faint idea of the sublime grand-
eur of their loneliness. Winding in and out their precipitous sides, one is deep down in a great cañon or gorge,
where rushing waters go dancing gleefully, or plunging over
great boulders, with ferns and drooping grasses dipping here
and there in the cool waters ; where nothing is heard but the
busy hum of nature, and the tramp of horses' feet or sound of
human voice seems hollow and out of place. Then, as if ascending Nature's spiral stairway, one is thousands of feet above
the level of the sea, and as far as the eye can reach rise peak
after peak and range after range of forest mountains, whose
tall pines seem mere shrubs in the distance. So one can journey on over the uneven roads for days, seldom finding a single
habitation, and at evening look back over the day's journey
and see only a purple haze veiling the great mountains of one's
admiration — an indistinct outline, a mist, as the day's pleasure or unhappiness is veiled in the past — a dream once realized.

These roads were originally Indian trails, where the children
of the forest went lazily, day after day, with their soft, catlike
tread in their moccasins, but leaving " footprints in the sands
of time,'' and unknowingly engineering with great nicety roads
and highways for their more learned pale-faced brethren. The
poor Indians will soon be among the things of the past. Cul-

tivation kills them; civilization annihilates them. Those who have been kindly taken into families and cared for, droop and die young; while those near villages work only *pour boire*. They all take with wonderful tenacity to alcohol, and will work for that when for nothing else, and it is rapidly and surely exterminating them.

Ben and Linda had taken a long ride. The horses were walking leisurely. The riders were lost in thought, when Ben broke the stillness by saying:

"Let us turn to the right. That is a shorter route to Nevada, and we can return by the other road."

"That would be delightful!" exclaimed Linda. "I think Nevada is such a pretty place."

"I do not," answered Ben, emphatically. "I never did fancy it."

Urging his horse on more rapidly, they continued their ride in silence. But long after, Linda wondered what strange premonition had caused him to speak of Nevada with so much bitterness.

They had ridden through Nevada, and were on the way to Grass Valley, when they were passed by two horsemen.

"One of those men looked very hard at us, Ben. Who are they?" asked Linda.

"I did not know either of them." Ben turned in his saddle as he spoke, for horses' hoofs were heard rapidly overtaking them.

The same men came dashing up, one on either side of Ben, each with a pistol in hand:

"If you have any arms, sir, give them up, and surrender yourself our prisoner," demanded one. Ben turned pale, but asked firmly:

"By what authority am I to yield myself your prisoner?"

"I am the sheriff," answered the stranger. "Here is the warrant for your arrest. Read it."

As Ben read, the color came back to his face, and he said politely:

"There is some mistake here, sir. I know nothing about this affair."

"Of course you don't," said the second man, insolently; and to the sheriff, "Did you ever hear tell of a thief who did know his own business?" Turning again to Ben, "Maybe I can tell you a little about this here story that you 've heard tell of before, young man."

Linda sat like one in a trance, not having power to speak. She heard all they said; saw Ben give up his pistol and surrender himself to their authority. Then he turned to her, and with trembling voice addressed the strangers:

"Gentlemen, consider my sister."

That aroused her, and she exclaimed:

"Never mind me. I will go where he goes."

"That is impossible, Linda," said Ben, decidedly; and turning to the sheriff, "In the name of God and humanity, do not tell her where I am going."

To comfort Linda, he added: "I am summoned to appear at court. The case being urgent, in which I am one of the chief witnesses, they have taken these extreme measures. These gentlemen will accompany us until we are near Grass Valley, then you must go home alone this time, little sister."

There was something so strangely pathetic in his voice, that Linda's eyes were full of tears as she looked searchingly into his face, and said pleadingly:

"I am afraid you are deceiving me, Ben. As I told you yesterday, I can endure more than you think. For Heaven's sake, tell me the truth."

"I really do not know any more to tell you now, but will write you to-morrow or next day, and the sheriff will see that you get the letter."

Linda raised her beautiful eyes full on the sheriff's face, and he had not the heart to deny her request, as she asked, softly, "Will you?"

"Yes, Miss, I will," he answered, with a respectful bow.

They were approaching Grass Valley, when he said quietly to Ben, "You can go no further."

Ben reined in his horse, and, giving his hand to Linda, said tenderly: "Good-by, sweet sister. There is something altogether wrong about this affair; but I am sure it will come out right. Try to forget it and be as happy as you can."

Linda kissed him and bade him good-by, with tears streaming down her cheeks. Slowly she went on her way, thinking: "There is more in this than Ben would tell me. How can I learn the particulars? To-morrow's paper will tell: it is the revealer of everything dreadful. But, surely, Ben has done nothing dreadful. There must be a mistake somewhere. No matter how it is; good it cannot be; but if it is bad, or even vile, I will serve my brother to the last. I wonder where they will take him. Oh, Ben, if I could only have gone with you! How can I wait until to-morrow! It seems a century off."

8

CHAPTER XVI.

"WAITING FOR THE VERDICT."

THE longest day must have an ending, the longest night must have its dawn, and yet the night seemed interminable to Linda, as she kept her solitary vigil. Not one thought of sleep came to her mind until the sun was peeping over the mountains, then from weariness she slept heavily.

When she made her appearance at the breakfast-table, her father, who had arrived at home the previous evening, after greeting her, asked: "What makes you look so pale, Linda? Are you sick?"

"No, sir; but I did not sleep well."

Mrs. Wetherell did not so much as look toward her daughter, and not another word was spoken during that morning meal, excepting the necessary demands at any table.

All day Linda wandered restlessly, awaiting the arrival of the evening paper, and, perhaps, a letter from Ben.

Evening came at last, and the stage brought the irrepressible Major Warren to the door. Linda watched him, as he came up the walk with his quick step and pompous bearing, and saw her mother meet him with charming grace and earnest welcome.

"My dear Mrs. Wetherell, how are you? and how is my fair future bride?" asked the Major, all in one breath.

"I am in excellent health, my dear Major, and your future bride —".

"Is as charming as ever," interrupted the Major.

"Yes, she is a charming girl, if she is mine, or rather yours," said Mrs. Wetherell, coquettishly. "She has finally consented

to your marriage on her eighteenth birthday, which will be in
a little less than three months, as you urged so strongly in your
last letter it should take place speedily."

"My dear madam, I assure you I will be the happiest man in
the world," said the Major, jubilantly.

"You must not expect too much, for she is a thoroughly
spoiled child. Still, you need have no doubts. I assure you
she loves you very fondly, and is delighted with her approaching marriage; only some girls have such ridiculous notions. I
fear, to all appearances, you will find her as arbitrary as formerly."

"My dear Mrs. Wetherell, fear nothing on my account. I
am a persistent man; and, as long as I have made up my mind
to marry your daughter, I will have her."

"I admire your force of character," said Mrs. Wetherell,
warmly. "You shall have my daughter with pleasure. You
are a genuine man, one after my own heart. Linda will be
with you presently. In the meantime, I will leave you to be
entertained by the Captain, whom I see coming. Perhaps it
would be well to broach the subject of your approaching marriage to him, as I have not thought it prudent to speak of it
until all your arrangements were finally completed."

Although Linda's door was closed, she could distinctly hear
every word that was spoken in the adjoining room. The effec'.
of that conversation can better be imagined than described. An
insupportable loathing for such foulness of purpose and vile hy-
pocrisy took possession of her, and she vowed again that death
would be preferable to a marriage with Major Warren.

She held in her hand the paper for which she had so anxiously
waited, but the arrival of Major Warren quite drove it from her
mind. Slowly she unfolded it, and began her search for what
might solve the mystery concerning Ben. Her first glance dis-

covered nothing, and thinking, after all, she had been uselessly alarmed, began reading an article headed, in great capital letters, "The teamster identifies the man who robbed him." Just below the heading her eye caught the sentence, "Ben Wetherell was arrested yesterday by the sheriff on the testimony of the teamster."

The paper dropped from her hands, and she fell back in her chair perfectly unconscious.

The family was seated at the table, and dinner served; still, Linda did not make her appearance.

"Bridget," said Mrs. Wetherell to the general housemaid, "go to Miss Linda's room, and tell her we are at dinner."

Bridget knocked at the door, but receiving no answer, opened it, and found Linda still insensible. In her horror she screamed loudly, which brought the party from the table into the room, and also aided in bringing Linda to her senses.

The Captain, from genuine alarm and anxiety for Linda, went for a physician. On his arrival, she said to him:

"Doctor, I am not ill. Nothing ails me but that," pointing to the paper. "But please let me remain in bed, and tell father and mother I must have perfect quiet and rest."

The Doctor readily granted her request, for she had a way of asking and commanding so pleasantly, it was almost impossible to tell upon whom the favor was conferred.

Bridget was very attentive, and when Linda refused to eat, said in her rough way:

"Remimber Mr. Ben, Miss Linda. Sure and ye can't help 'im a lyin' here on ye're back; and if ye won't ate, how do ye iver expect to git up?"

"You are right, Bridget; I must eat and I must act, and not lie here repining."

In spite of her good resolutions, the tears ran down her

cheeks. Ben had been her great hope, and now that he was taken from her, and in such an ignominious way, the poor girl felt crushed to the earth. What wounded her most deeply was the manner in which the affair had been commented upon in the dining-room immediately after she had recovered her self-possession.

The Captain seemed greatly shocked, but relieved himself of all responsibility by saying: "I did my duty by that boy; but he was an imp of Satan from his birth."

The mother exclaimed fiercely. "A thief! an outlaw, my son! I have no son! Captain, do you hear? We have no son! To us he is dead. Let the law take its course."

"You are right, my amiable spouse; we should never have had any son," said the Captain, earnestly. "I am glad you do not let your motherly feelings overcome your better judgment, and you can so firmly disown your son."

To Major Warren the Captain's words and manner implied simply what was spoken; but to Mrs. Wetherell they were of other import, and her face grew paler, and her black eyes burned with a dangerous light, as she steadily gazed upon the speaker's unconscious, saintly face, like a tigress ready to spring upon and annihilate her prey.

Turning to the Major, she said, with a strange, disappointed tone:

"I suffer for you, Major, with regard to Linda. You cannot think of uniting your most honorable position with that of one whose brother"—with much feeling—"is an outlaw."

"My dear madam, you misjudge me," answered the Major, with an imperious air. "No stain upon the family name of the woman I marry can reach me. Au contraire, madam, I am more anxious than ever to hasten our marriage. I feel I am performing an act of kindness in marrying your daughter,

8 *

and shall fear no further opposition on her part, knowing, as she must, few would marry her under the present circumstances."

"You are your noble self forever!" exclaimed Mrs. Wetherell. "I shall be only too proud to welcome you to my heart, instead of him who is gone, but whom I loved tenderly and well."

"Control yourself, dear madam," said the Major, kindly, taking her hand. "I pity you from the depths of my heart."

The Captain, who had been sitting quite apart, took up his gold-headed cane and silently left the room, to walk up town with the downcast air of a martyr, and call forth the sympathy of every one he met.

Major Warren led Mrs. Wetherell into the parlor, using all his eloquence to divert her mind and soothe her sorrow.

She had hard work to play the aggrieved parent to perfection, for her joy was complete, to think the rich old Major was still to be her son-in-law. Her only grief had been lest he would not care to fulfil his marriage contract with Linda.

In the meantime there had been a soft tap at Linda's door, and Mrs. Gray had entered in response to the gentle "Come in." Her sympathizing heart fully comprehended Linda's misfortune. She talked freely, without wounding, and Linda felt half the heavy burden was gone, in the friendly, confident manner she could talk and speculate on the probabilities and improbabilities of such an act on Ben's part. She seemed only to think of him in his trouble, and frequently exclaimed: "Pity him, Mrs. Gray! I know he is not guilty."

"I am sure not, dear," said Mrs. Gray, earnestly; "but you are the one I pity most. Walter and George both wished me to say, if there is anything in the world they can do for you, you are to call upon them unhesitatingly. They will be only too happy in serving you."

"How good and kind you are," said Linda, with tears in her eyes. "I thank you with all my heart. To-morrow I hope to hear from Ben ; then, perhaps, something can be done. In the meantime I shall remain in bed, to avoid Mr. Warren, who arrived last night."

That evening Nellie took her usual seat at George's side, to question him on the all-absorbing topic of Linda's trouble.

"George, dear, do you really think young Wetherell is guilty of that outrageous crime ?"

"It is hard to tell, Nellie ; but there seems little doubt, as the teamster has so positively identified him."

"It is shocking ! I never, in my life, felt for any one as I do for Linda."

"She is a noble girl, and very different from the rest of the family," added George.

"Yes, dear ; and she is so cheerful and hopeful in her trouble. Her father and mother deliberately disowned Ben as soon as they heard of this affair ; so the poor child has no sympathy at home. But, then, she never had from her mother. Oh, George, I think it would break my heart, if I could not think of my dear mother with holy reverence and love."

"Yes, darling ; it is a great source of happiness to recall those who are near and dear to us with affection, and have reason to cherish their memory when they are gone. You know how good mother always was. What a whole soul of love and tender anxiety she bestowed upon us ; and her thoughtful care is over us to-day as when I was a child."

"We have much to be thankful for in our family love, dear, especially when we see those around us yearning for such love. But can you not think of some way by which Ben might escape the full penalty of the law, for Linda's sake?"

"No, Nellie ; I do not think any interference would save him.

If this act was lightly passed over, it would very soon be re-peated; and the only way of quelling such lawlessness is in bringing the criminals to immediate punishment."

"That may be true, George; but think how our sweet friend we love so much will have to suffer.   You have no idea how her poor wounded heart is bleeding from this last blow of family dishonor, for she is extremely sensitive."

"Of course, it is a great sorrow and lasting disgrace.   George, dear," said Nellie, timidly, as she pressed her husband's hand tighter in hers, "did it ever occur to you that Walter was very fond of Linda?"

"No; he despises the whole family so thoroughly, he would never think more of her than as a friend."

"I am not so sure of that; and I have been very much bothered about Belle Burton, for I really think Walter loves Linda."

"Well, if he does, I hope he will marry her, and take her entirely away from the rest of the family."

"But what will become of Belle?"

"My opinion about Belle is not very flattering, Nellie.   She was always a gay, fashionable woman of the world, who made no effort to find Walter until about a year ago.   The truth is, she is no longer young, and does not exactly like the idea of being an old maid, after the score of admirers she has had. So she managed to open a correspondence with Walter, in hope of renewing their old relationship."

"Perhaps you do not quite understand the case," said Nellie, partly convinced, "but of the same opinion still."

"I would be sorry to misjudge her.   It certainly would be pleasanter to have Walter marry Linda, because we all know her and love her; but I think it will never be, especially now— Walter is so high-spirited, and thinks so much of family honor.

Not that he would think less of Linda, but it is doubtful if he would ever marry into such a family. My dear little wife," said George, fondly, "you are always worrying over some one's troubles. Especially, if there is the least chance of their getting married, you waste an immense deal of sympathy on them. One would think you had been shipwrecked on the shoals and reefs of matrimony, — that uncertain sea, so difficult to navigate, — and were trying to pilot others more safely."

"George, dear, how can you talk so?" and the little wife nestled closer to her husband. "It seems a sin for happy people to joke over others' misfortunes. You have always been such a good darling, we could not well be otherwise than happy."

"Indeed! is that it?" laughed George. "I always thought it was because you were so good."

"No, George. There must be a good husband where there is a cheerful, happy wife and mother."

"Exceptio probat regulam. In fact, there are exceptions to all rules, Nellie."

"There is no exception to this rule. A good woman may drag through necessary duties, as the wife of an unloving, uncongenial husband, with apparent cheerfulness and contentment, but in time her smile becomes forced, her eyes lack the fire of life, her cheeks lose their rosy tint, her step its elasticity; in fact, her whole appearance becomes a settled melancholy, when the labor of life goes on without the friendly companionship of an appreciative husband. Even her children's prattle grates upon her nerves, and their merry laughter drops heavily into her hollow heart, and each day grows longer and wearier as she plods on and on. But take me for an example of my rule. I am one who does the best she can, and although fa-

from perfect, expects her husband's kind smile and pleasant evening chat as the reward of the day's labor; while he, dear soul, will not let her sew on the children's aprons after dark, but rather play a game of chess and beat her to death; and thinks when his day's labor ends her's should. Such a husband will always have a good wife, because labor for those we love, and who love us, is one of the few pleasures that engender real peace and contentment."

"Is that your wise conclusion, after years of mature deliberation?" asked George, quite amused at her earnestness over what she professed never to have experienced. He continued, more seriously, "If you are convinced of your opinions, and I of mine, my dear little woman, we must be a wonderfully good couple."

"Not so good, dear, but what we might be better; but we do our duty as well as we know how, and that makes life easy. Besides, when troubles come, we explain them away, kiss and make up, and start on again, just the same. So our mole-hills never become mountains — they are only mole-hills, that make us laugh, after we are past them, that they ever should have been in our way."

CHAPTER XVII.

DESPERATE COMPANY.

THE next morning, when the first rays of dawn were breaking over the horizon, Linda arose, dressed herself quietly, and started out into the uncertain light. The roads were muddy, and the sticky clay, peculiar to that mountainous region, made walking very fatiguing. She hurried through the town, and taking the Nevada road, walked rapidly over hills and down dales until compelled to stop and rest. Fortunately, there were few persons on the road so early in the morning, and when she heard any one approaching, she stepped behind some friendly bush until they had passed. It was not yet seven o'clock when she reached Nevada. She stopped at a restaurant, the only one in the place, and asked for a cup of coffee. The proprietor, who was also head waiter, brought her the coffee and a steaming breakfast.

Linda expressed so much astonishment at the sumptuous manner in which her simple order had been filled, that she quite upset the good-hearted German, and he stammered a most awkward apology:

"Ich keeps a zimlich cheep restaurant, ma'am, und ven any pody cums lookin' hunrich, like you, by Got, Ich gibs 'em all dey can eàt, und says, Das ish fur der Lord. Das ish all die relichion Ich hab."

Linda fancied she must have presented a very hungry appearance, from the amount of sympathy she drew from that honest German's heart. She was so pale from her sleepless nights, and exhausted from the long walk to Nevada, that she did indeed appear in need of sympathy. She ate heartily, for the breakfast was tempting, and she was soon ready to undertake her difficult task. Upon offering to pay her host, it took considerable persuasion to induce the old German to accept the money; he seemed to think he had no business with it, as it interfered with his charity.

It was but a short walk from the restaurant to the jail. There was no one in sight, so Linda mounted the steps and knocked at the iron-barred door. The jailor immediately made his appearance at the grating, and asked, "Who is there?" When he saw it was a woman, he said, roughly:

"What do you want?"

"I would like to see Mr. Wetherell, if you please," said Linda, quite afraid of the rough specimen of humanity peering through the grating.

"But I don't please; not if I know myself, and I think I do," said the man, yawning.

"Can I not see him for one moment?" pleaded Linda.

"Let me introduce to your respectful notice, Mr. Jacob Sniffens. When you know Jake Sniffens, you know a man what is a man — a man as keeps his word."

Linda felt discouraged, but asked again imploringly, "Can I not speak a few words to him through the grating?"

"Can you hyer, or can't you hyer?" said Mr. Jacob Sniffens, fiercely. "I never could get along with petticoats. Them and me don't hitch somehow. When I says no to a man, he walks off in a style becoming so high a functionary as a pair of pantaloons; but when I says no to a woman, she stands there a blubberin', and teasin', and tormentin' of a fellow as natural as if she had a self-acting pump inside o' her."

The tears rolled down Linda's cheeks, and it was with great effort she asked: "Where can I find the sheriff?"

"Well, I think you can't find him," said Mr. Sniffens, coolly. "He's went to Sacramento after that ere other cuss in the same line of business as your sweetheart; only he robbed the stage — a darned site decenter job."

"When will he be back?" asked Linda, without appearing to notice his insulting remarks.

"He won't be back afore day after to-morrow, and maybe not then. Have you got any more questions to ask?"

"No, sir; but will you please tell Mr. Wetherell his sister came to see him, and was not admitted?"

As Linda went away, she heard the insolent fellow laughing.

"Sister! That's good! That's excellent! Them women folks must think Jake Sniffens is green."

When Linda was out of hearing, he said, after considerable reflection: "I guess I'll not trouble that ere young devil with that ere message, for like enough he'd try to get out, and the sheriff bein' away, Jake's head might come to grief. I wouldn't trust that imp of Satan if he was reposin' in Abraham's bosom."

Linda had no alternative but to retrace her steps. She knew Bridget would miss her, but had arranged that by saying she might go to Mrs. Gray's.

The kind German's breakfast was a lucky deed of charity, notwithstanding it was paid for. Linda's disappointment at not seeing her brother, after the fatigue of the morning, almost prostrated her. She longed to rest in some quiet place, but the dread of being interrogated and stared at, prevented her entering a strange house, so she wearily went on her way. When some distance from Nevada she noticed a by-path, which seemed a nearer road to Grass Valley. She followed it through the thick chaparral until she came to a little eminence, from which she saw the smoke from a chimney of a log cabin. It was not far distant, and she hailed it with delight, thinking the humble inmates might be kind enough to let her rest there. She had no sooner approached the cabin, and stepped upon the great log steps, and taken one glance at the interior, than she comprehended her position and mistake. There were three men lying in bunks, who started at her approach; and one of them, with long, black, curly hair, who proved to be the famous "Curly Smith," exclaimed:

"Hellow! Where the devil did you come from? Walk in, sis. You've struck a good camp. We are in need of petti-

9   G

coats, since Jennie on the Green went down to Boston Ravine to live."

Linda started to run, pale as a ghost, and almost fainting from fear. Curly Smith jumped to the floor, calling, "Come back here, or I'll bring you back."

Just then, a man who was lying on some straw in what seemed a dog kennel, only larger, and like a small addition to the cabin, said to Linda, in a loud whisper, as she was passing, "Take this."

As a drowning man will grasp after a straw, Linda grasped the pistol the stranger offered her. She had never fired one, although she had handled them and understood how to use them; for the country was so wild, almost every one carried weapons of some description. As Curly Smith was determined to pursue her, she knew running was out of the question. She turned suddenly, and raising her pistol, said, with the firmness despair only brings, "Stand off, sir, or I'll shoot!"

"You will, will you?" said Curly, with a contemptuous sneer. "Two can play that game. My kitten, you will find yourself in a lion's paws before you get through."

"Hold," said the man coming out of the kennel. "If you touch that girl, I'll spill your vile blood for you." He immediately drew another pistol from his belt, and, aiming it at Smith, stood at Linda's side.

The two men in the cabin had come out in the meantime, and both with one voice said, "We'll back you, Bob; sail in."

The plot of ground where this strange group stood was brown and seared from the scorching summer sun. They were completely hedged in with chaparral and underbrush on all sides, only relieved by the brown cabin to their right, with its blue smoke wreathing toward the purer blue of the mountain sky.

Beyond the cabin, the pine-covered mountains seemed to touch the very heavens, while down to the left rushed a foaming stream, almost lost in the labyrinth of luxuriant greens. There seemed to be no outlet to the place, it was so isolated from human habitations, and so thickly woven in the mountain forest.

Linda looked superbly beautiful, as she stood there, pistol in hand, ready to shoot at one of the most desperate villains the Sierra Nevada Mountains ever knew. Her slight, maidenly form seemed little in accordance with her position. Her hat had fallen back, and her soft brown hair was dishevelled; her face was perfectly colorless; but her large, luminous eyes blazed like flashes of fire, as she cast eager glances at those desperate men in whose hands her destiny lay.

Curly Smith was dressed in black pants and a gray flannel shirt. He wore a broad leather belt around his waist, which contained a second pistol and a knife; and his companions were all similarly attired. Curly would not have been a homely man, but for the fiendish expression of his small, black eyes. His hair, which was jet black, hung in a mat of small curls about his neck and over his shoulders, from which peculiarity he received the cognomen of "Curly Smith." He was a desperate-looking man, and one of the most dangerous and unrelenting in the mountain gangs. On one side of Linda stood her friend of the kennel, a man with a handsome, benign countenance, quite out of place in a desperado. On her other side were the two who had come out of the cabin, and apparently equal companions with Curly Smith, although, by some strange influence, entirely controlled by the milder man.

Smith laughed a low, fiendish laugh, as he said, in a deep, discordant voice:

"Is this the way you miserable drones respect my laws? I'll show you what Curly Smith says shall be done, and if words

won't do, I'll put a hole through you that will make you remember." Saying this, he aimed at Linda's first friend.
There was a click of pistols, and four were pointed at Smith.
Linda, in her excitement, bore a little heavily on the trigger,
and her pistol went off, the ball passing through Smith's sleeve.
He was said to have known no fear, but he dropped his weapon
as the ball grazed his arm, saying, doggedly, "Four against
one is not fair play."

The men were astonished at Linda's shooting. Thinking
she had done it intentionally, her first friend said:

"She is a trump, by George. Curly Smith, if you, who
dote on courage, can beat her, you may fight her."

"I move," said another, "that we three escort her to the
road."

"Escort her to ——, if you like. Such spoonies as you
would make a fine howling congregation," said Curly, as he
disappeared within the cabin.

One of the men said to Linda's first friend, "Bob, you can
have the pleasure of seeing this young lady home ; but be back
by dark, for we will want you."

The two men then followed Curly into the cabin. Linda and
her friend went quickly along the narrow path for some distance
without exchanging a word, Bob leading the way, and Linda
following closely. Finally, feeling quite faint after her unnatural excitement, and coming into a more open country, Linda
asked, wearily :

"Can I not sit down on this log and rest a while? I am so
tired."

"Yes, certainly," said her escort, stopping at once, but
keeping at a respectful distance. "We are so near the main
road here, there is no danger. I hurried to get as far away
from the cabin as possible, for, if Curly Smith had taken a

notion to come after us, he would have come. How in the world did you chance to come to his cabin?"

"I was on my way from Nevada when I saw the path leading off toward Grass Valley, and thinking it a shorter route, followed it. But who is Curly Smith?"

"He is one of the most desperate, daring villains in these mountains."

"How can I ever thank you for your kindness to me this day?"

"Do not thank me at all. I am not overly tender or gentle, Miss; but, somehow or other, the moment I saw you, to-day, you brought back to my mind so forcibly one who is gone from me, that at first sight of you I would almost have sworn it was she. She had brown eyes and hair like yours, and if she had only lived, Bob Rivers would have been a different man. I can be bold and daring with the rest of them until I think of my lost Fannie, then I weaken. You can thank Fannie, the sweetest angel in heaven, for taking care of you to-day, and not me."

"Let us hope that her holy influence may yet take as good care of you, and bring you out of trouble to peace as safely, as it has done me to-day."

"Safe?" asked Bob Rivers, bitterly. "You think you are safe, do you?"

"Yes, with you I feel I am perfectly safe," said Linda, earnestly. "How could it be otherwise, after your kind protection to-day? Notwithstanding you attribute it to my likeness to Fannie, I am sure it was due more to your own noble sense of honor."

"Really, Miss, you make me feel more like a man than I have felt for many a long day. You are safe with me, but there are few men, let alone young girls, who would consider them-
9*

selves safe on this lonely mountain path, hedged in on all sides with thick chaparral, in company with Bob Rivers."

"Is Bob Rivers, then, so desperate a character as he is pictured by himself?" asked Linda, kindly.

"Bob Rivers," continued her companion, "was once a gentleman; but a calamity befell him, and he is living to redress it. I told you I owed Curly Smith a grudge.   It is a little thing, perhaps only the loss of peace and happiness."

"You are not half so bad as you think, or you could not so clearly define your own position.   You are not lost to all sense of goodness, and I hope to hear better things of you in the future.   Have you ever heard of Ben Wetherell, who is under arrest for having robbed a teamster?"

It was with great effort Linda asked that question of her companion, but it occurred to her if Ben was guilty, such a man would likely know it.

"Yes, I knew him by sight.   He was a fine, brave fellow; and I don't see how he got into such a mean scrape.   He was a great hunter, and used to go all over these mountains.   Everybody knew who he was, and liked him, and no one molested him.   Once, a couple of our men, just from over the mountains, were out on a lark.   They stopped Wetherell, and politely asked for his purse.   He turned on them, and they faced about and left in double quick.   He was a brave fellow."

"Do you think he is guilty?"

"Guilty?   To be sure.   The teamster swears to his identity; and that very afternoon I saw him out hunting, dressed just as the teamster described him.   His partners, poor fellows, feel dreadfully cut up about it, and think him perfectly innocent; but they say he was out hunting that afternoon later than usual, and was still away at the time the teamster was robbed.   Great

God! what ails you?" and Bob sprang forward just in time
· to catch Linda in his arms as she staggered and fell.

The excitement of the day and her bodily fatigue had quite
exhausted her; and this final blow, this man's positive asser-
tion of Ben's guilt, felled her to the ground.

CHAPTER XVIII.

THE DISCARDED DAUGHTER.

BOB RIVERS had never before seen a lady faint, and his
first impression was that she was dead. He did not dare
go for assistance, lest it might be thought he had been the
cause of her death; still, he could not leave her there alone.
Finally, it flashed upon him that some delicate persons became
unconscious and still lived. With that idea, he rushed through
the thick brush to the running stream, saturated his handkerchief and filled his hat with water. When he returned, and
found her still insensible, he quietly, and gently as a woman,
bathed her face and hands, and moistened her colorless lips.
Soon she moved, gasped for breath; then opened her eyes and
stared wildly around. Bob's reassuring words that she was
safe, soon brought her back to a perfect realization of her
position.

It was some time before she was able to undertake the remainder of her journey, although Bob assured her it was not
more than half a mile. Grass Valley was a country town and a
long town, the principal part being built on two streets that
formed a perfect right angle. After reaching Main Street, where
the settlement began, it was fully half a mile to Linda's home.

Her feet were wet, her dress muddy, her hair in disorder, and her whole appearance so remarkable she dreaded the prying eyes of the villagers.

When she recovered herself sufficiently to continue her walk, Bob kindly offered her his assistance. She took his arm, and was thankful for his strong support, until they reached the edge of the town, when he said:

"I am sorry, but I must leave you here, Miss. I dare not go any farther."

"I am sorry, too, my friend," and Linda offered him her hand. "I cannot thank you enough for your kindness to me to-day. If my humble prayers can avail you anything, they shall be offered up nightly, that the remembrance of Fannie may yet bring you back to the paths of rectitude. Here is the pistol you so kindly gave me. I almost forgot to return it."

"Please keep it," said Bob, beseechingly. "Carry it; if you should ever go alone again, it may serve you."

"I will not deprive you of it."

"I have more; and if you will only honor me by accepting such a poor gift from so unworthy a personage, you will make me happy."

"Then I will keep it, and the giver shall always be kindly remembered."

"May I not know the young lady's name I have had the pleasure of escorting to-day?" asked Bob, with all the deferential grace of a polished gentleman.

"I am Linda Wetherell, Ben's sister. I went to Nevada to-day to try and see him, but was unsuccessful."

"Mr. Wetherell is fortunate in having such a sister. If he is worthy of you, and I believe him to be a good fellow, you may yet save him."

"Thank you for those comforting words. I hope we may

meet again." She was turning to go, when Bob delayed her by saying:

"If you ever have occasion to wander in the mountains, and are in danger, mention my name; and if I can be found, I will be your obedient servant."

A buggy went dashing past, containing a lady and gentleman. It was her mother, with Major Warren. Linda started as if shot. She knew her mother's piercing black eyes had seen her bidding Bob Rivers good-by. Fortunately, Mr. Warren's attention was so entirely engrossed by his unruly horses that he noticed nothing.

The shock seemed to strengthen Linda for the remainder of her walk home. She hurried along, meeting few she knew, and no one appeared to take especial notice of her. On reaching home, she went quietly to her own room, arranged her toilette, and called Bridget, to find out whether her mother had been inquiring for her.

"To be sure," said Bridget, "yer mither was after askin' for ye; for, bless yer swate sowl, the grand Major was after wantin' to take ye ridin'. So I tould 'er ye were at Mrs. Gray's; and she wint there after ye, but come home and jawed me up and jawed me down; said I was a liar, and in wid ye, and if I did n't moind me ane business, I might take mesilf off, bag and baggage, the first of the month."

"I am sorry it caused you so much trouble," said Linda, kindly; "but I hope it will not prove serious."

"Sure, ye nade n't bother yer dear sowl about me," said Bridget, apparently not bothered about herself. "She'll not be after sindin' me off in a hurry. Faith she can't find another that 'd put up with her impudence."

"Bridget, you forget yourself sometimes. You must speak more respectfully of my mother," said Linda, firmly.

"Disrespictful! Is it me ye would call disrespictful? Be the stick, I niver said a disrespictful word of a livin' craythur, espichially of yer mither, for she's a foine-lookin' lady, if she is the biggest divil I ever saw. How she iver begot such a swate little craythur as yersilf, Miss Linda, faith it's beyand the power o' mortal to tell; but I'm after thinkin' the blissed angel Gabriel smoiled on the divil about that toime."

Bridget was perfectly incorrigible, and Linda wisely concluded to let her chatter in her harmless way. The twig had not been properly bent in girlhood, and the sturdy tree withstood all attempts at improvement and cultivation.

It was quite late in the afternoon when Linda had a delicate lunch, after which she laid down, and slept sweetly, until awakened by Bridget, who came with a message from Mrs. Wetherell requesting her to be present at tea that evening.

Linda accepted the request as a command, and hastened to comply. On entering the supper-room, Major Warren came toward her to shake hands, but she gave him a stately bow, and passed on to her seat.

"Your mother assures me we are to be the best of friends now, Miss Linda," said the Major, with a simpering smile.

"You should not hold the daughter accountable for what the mother may say, Major Warren," replied Linda, coldly.

The Major's countenance darkened, but he did not reply. It was the first time Linda had ever spoken disrespectfully of her mother, and Mrs. Wetherell's face showed she felt it keenly. Perhaps it was the loss of her power over Linda she felt. It was only an instantaneous flash, but Linda's quick eye read it, and her own face was suffused with blushes.

Mrs. Wetherell never allowed her feelings in any way to betray her, and while the spasmodic indication of annoyance flashed over her dark, oval face, she darted an angry glance at

Linda, and changed the conversation in a sprightly, racy manner, that can only be done by a shrewd woman of the world.

'There are many modest tea-tables, where the frugal meal begins with grace and ends with a blessing, whereat are played
finer plays and better acted than often appear behind the foot-
lights of the world-famed theatres. Mrs. Wetherell's whole
life seemed to be one studied part, in which the real woman
seldom appeared.

After the evening meal, Captain Wetherell asked Major Warren to accompany him up town, to which he assented, much to
Linda's relief; but it only proved a respite from one terror to
encounter another. She was going to her room to pass the
evening alone, as was her habit, when Mrs. Wetherell called her
back.

"Linda,.I wish to have one more conversation with you in
regard to your marriage with Major Warren, which is to take
place a little more than two months from now. You must give
him your answer in person. You should feel flattered to think
he would marry you, disgraced as you are by your brother. As
I have already told you, in marrying him you will be independ-
ent financially, and in becoming Mrs. Major Warren the old
dishonored name of Wetherell will be lost, and, it is hoped,
forgotten. You do not know your own good; and I ask you
again kindly, hoping you have wisdom enough to decide to
your own future advantage."

"I have decided, mother," said Linda, firmly but respectfully. "I decided in the beginning. I told you then, and
repeat it now, I never will take sacred vows upon myself I positively can never fulfil, or be the wife of any man so thoroughly
obnoxious to me, were he as rich as Crœsus."

"Is that your final answer?" hissed Mrs. Wetherell between
her teeth.

"Yes, mother, that can be my only answer," replied Linda, while her soft brown eyes pleaded more eloquently than words.

"Then, undutiful girl, you shall be nothing more to me!" and Mrs. Wetherell paced the floor rapidly. She looked a fiend in her grand rage. Suddenly stopping before Linda, she exclaimed :

"Go from my presence. Before to-morrow noon you shall be on your way to Nevada, where you can remain near your well-mated brother. Anything to get you out of my sight! I am, indeed, blessed in *my* children — one a highwayman, the other an outcast! I will see that your board is paid and you have clothes to wear, but I never wish to lay my eyes upon your face again, unless you change your present decision. So long as you persist in your wilful course, you are no longer my daughter."

"Oh, mother," pleaded Linda, but her sobs choked her further utterance.

"Go, I say; I hate your very presence!" and Mrs. Wetherell stood cold and unbending, pointing toward the open door, until Linda, with her head bowed and weeping bitterly, passed submissively through the dining-room into her own quiet chamber, where, unmolested, she could pour forth the bitterness of her sorrow, and reflect upon her cheerless future. Her mother never threatened without executing, and she knew, before the close of another day, her home would be among strangers.

The Major had received a telegraphic despatch to return home at once. The midnight stage would take him away, and she had no fear of her mother seeking her under any circumstances; so, endeavoring to conceal the traces of grief her weeping had made, she went out into the friendly darkness, and was soon at the cottage.

Nellie, with her gentle, warm heart, was always ready to greet her. George and Walter were also there to welcome her, and they saw, by the pale, haggard face and bloodshot eyes, what struggles the poor girl had passed through.

"Linda," said Nellie, "your mother was here this morning inquiring after you, but I could not give her any account of you. About noon I went over to see you, but Bridget said you were not at home. Your bed was tumbled, but you had evidently not slept in it last night. You must tell me where you have been, little truant."

Linda's face flushed as she thought of her venturesome day. "I will some time, but am too tired to-night. I came to say to you," and she drew her chair closer to Nellie's, as George and Walter were talking over some business arrangements, "that I must leave you to-morrow."

"Leave us to-morrow?"

"Yes." Linda tried to suppress the tears that seemed ready to flow continually in her long days of grief. "I must leave you, my best, my only friends. Mother has told me I must go to Nevada to live, but I have no idea with whom."

"Why are you to go there?"

"The same old feud — because I will not marry Major Warren."

"You poor child!" Nellie's eyes were filled with tears. "Could your mother be persuaded to let you stay with us? We would be so happy to have you. Would we not, George?"

"Yes, my dear, if you say so," answered George, smiling; "but I have not the faintest idea what you are talking about."

"Linda's mother says she must leave home, and I want her to come and stay with us."

"Certainly, Linda. We will be delighted to have you," said George, warmly. "If our little nookery is not big enough,

10

we will gladly enlarge it for such a valuable addition as your-self."

"You are very kind. I thank you with all my heart; but you know father has business near Nevada, and is there quite often —besides," her voice trembled slightly as she added, "Ben is there."

No persuasions would avail to change her purpose, and she left the little cottage, where she had spent so many happy days, with a heavy heart. Walter had been unusually quiet all the evening, and Nellie told her he had been as blue as an in-digo bag ever since she stopped coming there, and if she ceased her visits altogether, she feared he would soon become as dis-agreeable as all other old bachelors.

After affectionate good-nights, with a promise from Nellie to be with her the next day before she went away, and also assur-ances of frequent visits, wherever her future home might be, Linda left the cottage, accompanied by Walter. As they went out into the street, he said :

"If you are to leave us to-morrow, Linda, will you not grant me one parting favor?"

"Yes, certainly, if I can," answered Linda, frankly.

"Then you have said 'yes,' for you can as easily as not. I want you to take a roundabout way to get home. The evening is pleasant, and I want to have a talk with you before you go away. It seems an age since I last saw you, yet it is only a few days. You must not leave me for an indefinite time without some assurance that my hopes are not in vain. Linda, you do not know how dear you are to me. I cannot live without you."

We are all weak, human creatures—often when the spirit says "no" the yielding flesh goes astray. Linda did not in-tend to give Walter this opportunity to address her, but she loved to be with him. Besides, it was her last evening there, perhaps for a long time, and that meant the last of her happiness. "Why not be as happy then as possible?" So they walked and talked over all Ben's troubles and their own future happiness. Finally, Walter asked her why she was going to leave home, and she unhesitatingly told him the cause.

"Go, then, dear Linda. In a few weeks I will bring you proofs that Belle Burton has no claim upon me, and asks none, and you shall be my wife."

Linda's hand trembled within his arm, as she said, quietly:

"It is a great happiness to talk of and hope for, but there seems to be an evil fate that governs my every effort, and all my dreams of happiness are followed in reality by horrid nightmares. Do not talk to me any more, Walter, of love or marriage. When you are free, come; but even then I will dread your coming, for my mother has cursed my union with any other person than Major Warren."

"My poor little girl!" said Walter, tenderly. "A mother's curse should not be feared, when you are innocent and she guilty. So long as you do that which is right, you will not suffer from her ambitious designs."

"But, Walter, she will make it her life study to make me miserable. You cannot understand the unnatural feelings she has towards me. It seems contrary to all laws of consanguinity. I have longed so for her love and affectionate caresses, and instead I have seen a shudder pass over her frame at my touch. If she knew you loved me," said Linda, timidly, "mark my words, she would turn your love to hatred."

"Never!" said Walter, firmly. "No one shall influence me against the woman I love. If you say but the word, to-morrow shall be our wedding-day, and Walter French will be the happiest man in Nevada County."

"No, Walter, no. You are noble and good, but you must wait until your future wife's brother is out of jail. I would make a sad bride, and be entirely selfish, if I could not now devote myself to poor Ben."

"Then, darling, you can choose your own time, provided it is not too long, and at last I can claim you as my own little wife."

"That you shall, Walter. If you can love such a sorrow-stricken creature as I am, you are welcome to me."

Walter's arm was about her waist; her head nestled on his breast; his lips touched hers, and the plighted hearts beat in ecstatic unison. Nothing but the dull thud of the distant mills broke the stillness of the calm night. Nature seemed hushed in reverence of happiness so full, so sweet, so silent. The very pines ceased their moaning, and when the cold moon peeped from behind the far-off mountains, she seemed a relentless intermeddler, exposing Linda's blushes and Walter's triumphant smiles.

Ah, Linda, a week ago you would have said, "Not until you have heard from Belle Burton!" But Linda was a sad, lonely girl, and she loved Walter. What was Belle Burton to her then?

Weary, but with a happy heart, Linda sank to rest. The old prayers came back in all their freshness, and she thought bitterly, "I can always kneel and pray when I am happy, but grief deadens my senses, and seems to come between me and everything heavenly. The time when all good people say they feel drawn toward God, I am farthest away."

CHAPTER XIX.

MRS. NEAL.

"The life of woman is full of woe,
· Toiling on and on and on,
With breaking heart and tearful eyes
And silent lips, and in the soul
The secret longings that arise,
Which this world never satisfies!
Some more, some less, but of the whole
Not one quite happy, no, not one."
                        Golden Legend.

ON entering the dining-room the next morning, Linda found the breakfast-table arranged for but one. "Ah," she thought, "mother is off already in search of my new home."

"Gude mornin' to yez, Miss Linda," said Bridget, entering with the breakfast. "I hope yez have a gude appetite this mornin'."

"From the number of delicacies you have prepared, you surely expected I would have, Bridget."

"Well, Miss Linda, yer mither tould me to give yez yer breakfast, and thin hilp yez pack yer trunk. Now, that cartainly maines lavin'; and if yez be goin' to lave us, Bid 'll give yez all yez can ate the rist o' yer stay. It's not for me to be axin' questions, but if yez be goin' to lave us, bad luck 'll cum to this house."

"Oh, no, Bridget; there will nothing serious happen. I am only going to Nevada for a while."

"Now yez mark me words, something will happen! Yer

mither got to the gate, and she forgot her gloves, and back she cum. This be Saturday mornin', and bad luck cums to all thim as turns back on a Saturday mornin'. Yez may smile, Miss Linda, but I 've lived to see it mesilf. There was me Uncle Pat Mallerry's boy. He started to work on a Saturday mornin', and whin he got to the door he cums back, and says he: 'Mither, I forgot to tell yez, I think the dapple pony's gettin' a corn on his right fore-foot.' 'Be off wid yez, ye young spalpeen, that yez would turn back on a Saturday mornin' to tell yer ould mither that the dapple pony's gettin' a corn. Bad luck to yer brainless pate, that yez have no better sinse than that,' and, will yez belave it, Miss Linda, before the sun had set that day, Barney Mallerry cum home with his neck broke short off, and it was the dapple pony as throwed him on a pile o' stones. If it don't cum to-day, nor to-morrow, the bad luck 's overtaken yer mither, and ye 'll live to see it.''

Bridget's eloquence was interrupted by the appearance of Nellie Gray's smiling face at the door, with her habitual pleasant greeting:

"Good-morning, Linda. I have come to stay with you until you leave us, dear; that is, if you are still expecting to go to-day."

"I know nothing more than what I told you last evening, excepting that mother left home early this morning," answered Linda, warmly returning Nellie's affectionate embrace. "I imagine she has gone to Nevada in search of my new abiding place, and shall make my preparations for leaving as directed. She seldom changes her mind."

"Then, if you ·must leave us, I will assist you all I can, although I would so much rather you were not going. We will miss you sadly."

While they were arranging for Linda's departure, a carriage

drove up to a cottage on the outskirts of Nevada, which stood in the midst of a neatly-kept garden. A few words from the driver, and Mrs. Wetherell alighted, hastily approached the door, and rapped loudly. In an instant it was opened by a trim, motherly-looking woman in deep mourning. Mrs. Wetherell gave a searching glance of admiration before speaking; so did every one, for the first time seeing Widow Neal. She was of medium height and stout, with quite a round face; her complexion still transparent and her cheeks rosy, notwithstanding forty years of cares and sorrows were indelibly stamped upon her sweet face. But the great feature, that made all look twice and thrice, was the profusion of wavy white locks, loosely but neatly caught back with a band of black velvet.

"Mrs. Neal, I presume?" asked Mrs. Wetherell, very respectfully.

"Yes, madam, I am Mrs. Neal."

"I was told you wanted a lady boarder. Was I rightly informed?"

"Yes, madam, you were." Mrs. Neal spoke slowly, and her voice was very sweet—not one of those simpering, lisping, drawling vocal instruments in use by many women who play at being sweet and fascinating for company or holidays, but a full, clear, well-modulated voice, that was always in tune and never jarred.

Mrs. Wetherell looked steadily into Mrs. Neal's honest brown eyes, as she said :

"I have a daughter, almost eighteen years old, whose health has not been very good in Grass Valley. If I can find a desirable place in Nevada, I wish her to remain here a few months."

"Although I would be very happy to have a young person in the house with me, I fear my home would not be desirable for her. She might find it lonely, as I go out seldom, and am a stranger here."

"That is rather an advantage than otherwise in this case. My daughter is naturally quiet and not inclined to visit a great deal. I was told you were a widow; have you no children?"

"No, madam."

The eloquent regret expressed in those two words did not even escape the hard-hearted, impenetrable Mrs. Wetherell.

"I had an adopted son, who was to have met me here, but my coming was delayed by the illness and death of my mother. Although I have been here two months, and made every effort, I have not yet been able to find him."

Mrs. Wetherell was little interested in others' disappointments or troubles, and thinking Mrs. Neal about to give her a detailed account of family distresses, at once entered upon the business of her visit, and everything was soon satisfactorily arranged.

Agreeing to send her daughter that day, Mrs. Wetherell arose to take her departure. Handing Mrs. Neal a card, she said: "I leave you this, that you may know the name of the young lady you are to expect." With a stately "Good-morning, madam," she took her seat in the carriage, and was soon out of sight.

Mrs. Neal closed the door quietly, thinking, "I am almost sorry I agreed to take that woman's daughter. There is something terribly cold and repellent about her; but then the daughter may be quite different. It is to be hoped so, at least. There is little in a name; still, let me see. 'Mrs. Richard Wetherell.' Can it be possible?"

The card dropped from her hand. It seemed as though an adder had stung her to the heart and drawn all the life-blood, she sat so motionless, looking into space — the space of many years. Instead of the rosy, cheerful Mrs. Neal of the few minutes before, there sat a spectre, whose pale and anguish-stricken countenance told how the hair became so hoary long before the time for frost on her brow. Over that scrap of paper on the floor passed volumes of unwritten history — panoramas of years.

"What a relentless fate!" said the widow, solemnly. "Can there be no mercy in my God? I thought my hopes and joys and very life had been rotting in the past. So many years their ashes were scattered to the winds, that not a trace even of sorrow at their having existed could be found on the earth. I awake to find the outer man and the inner man may change, but the feelings, though changed with all the changes, vibrate to the old touch and shudder at the old agony.

"The Agnes Neal of twenty-four years ago has long been forgotten, and who would recognize her in the Widow Neal of to-day, with these gray locks? Still, there is an elastic cord between the young Agnes and the old — the past and the present — that bends to all oppressions, and stretches over every curve, yet never breaks.

"I thought my happy young life was buried forever, and out of the fragments of what was once lovely I could make a new woman, known only to myself — nobler and better, if possible, from much endurance and hopeful resignation; but I find no workman, however skilful, can tear down a noble edifice and build another of the old materials, and make it strong and beautiful as it was in the beginning.

"After all my studied self-control, my patient longing and waiting for forgetfulness of the past, a simple scrap of paper tears open my heart wounds as if it were but yesterday they were lacerated, and in my desolate future leaves Hope a bleeding corpse as my companion.

"How can I take their child into my house? *Their* child!

How can I prevent her coming? I have no messenger, and if I had, where could I send him? My promise is given; I will keep my word. It may not be for long. If it should be the daughter of the old Richard Wetherell of years gone by, he will never recognize me, perhaps never see me."

The widow passed into a cozy little bedroom and mechanically arranged it for Linda's reception. She was still pale, and the tempest that had swept over her soul had left deep traces; but those who battle always with storms brave the tempests, too. Mrs. Neal's face, though paler and sadder than usual, again wore the peaceful calm of Christian resignation.

CHAPTER XX.

EYES THAT BESPEAK STORMS.

IT was past noon when Mrs. Wetherell alighted at her own door. On entering the house, she spoke politely to Mrs. Gray, and also to Walter, who had come to say good-by. To Linda she simply said:

"Linda, the carriage is at the door, and the driver knows where to take you." then passed into her own room.

Mr. Gray, with the little ones, was at the gate to meet them; and a stranger would have thought Linda the pet of a loving household, about to leave home, rather than a sad-hearted girl forcibly sent away. Although they did not see her, Mrs. Wetherell stood at the window watching the group so attentively that not a single glance escaped her hawk-like eyes. She noted every movement with greedy pleasure, particularly the long pressure of the hand and tender good-by of Walter.

Well for them they saw not the flash of her black eyes, and knew not a storm-cloud was gathering to burst with all the fury of a vengeful woman over their happiness. May the gentle winds of heaven waft it beyond their heads.

The ride seemed interminable to Linda, not knowing her destination; and she was too proud to expose her ignorance to the driver by asking questions; so it was with a strange mixture of relief and dread she ascended the steps of her future home. Before she had time to rap, the door was opened by Mrs. Neal. For an instant, they silently regarded each other, and during that interval, by one of those strange, magnetic influences most of us experience, but none can define, they were friends.

"I am glad you have arrived, dear," said Mrs. Neal, putting her arm affectionately about Linda, and kissing her as quietly and motherly as if she had known her always.

Sometimes pleasant surprises are as great a shock as unpleasant ones, and Linda, who had expected only unhappiness after her removal from home and friends, was so overcome by the kind greeting, that she burst into tears as she returned the motherly embrace.

"My dear child, do not cry," said Mrs. Neal, as she led her to a sofa, and drew her head upon her shoulder. "I can readily understand; you must feel badly at leaving home, and I fear you will not be happy here. It was unfortunate your mother insisted upon your coming. My humble home will be entirely too lonely for you, with no one but me."

"No one here but you and me?" asked Linda.

"No one, my dear," answered Mrs. Neal, in her sadly-sweet way.

"Oh, how delightful that will be!" exclaimed Linda, smiling through her tears.

Mrs. Neal, in amazement, asked: "Did your mother not tell you how lonely this place would be?"

"My mother told me nothing. I had no idea where I was going until I arrived."

"That is strange," said Mrs. Neal, thoughtfully, raising her anxious eyes to Linda's face.

"It is not half so strange as many other things she does," said Linda, bitterly. "Did she tell you she was sending me away from home forever?"

"No, dear, she did not."

"Then, before you open your noble heart so generously to take me into your dear little home, it is only just to tell you why and how I am sent here."

Linda did not usually form sudden attachments, but with Mrs. Neal it proved a case of love at first sight. Not a strange thing either, for every one who knew Mrs. Neal loved her.

The clock struck six when she withdrew her hand from Linda's and imprinted a motherly kiss upon her forehead.

"You are young, child, to have such sorrow; but you will bear it bravely, for you have real womanly nobility of character. Troubles kill weak women, but they strengthen the strong. Those who suffer intensely enjoy intensely, and can better comprehend this wonderful world, with its multitudes of human beings, all suffering and enduring. It is a divine gift, to be able to suffer and accept it as the chastening rod of a merciful Father. If the burden is heavy, the reward is great. It may be long in coming, but it will come, although how or when we can none of us tell. At thirty years of age, my hair was as white as it is to-day. Some time I will tell you what made it white, for one's troubles are easier borne when one knows others have suffered more. I have always been very grateful that my hair alone was changed and my mind left active and vigorous.

No matter how hard our trials or numerous our afflictions, we can always find something left to be grateful for ; and the little blessings hidden away from human sight by sorrows are doubly sweet."

"Oh, you are so noble and good ! " burst forth Linda, grasping both her hands. "Everything seems easier to bear already. And you have no one to care for but this adopted son, and you cannot find him. Will you not let me love you, and be a daughter to you? and please love me a little in return. I have always yearned so for a mother's love."

"Yes, dear, you shall be a daughter to me in my loneliness, and I will be a mother to you."

The promise was sealed with a kiss and embrace ; and as Linda raised her head from her new mother's shoulder, she asked, timidly, "May I call you Mother Neal?"

"Yes, child, what you choose ; but it is past our supper hour, my dear, and I will leave you to amuse yourself while I go to prepare it."

"But if I am to be your daughter, you must let me share your labors."

"As you like, my child," said Mrs. Neal, smiling. "My daughter must feel perfectly at home, that she may never weary of her humble choice."

So sweetly began Linda's residence with Mrs. Neal. Her first letters to Walter and Nellie, instead of being homesick, tear-stained epistles, were simply happy eulogies on Mrs. Neal and her new home, ending by saying: "I know you will love her, too, for you cannot help it."

Not a week had yet elapsed when Linda was surprised by a visit from her faithful friend Mrs. Gray, accompanied by Walter. Mrs. Neal's welcome to them was so quiet and sincere, every movement and every word so subdued and ladylike, that

11

Walter and Nellie did just as Linda said they would, "loved her too."

As soon as Nellie and Linda were left alone, Nellie put her arms about Linda and embraced her warmly, saying: "Walter has told me all about it, dear, on the way coming up here, and I am so delighted. I will visit with Mrs. Neal, who is just as lovely as she can be; and you shall take a long ride with Walter. I told him so before we arrived; so it is all arranged. I am very happy to welcome you to my heart, no longer as one of the sweetest and best of friends, but as the truest, tenderest of sisters."

There was nothing definite about Ben's trial, and, as Walter had advised Linda, she had taken no further measures to see him. Walter's visit to Nevada was as much to the sheriff as Linda, to get permission for her to visit her brother. This he readily obtained, but was told the keeper of the jail must be present during the visits, as the building was a poor structure, and almost any simple carpenter's tool would be sufficient, if dexterously used, to effect an escape. They could not keep too strict watch, and he would not show any favors.

Linda could visit Ben once every week, and she was delighted with the privilege on any terms.

After the errand to the sheriff was accomplished, Walter took her for a short ride over the mountain roads, but it proved, as Nellie had previously told her, "a nice long one." It was a glorious day to Linda. The air was so balmy and fresh, as they swept along the mountain side, that it wafted all weariness and sadness from her heart.

We will not mock the sweet felicity of our lovers, by recounting the many nothings that, combined, made up their perfect happiness during the fleeting hours, as they wound in and out of those romantic by-ways in the mountains. Lovers' talk should be as unintelligible as the cooings of turtle-doves, for they will say silly things sometimes. Yet they are wise in their silliness; for, after all, true wisdom consists in being happy — in extracting happiness from all the sweets in life, and casting aside the bitter. Many seem to hunt out the bitter drops and let the sweet ones go untasted. To love deeply and fondly may be silly, but the wise who ignore such foolishness, lose the real essence of life, for the only approach to perfect happiness is the repose of two souls blended into one by pure, unalloyed affection and deep, tender sympathy.

Linda's mother had sent her away from home, and refused to see her. Her father was at his mill, a few miles distant from Nevada, and had not yet visited her in her new home. Her brother was awaiting the judgment of the law for the crime which he was accused of perpetrating. Walter argued eloquently that her lonely position was not befitting a young lady of her age, and wished their marriage hastened on that account. He told her he was building a cottage near George's, and they would be ever so happy and contented there. Still, Linda would not consent to an immediate marriage. "Wait, Walter, until Ben is liberated," was her constant plea.

When evening twilight crept over the earth, Linda was once more alone, looking out over the dull little town, surrounded by its lofty, wild mountains. She felt lonelier than ever. Sometimes, when happiness pays us fleeting visits, it leaves us all the more wretched after it has gone.

She went softly to the sofa, where Mrs. Neal had lain down, and crept closely to her side. That wise, good woman knew Linda's heart better than she did herself, and, as she gently caressed her, talked of her absent friends, that she might pour forth the weight at her heart. When absent from those we love, it seems to bring us nearer, when we can talk of them freely.

CHAPTER XXI.

IN PRISON.

THE sheriff had granted Linda permission to visit her brother the next day. Accompanied by Mrs. Neal, she carried the treasure in her hand, addressed to Jake Sniffens, that was to admit her that day of each week to see Ben.

She dreaded meeting the rough Jake, who had so grossly insulted her on her previous visit; still, her heart beat lightly, as she ascended the steps and knocked at the iron-barred door. The same rough voice called out from behind the grating:

"Who's there? What do you want?"

Linda trembled at the very sound of the voice, but answered firmly:

"I have permission from the sheriff to see Mr. Wetherell."

"Certainly, Miss," said Jake, politely, taking the permit and reading it. "Walk in."

"You were not so accommodating last week," said Linda, smiling.

"No?" asked Jake, astonished. "Oh, I'm always accommodatin' to the ladies. If any fellow wouldn't let you in last week, it wa'nt Jake Sniffens, or I'm a Dutchman."

Linda made no attempt to convince him of the veracity of her statement, but was pleased to find the present Jake so much more amiable than the former — owing, of course, to the sheriff's pass. She thought truly, "Telle est la vie."

Jake went on talking. "You know the regulations, I suppose. I have to keep my eye on you all the time you are visiting him."

"Certainly. I expect that," answered Linda.

Jake disappeared, but soon returned followed by Ben. It was a sad meeting. He and Linda both wept like children, and but for Jake's rough comfort they would have had a mournful visit. After he thought they had wept about enough, he burst out in his rough way:

"Here! no more of that nonsense. That's the worst I ever did see."

It was not delicate sympathy, but it had the better effect of bringing them to their senses. Mrs. Neal sat apart, and tried to entertain Jake while Linda talked with Ben, who was so low-spirited that it required all her self-possession to divert and cheer him. As she rose to leave, he said:

"I wish they would take me out and hang me, Linda. I am a living disgrace to you."

"Don't talk so, Ben," she answered, tenderly. "This, I am convinced, is your misfortune, and not your fault. I know you are innocent, and no matter about the disgrace, dear. You will soon be liberated, and then all the world will know of your innocence."

"Oh, Linda, you know little of the law and the courts. Innocent or guilty, the man has sworn that I robbed him. Unfortunately, I was out hunting at the time, and I can bring no evidence in favor of my statements. All is against me. I will be tried, found guilty, and sent to State's prison for life, or until life is not worth having."

"Do not be so desponding, dear brother. Can you not get away?" This was asked *sotto voce.*

"I might, Linda; but I would not go if the door was left open for me."

"Think it over, dear, and I will come to see you every week, on this same day."

"Here!" exclaimed Jake, "that whisperin' won't pay. You

11 *

two can't put yer heads together, and plot treason against Jake Sniffens, with him a settin' here a lookin' you out of countenance."

In a low whisper he added, "A fellow must say sweet things sometimes; but I think the resurrection would overtake me, a settin' here a starin', if I had to stare that ere hard crust of Satan out of countenance. He's the worst I ever did see — he plays so innocent like."

Jake heard all the rest of the conversation, and the visit was finally ended. With a promise to return the same day the next week, Linda took her leave.

CHAPTER XXII.

THE ANONYMOUS LETTER.

WHEN Walter returned to his office after his visit to Linda, he found a letter addressed to him lying on his desk. He tore it open hastily, and read:

MY DEAR FRIEND: — True to her family instinct, your sweetheart, Linda Wetherell, is false to you. She is wholly unworthy of you. Within ten days she left her home, was gone all night and until a late hour the next day, when she was seen, by the writer of this, parting from her lover at the outskirts of Grass Valley. I write you this because I am

YOUR FRIEND.

After reading it, Walter threw the note down, as if it was unworthy any notice. He asked himself: "Why should I regard such a vile, little, nameless epistle, when Linda is my betrothed wife, and we are soon to be married? Have I not known her better than any one else, and watched her closely, too, for over a year, and she has proved herself as pure, good, and unselfish as any woman possibly could ? ''

He took up the note and read it over again. He paced the floor, trying to think of Linda and his approaching marriage — hoping those bright thoughts, that had so completely filled his mind one hour previous, would dispel all gloomy doubts; but, no ! ever and anon the contents of that note would flash across his mind. He tried to think when Linda could possibly have been away from home in that manner, when suddenly he remembered that Mrs. Wetherell had been in search of her at the cottage one morning, the week before, and greatly annoyed Nellie by insisting upon her being there.

"Of course Nellie knows where Linda was," he said, half aloud. "I will go up immediately and ask her, for this thing annoys me more than I like to admit."

He hastened to the cottage, and assuming a careless tone, asked :

" By the way, Nellie, did Linda tell you where she had been that day her mother came here in search of her ? "

" No," answered Nellie, carelessly, and went on with her reading.

Walter felt more annoyed than ever. He walked to the window and stood nervously tapping the glass.

Nellie noticed his uneasiness, and laying aside her book, asked :

" Why do you wish to know ? "

" For no reason in particular," he said, shortly; but his manner and tone belied him.

" Yes, it is something in particular, Walter, for you look very unhappy. Can I not help you ? "

Nellie had a fond way of saying things that comforted one

amazingly. Walter drew the note from his pocket, and handed it to her, without saying a word.

After reading it, she looked up and smiled, as she asked : " Is this all ? "

" Is that all ! " said Walter, astonished.

" Well, Walter ! I thought you were more of a man. If I were engaged to Linda Wetherell, and received a hundred such miserable, intriguing notes, from a hundred different persons, I would burn them all, and go and ask Linda where she had been, and feel sure she would tell me the truth."

" But, Nellie," persisted Walter, " the one who wrote that note seems to know more of my future wife than I do."

" Walter, her mother wrote that note," said Nellie, decidedly.

" Impossible ! Nellie. I know her mother is a very bad woman, but she surely could not be such a fiend as to interfere in that unprincipled way, when she must know her daughter is honorably engaged to be married. On the contrary, I should think she would be pleased to get rid of her."

" She has cast her out already, and considers she has got rid of her," answered Nellie. " Besides, Linda told me long ago her mother had said she would make her miserable all the rest of her life, if she refused to marry Major Warren. Linda answered, she would be as miserable as she possibly could be if she married him ; so she preferred being made miserable by her mother. Mrs. Wetherell said, you shall be miserable enough, if you leave it to me."

" I wish Linda had told me that," said Walter. " I do not feel quite satisfied about this matter."

" Then go to Linda to-morrow morning, and have her explain her absence. If she cannot explain it satisfactorily, then there will be sufficient time to doubt her."

"I will do as you advise, Nell," said Walter, better satisfied. "I believe you have more good sense than any other woman in the world."

"Excepting Linda," smiled Nellie. "You will find her as sensible, faithful, and true as any woman in the world can be."

The next morning, when Walter awoke, sweet sleep had entirely dispelled the gloomy doubts of the night before, and he felt heartily ashamed of his foolishness. He told Nellie so, and requested her, as a special favor, never to mention the subject to Linda, nor question her with regard to her absence. He felt he could and would trust her implicitly, but if ever anything else disturbed his peace of mind, he would go to her and have her explain all.

CHAPTER XXIII.

THE LOST WIFE FOUND AND LOST.

LINDA had gone to spend a few hours with Ben, for Jake Sniffens had become very lenient, exercising great patience toward her, in permitting her visits to be prolonged into hours.

Mrs. Neal's door stood open, and the soft breezes, laden with the perfume of honeysuckles and roses, pervaded the cottage. There were footsteps on the gravel walk, then the shadow of a man, and Mrs. Neal, raising her eyes from her work, saw Captain Wetherell standing in her cottage door. She had often seen him without being seen, and had so dexterously avoided all possibility of meeting, that she had ceased to dread it. Now, from her far-off dreaming and security, she was suddenly

I

recalled by the presence of that man, face to face, in her cottage door. She gave a low cry of anguish, sprang to her feet, and the ashen lips said, slowly:

"Richard Neal!"

The Captain stood aghast. He staggered to a chair and dropped into it heavily. His eyes never left Mrs. Neal's face — they stared blankly, apparently seeing nothing.

Mrs. Neal, with the pallor of death, stood confronting him. Recovering herself, she said mechanically:

"Captain Wetherell, Miss Linda is not at home."

She was leaving the room, when the Captain sprang forward and grasped her hand, exclaiming:

"Agnes, for God's sake, stay."

She tried to free herself from his firm hold, but he was the stronger, and held her like a vise, as he hoarsely whispered:

"Agnes, I have searched the world over for you. Listen to me one moment."

"Captain Wetherell, I cannot listen. You and I parted years ago — parted forever! You betrayed me; you acted a coward's part. No explanations will avail. All reference to that wretched past is inexpressibly bitter. Let it rest."

"I know I did wrong, Agnes, very wrong. I admit it all."

"Wrong!" said Mrs. Neal, bitterly. "Wrong is too mild a term for a crime like yours."

"Crime? What do you mean by that, Agnes?"

"How can you stand face to face with me, Captain Wetherell, and blandly ask what I mean by terming your villany crime? You, who came to my father's house, received his hospitalities, won his daughter's love, and took her before the altar to have that aged man bless his child as your wife; then, on pretext of business that kept you roaming about, left me at home, in our out-of-the-way village, until my father died, when you took us to New Orleans. I was your happy, trusting, loving wife, and bore you two children — and then — and then — I discovered you had another wife, and other children who bore your name, and I and mine were aliens.''

"Stop!'' cried the Captain, fiercely. "I did act like a scoundrel, but not toward you. You were, and are, my wife. My name is Neal — Richard Neal. There is a Mrs. Wetherell, but there is no such person as Richard Wetherell.''

Mrs. Neal shuddered at the thought of being that man's wife — the man whose very name had become synonymous with everything wretched and vile, the destroying demon of her peace and happiness. She knew not what to think, much less to say ; besides, she could not place any confidence in a single word he uttered.

"No such man as Richard Wetherell?'' she asked, dreamily, as if she had not heard distinctly.

"No such man,'' echoed the Captain. "You shall know what you should have known when we were married. What I told your father, although I did not quite tell him the truth — ''

"Scoundrel! to lie to my unsuspicious old father!'' A fire was kindled in the mild woman — a fire doubly dangerous from the smouldering cinders underneath the blaze.

The Captain, at all times a coward, instinctively retreated toward the door. He remembered her a sweet, mild, loving girl — he met a wronged woman.

"Hear me, Agnes, hear me,'' he pleaded. "My name was and is Richard Neal. My parents died when I was young, and left me to the care of an uncle who was cruel and harsh with me. My father had left me quite a sum of money in a bank, subject to my uncle's control until I was of age. He had a son, an only child, and I fancied sometimes he would liked to have killed me, to bestow my wealth upon that boy. There was always jealousy between us, and my uncle being poor, felt bitterly toward my father for not having left him anything, excepting the sum for my board, which was drawn quarterly from the bank ; and I was always the messenger sent for it. My home was hard and unpleasant. I was compelled to work like a day-laborer, notwithstanding my expenses were paid. I could not endure such a life. My father had been kind and gentle, and left me a fortune, ample for my education and comfort.

"I was sixteen years of age, and had still five years more of slavery before I could control what was justly my own. When the time came again for the quarterly payment, I wrote a check myself, for I had labored until I could imitate my uncle's signature to perfection. It happened, very propitiously, at that time there was an estate for sale that had a good rental, and the banker, an old friend of my father, tried to induce my uncle to buy it for me, as it was the exact sum of my bank deposit, and he argued it would double in value by the time I was of age. My uncle would not hear of it. He could not make me richer than his son, and from that time his dislike to me became absolute hatred. The time approached for the sale, and I signed a check for the full amount, telling the banker my uncle had changed his mind and had purchased the property. I had always been so upright and reliable in my transactions for years, that I had the perfect confidence of the banker, and he gave me the money.

"I left that part of the world, and have never been there since. I only took what was justly my own, but I dreaded the result of my uncle's anger, and fled westward under the name of Wetherell, and, becoming identified with that name, never changed it. I told your father I had changed it to get some money an uncle had left me on that condition, for I loved you, Agnes, and our marriage, to be legal, had to be solemnized under my real name. Then fate threw in my way a dashing beauty. When I look back, she seems like one of those enchanted devils one reads about. I had always led a fast life, had met and won many handsome women, but this one was by far the most brilliant creature I had ever seen. I was her slave, and, but for our marriage, would have married her. She led me so gently, so surely, that I made a vow to possess her. She was proud and fiery, and as no one knew that my name was not Wetherell, and I could not win her any other way, I went through a ceremony of marriage that I soon had deep cause to regret, for she was a full-fledged devil. She discovered our marriage — God only knows how — and threatened me with State's prison for bigamy, if I would not leave the country. So I agreed to go to India for ten years.

"You know with what a sad heart I left you, Agnes, for, although I had been false to you, I loved you, and you alone, of all the women on earth. I kept writing to you continually, but when eight years had passed, and I had never heard from you, I could endure my exile no longer. I came back, and searched for years in vain for you. My life has been a pitiable failure without you. I have no home, no resting-place on earth. That woman and I have never lived together since she discovered the fraud practised upon her; yet her selfish pride induces her to keep up the appearance of family ties. All these years I have wandered over the earth, peering into every woman's face, seeking and never finding you till now."

"Sir, I am nothing to you. Mrs. Wetherell has passed for your wife so many years, she is entitled to the honor. I am dead to you."

"Agnes, I will break every tie, brave every danger, if you will only be mine once again — my long-lost wife, my love."

"Captain Wetherell, I disclaim all relationship. Your own

12

conduct broke the bonds that bound us. Your cruelty turned my love into bitterest hatred and contempt. Nothing can ever soften my heart to you."

"Not even our children, Agnes?"

Mrs. Neal trembled visibly, but made no reply. The Captain noticing her distress, asked:

"Our children, Agnes, where are they?"

"Where, indeed?" said the agonized woman, in tones of deepest despair.

She turned suddenly upon the man who had been her husband, and, with a ghostly smile that seemed only the action of the muscles that had no connection with her innermost self, hissed from between her set teeth:

"They are dead! And there is not a living creature to bind together the past. I am a stranger to you, Captain Wetherell, and my house is not open to you in future. Good-day, sir."

"Good-by, Agnes, if you say it must be; but think it over. Remember my years of penitence, my desolate future, and ask me to come again, and be what I am before heaven, your husband. I will obey you, Agnes; only be merciful."

CHAPTER XXIV.

TEMPTATION CLOTHED IN LOVE.

"Nor should Apollo, with his silver bow,
  Shoot me to instant death, would I forbear
  To do a deed so full of cause so dear." — *Homer.*

TWO months had passed, with nothing to disturb the monotony of Linda's life, excepting the regular visits from Walter and Nellie, and her unfailing attendance at the prison.

Mrs. Neal was the same sweet, motherly friend; if anything, lovelier, and fonder of Linda, who found her a wise counsellor, and returned her love with devotion. Their time was passed in sweet communion, never wearying of each other, but daily becoming more essential to each other's happiness.

Linda had but one secret from her adopted mother, and sometimes that weighed heavily upon her mind. She had determined, if possible, to liberate Ben, and in that she knew she would meet with opposition in the conscientious Mrs. Neal; so she resolved to keep the secret until she could tell the result.

It was the day for her regular visit to Ben. Mrs. Neal had gone to a cabin some distance off, to carry some broth to a lonely, sick miner, and Linda knew it would take her some time, as she was ministering angel to all in need for miles around. She leisurely arranged her toilette, and, smiling to herself, slipped a carpenter's chisel up one sleeve and a file up the other.

"This is desperate business," thought she, "but I am sure

the means will overcome Ben's scruples, and he will at least make an effort to escape. I saw him at the grating watching for me last week, so I know in which cell he is confined. If Jake Sniffens is half as careless to-day as he was last time, I will have no trouble."

She felt lighter-hearted than she had for a long time before, as she hurried along to the prison. Much to Jake Sniffens's comfort, there was no "blubbering" on that occasion. They sat down and talked pleasantly together, so that he could hear every word. He did not notice how long Linda held Ben's hand in hers; but she almost always held his hand, so there was nothing strange in that. Jake shortened the visit by the announcement that some one was knocking and he must go, which meant that Linda must go too.

As she bid Ben good-by, she whispered, pleadingly: "Please try, Ben, for my sake."

He could not withstand the temptation, clothed in love as it came, and he answered, softly: "Be under my window at eleven to-night."

That was all, but it made Linda's heart bound with joy. She was confident Jake Sniffens had not noticed anything peculiar in her visit, nor heard the whispering; so far, all was well.

Ben was taken back to his cell, the heavy iron door was closed and locked, and Linda went home anxious but hopeful.

Mrs. Neal had accompanied Linda several times in her visit to Ben, and felt great interest in his welfare. She was at the door to meet her on her return to inquire after him, and noticing her flushed cheeks, asked anxiously:

"What ails you, dear child? Is there anything wrong with Ben?"

"No, good mother, Ben is just as usual, but I have a wretched headache," which was really the case.

"You must lie down, dear, and I will bring you a nice cup of tea," and Mrs. Neal stroked Linda's aching head.

Linda did as she was bid, and Mrs. Neal brought the tea with a steaming piece of toast, then sat long by the bedside while Linda slept. She seemed to take great pleasure in her task, for often, as her eyes rested fondly on the sweet face before her wrapt in peaceful slumber, a smile of real contentment passed over her usually sad face.

The striking of the clock startled Linda, and she raised up hastily, exclaiming:

" Nine o'clock! How long I have slept!"

Seeing Mrs. Neal still by her side, she exclaimed: " Mother Neal! It is just like you, to have sat here all this time. You must be tired. Please go to bed, now. I am quite well again. The pain in my head is all gone."

"I am glad. I knew you were better, you slept so quietly. If you should feel sick during the night, or require anything, call me, dear. . Good-night, child, and pleasant dreams."

"Good-night, darling Mother Neal," and Linda embraced her fondly.

When the door was closed, she exclaimed, with a yearning appeal: "Oh, you darling, good woman! If I could only tell you what a task I have before me this night! May the angels of peace, that have made you such a perfect being, wrap you in slumber so profound that I can go out into the darkness to-night as undisturbed as if I were spirited away."

She knelt down and prayed earnestly—a strange, inconsistent prayer, like many offered to the great shrine on high—a prayer in which she pleaded for help in doing wrong—a prayer for forgiveness before the sin was committed, with the full determination of committing it. Half the praying world is quite as inconsistent. Few Christians, so called, seldom return

12 *

thanks for past blessings, but kneel regularly to go over their vocabulary of wants.   They pray to gain something — what; they do not know themselves — but on general principles.   If there is a God, it is well to be on the right side of Him.   If there is a future, it is just as well to be prepared for it.   Linda was in danger and afraid, so she prayed for God's blessing, and expected it as much in doing wrong as in doing right. We cannot understand, when we are bidden to " ask and it shall be given unto you," that our prayers are not always answered, because we are incapable of judging what is best, and ask for wrong things.   So the doubting world sneers at the efficacy of prayer.   If we have a delicate child, who pleads and entreats for something we know would positively do him bodily injury, we refuse the request, although our severity grieves him at the time.   He does not know what is best, so we must exercise our maturer and better judgment — not that we cannot grant the request, but will not, and in the far-off future the child will be all the better for that act of self-denial.   So our foolish, impulsive prayers go unanswered for our own future good.   With all our conceit and vaunting pride and power, we are only a family of children, under the perfect control of a Great-and Wise Power—that the most learned can neither comprehend nor influence one atom.   We are bubbles on a mighty ocean, sparkling and dancing in the sunlight, to be washed on the beach in a mass of foam at evening, and sink into the thirsty sand.

As Linda sat waiting for the ticking clock to tell the houɪ, for starting on her dangerous errand, her thoughts went flying off to that family circle in Grass Valley ; and most delightful of all, she was soon to be one of them, and Mother Neal was to go with her.   It was the happiest dream of her life to repose in the love and care of such a united home.   The little clock struck ten—she started nervously. "Only one hour more, and I· must be under the prison window. Come out from your hiding place, my only protector," she said, taking a pistol from a little casket. "A blessing on Bob Rivers for this! Without it, how could I venture out at half-past ten o'clock this dark night alone? With it, I can dare almost anything. How I longed to tell Walter all about my intentions with regard to Ben. How happy I will be if successful, and what will I not suffer if I fail? Could I but pace up and down this little room, the time would not seem half so long; but the slightest sound might awaken my anxious, slumbering Mother Neal. So I must sit quietly, while my thoughts fly in quick succession, like autumn leaves before a gale. Half-past ten — thank God! I must be off to the prison. Prison! the very name makes me shudder. Ben in prison?—yes, and so am I. My body is free, but my soul—and oh, I fear my happiness is enchained in a living tomb. How I tremble. Eighteen years old to-morrow, and going alone at midnight to release my guilt-stained brother from prison—to break the laws of State. Oh, Ben! Ben! if you knew what all this costs me. And Walter, will he love a woman who dares so much? Will he not fear me instead of loving me, coming, as I do, from such a strange family? Oh, God, if there is any mercy in heaven, have mercy on me."

She went 'softly and timidly out in the dark night. Veto, the watch-dog, snarled and growled, but Linda's friendly voice quieted him at once. She tried to make him stay at home, but he would not pay the slightest attention to her pantomime, and persistently followed her.

Linda reached the prison at the appointed time, and whispered tremulously, "Ben, I am here."

"All is well," was the reply. "We will be free by one

o'clock. You must not remain there. Go down the Grass
Valley road about half a mile, where a cross-road leads off to
the left. Wait there; I must see you. Keep in the bushes.
If you hear any one approach, be silent. When I come I will
call your name; reply to nothing else."

"God bless you in your task to-night, Ben, but my heart is
faint and full of doubts."

"Fear not!" said the voice from the dark cell. "I would
give the world to be free, if I could only be your slave."

Linda went carefully away toward the road, with Veto following closely.

"Thank you, Veto, for your company," she said, patting him
on the head. He wagged his tail and licked her hand, as if to
say, "I knew you would want me."

As her eyes became accustomed to the darkness, she could
see the rough, uneven road distinctly; but at midnight, alone
in the mountains, with her footsteps resounding like ghostly
pursuers, the half mile to where the road led off to the left was
a long journey. When they finally reached the spot, she sat
down under a thick cluster of manzanita bushes, and Veto,
crawling closely to her side, put his head in her lap. It grew
darker every moment, and great rain-drops began to fall. The
wind rose higher and higher, until it whistled and howled all
around them, like a wild beast, in those lonely mountains. The
tall pines lashed each other and moaned pitifully. The rain fell
faster and faster, until it seemed to have spent its fury, then
gradually subsided, like the sobbing of a child after weeping.

Under the shelter of the thick manzanita bushes, Linda was
quite shielded from the storm; but the moments were hours,
and the hours an eternity to her. After she had waited long
and patiently, she heard the sound of approaching voices.

Veto growled, but she put her arms around his neck and patted him. She whispered something in his ear; he seemed to comprehend it all, for he did not stir again.

Poor Linda was almost paralyzed from fear, lest any instant Veto would make their hiding-place known. On they came, nearer and nearer, until she heard a rough voice say:

"That was a fine piece of business in Curly."

"Yes, Curly acted the traitor there, sure," was the answer. "What in thunder had he against Bob Rivers, anyway? Bob was the best fellow that ever made an honest living in these mountains."

"Honest, be d—d!" said the first speaker. "What's gettin' into you, Ned? Who wants to be honest when he's gettin' on well?"

"But what about Bob Rivers and Curly?" asked the second speaker again, paying no attention to his friend's taunt.

"I don't exactly know," was the reply. "It was something that happened long ago, I believe. Bob was in love with a girl, and they were going to be married, when she disappeared all of a sudden, and has never been heard of since. Some say Curly took her off by force to one of his cabins, and the girl died of grief for Bob."

"The devil!"

"Yes," resumed the narrator. "Her name was Fannie West, and a devilish pretty girl, I've heard."

"If I'd been Bob," said the other, "I'd have killed that wretch."

"So would Bob, I guess, if he could prove he did it. Thompson told me he was down at Curly's cabin not long ago, when a blamed pretty girl came along that way by some mistake, and if Bob had not given her one of his pistols, and taken her part, it would have been another Fannie West case. Whoever she was, she owes a heap to Bob Rivers, for, after taking her part, he saw her safely on her way home. The boys were going down on a lark to Grass Valley that night, and when Bob got back, he found Curly very much out of humor. Thompson said he tried every way to get up a fight with Bob, but Bob was unusually quiet. That made Curly so mad, when they were near Grass Valley he deliberately turned and fired at Bob. He missed his aim, but it brought a lot of men out of a saloon near by. Curly walked up to them, and said, 'Gentlemen, this is that other stage robber that has been missing so. long — arrest him;' of course they nabbed Bob. Bill Brown was with them, and he drew off and shot Curly, saying, 'Take that for your treachery.' They nabbed Bill, too, and sent him and Bob up to jail. Curly is pretty bad, but the boys have changed mightily if they let Bill swing for killing — "

The last words of the sentence were inaudible, although Linda held her breath to catch every sound. She thought long over that strange dialogue, and felt greatly depressed, when she fully realized how much sorrow had come from that single act of humanity on the part of Bob Rivers toward her.

"Oh," she exclaimed aloud, "what a singular life I have allotted me in this strange world! It must have been the wind, but I thought I heard a human voice — there, I hear it again; if it is only Ben!"

Veto started again, and it required all her powers of persuasion to keep him from rushing off. Nearer and nearer came the voices, and in great haste it seemed; as they approached her hiding-place, her name was called softly, "Linda."

"Here I am," she answered joyfully, springing from her hiding place; but, seeing two men, she stopped suddenly, and asked: "Which is Ben?"

All was silent for an instant. Then the same voice that had answered her from the prison window said, pleadingly, "Forgive me for this deception. Ben is not here."

"Not here?" gasped Linda. "Not free?"

She staggered as if shot, and would have fallen, but for the strong arms that caught her. It was only momentary, and she asked pitifully: "Who are you, and how did this terrible mistake happen?"

"I will tell you," answered the same person, kindly. "In the first place, that you may not fear me, I am Bob Rivers. Perhaps you remember, I went part way home with you from Curly Smith's cabin about two months ago."

"Yes, I remember," said Linda. "I would be heartless, indeed, if I could ever forget your kindness. I am glad you are free, even though poor Ben is still a prisoner, as I feel sure he is."

"I am sorry to say he is. But we must not remain here," said Bob, nervously. "Let us walk along this side road. I have considerable to tell you, and we are not safe here."

CHAPTER XXV.

THE FATAL MISTAKE.

YOUR brother, Bill Brown, this friend of mine," said Bob, pointing to the man by his side, "and I were all confined in one large cell, facing the road, where you saw Ben to-day. After you went away, your brother brought in those tools. They were safely secreted, and all the arrangements made for to-night. As bad luck would have it, the sheriff visited us this afternoon, and told Jake Sniffens Ben's

trial was to take place next week, and ours the week after.   He
ordered Ben put in a cell by himself, because he thought he
would be more comfortable.   The sheriff did it out of kindness, but it almost broke Ben's heart to go.   Jake was going to
change him immediately, but some one called him away, and
he did not come back for about an hour.   In the meantime Ben
told me what I was to say to you.   You see, during those long
days in prison, knowing he was your brother, I told him all
about the day you went to Curly Smith's cabin by mistake, and
how brave you were, and afterward about my going part way
home with you—how you fainted when I said I thought he was
guilty, and how I could have cut my tongue out the moment
afterward, for I knew that was what almost killed you.   The
poor fellow cried like a child, and said:

"'Poor Linda!   What she has to suffer through me!   If .
she only knew how innocent I am of this charge, it would be
lighter to bear.   I am very much afraid of the result of my
trial, and then what will she not have to endure?   Bob, if you
are freed and I am not, if you have one spark of humanity left,
do look after Linda a little, for you don't know how much she
needs some one to protect her.   I could bear to be torn limb
from limb and piece from piece, if I could undo this wretched
wrong, and lift this load of sorrow from her heart.' "

Linda was sobbing and crying like a child, and Bob, thinking
he had added another bitter drop to her already overflowing cup,
almost wept too.   They had walked along in silence some distance before he continued:

"Ben wanted Bill and me to make the most of our chance
and get away.   He thought there was no hope of escape for him,
but he was innocent, and, perhaps, it would be as well to let
the law prove it.   He told me what to say at the prison window,
and not let you suspect anything was wrong, for he had an ob-

ject in having you meet me out here. He wanted us to go along this road about a mile until we came to a cabin, on the right hand side, where the road seems to be lost in the bushes. He said we would know it by a light in the first window. He told me to take you there to see his wife and baby."

"Did you say Ben's wife and baby?" asked Linda, as if she had not heard aright.

"Yes, Miss, Ben's wife and baby. He wanted me to ask you to forgive him for not telling you. He was married a few weeks before you arrived from the East. His wife's father and mother had been killed by the Indians a short time before, and she had no relations in this country — not even friends. Ben had not known her very long, but he loved her, and she loved him, and was willing to live with him in the humblest manner; so they were married. He said the reason he had not told you was because his family were all at war with one another, and such an announcement would only have added fuel to the flames. Besides, his father would not be likely to recognize his wife, as he would have nothing to do with him, and she was poor, like himself, so his mother would not be pleased with the addition to the family. He was working industriously, and doing well, and had hoped soon to have a pleasant home in which to receive you. His wife understood the circumstances, and was willing to wait patiently. He has sent her two letters telling her all about his troubles, but thinks she never received them, as he has not heard from her."

"This is all very strange," said Linda, thoughtfully. "Did you ever see his wife?"

"No," answered Bob. "I never knew he was married until he told me. He thinks the world and all of his wife, and asked you to be kind to her for his sake."

13   K

"How far do you think it is from here?" inquired Linda, anxiously.

"It cannot be very far, for he said it was not quite a mile from the main road."

They were continuing their walk in silence, when Bill Brown, who had not said one word during the entire conversation, exclaimed, excitedly, "There is a light in a cabin window!"

Sure enough, there was the talisman that was to guide them. As they approached the cabin a dog barked fiercely within. Instantly a sweet voice asked, "Who is there?"

"Friends," said Bob, and his voice trembled perceptibly.

The cry of joy that burst from the frail creature who opened that cabin door brought tears to every eye, and it had been long since Bob Rivers and Bill Brown had shed tears.

"Oh, Ben, dear Ben! I thought you must be dead!" cried the expectant wife. Then, seeing so many strangers, she became bewildered. No one could speak the first bitter words of disappointment.

Linda regarded her new sister an instant, with her streaming blonde hair and soft blue eyes. She had made up her mind to love Ben's wife because he loved her, but her quick eye read that gentle creature, and like lightning the thought flashed through her brain "I can love you for yourself." She sprang forward, threw her arms about her neck, saying:

"I am Linda, your sister, and I have come to tell you of Ben."

"Then, he is —"

"Not dead," said Linda, earnestly; for Lucy, as Ben had sent word to call her, seemed unable to finish the dread question.

"Then he is not with you?" asked Lucy.

"No, he could not come; but here is a friend of his, Mr. Rivers."

Lucy bowed coldly to Bob. She could not recover her self-possession after her disappointment.

"Lucy, I have come," said Linda, with a voice full of sympathy and love, "to be your friend until Ben can come to you. He is in great trouble."

"You are fortunate, Mrs. Wetherell. Who ever can claim Miss Linda's friendship, has not only one of the most faithful and truest friends in the world, but a perfect angel to take care of them," said Bob, earnestly. "Two hours ago I was in jail, and she liberated me. My life is at her command."

"Do you mean that?" asked Linda, seriously.

"I do," answered Bob, emphatically.

"Then I command you," said Linda, earnestly, "to let the dead past bury its dead, and henceforth make your life a noble one."

Bob raised his hand and said, solemnly, "I swear to you, I will."

They had quite forgotten Lucy, who stood by deathly pale. She turned her soft eyes to Linda, and asked, quietly, "And Ben, is he in prison?"

"Yes, he is still there," answered Linda, with pity in her great brown eyes; "but I hope and pray he will soon be free."

As may be expected, Lucy had heard nothing from Ben. His two partners had been very kind and attentive to her; but thinking he was innocent and would be speedily released, they had kept her in utter ignorance of the real state of affairs. They told her, when he was first arrested, that while visiting his sister he had been subpoenaed as witness in an important case in San Francisco, and might be absent some time. They thought at first he might be gone two or three weeks, but when two months went by, and still he did not come, she became greatly alarmed. She was fearful some accident had happened, or she

would at least have heard from him.   But with all her conflicting thoughts, she had never once dreamed of dishonor.

Bill Brown would not enter the cabin ; he was very sullen and
morose, considering he had just escaped from prison.   He sat
outside in the rain awhile, then mentioned a place of rendezvous with Bob for the next morning, and left.   When he was
gone, Bob remarked, " That fellow acts as though he was sorry
he had left jail."

Linda and Bob related all the particulars of Ben's imprisonment, with Linda's efforts to release him, and the result.   They
expressed their firm belief in his innocence, and positive ex-
pectation that he would be restored to his anxious wife the
following week.

It was a long night of trial for Lucy, but Linda was a good
comforter, and had suffered and become quite resigned through
the same trials that Lucy had to undergo.

The rain poured down in torrents, and as Bob had no other
place to go, he remained in the cabin.   He was very uneasy,
for he wanted to leave Linda and Lucy alone to talk over their
troubles in their own womanly way.   After he had thought of
a great many plans, it occurred to him that Linda must be faint
and hungry after her night's exertions, so he said in a very
modest way, for a mountain desperado, "If Mrs. Wetherell
would let him, he would go into the kitchen and make a cup
of coffee.   He assured them Miss Linda needed something
after her long walk and exposure to the rain, and he had kept
bachelor's hall so long, he was fully competent."

Linda was obliged to go home early in the morning, for she
knew how anxious Mrs. Neal would be about her ; but she
promised to return the following day and remain with Lucy
until Ben was released.   It was seven o'clock when she started
for the main road, accompanied by Bob Rivers.   After they
had gone a short distance, he said : ·

"I have some business out here, about a quarter of a mile from the road; that is why I remained last night. I should have been a good ways off from here by this time, for those hounds scent a fellow within ten miles. My business is in an old tree not far from here. It serves as my banking-house, and this is my pass-key." He drew a small coil of rope from an old stump by the roadside. "I want you to remember where I keep that, and also the tree I am going to show you. It has two peculiar chips of bark cut out of it, and the top was burnt off some years ago. About eight feet from the ground a great arm branches off, but the main trunk is perfectly hollow, and will hold a man very comfortably. I have some money deposited there. The interest is decidedly small, but the principal is safe. There, that is the tree."

"Hark! did you not hear voices?" asked Linda, in alarm.

"Yes, I do. If I can only gain that tree."

"Leave me; go quick!" whispered Linda.

"Have no fear on my account; I can get along."

The voices approached nearer every moment. Linda stood in breathless anxiety. Bob gained the tree, threw the rope over the branch, swung up on it, and in an instant was out of sight. He was pulling in the last of the rope, when Veto barked, and sprang forward to meet four men, who came in full view of Linda. The last of the rope disappeared, and Linda leaned against a tree for support.

"What is that woman doing out here this time of day? Bring her this way," said one, who seemed to be the leader.

The man nearest to Linda took her gently by the arm and led her to the roadside.

"Who are you, girl?" asked the leader.

Linda, in her alarm for Bob, could not answer immediately. One of the men, who had not appeared to take much interest in

13 *

her, came up and looked her full in the face, gave a long whistle, and exclaimed: "The devil! If that there is n't the soft-eyed, tender, blubberin' sister of that there scapegrace that's in jail up there, and was only moved out of that there cell yesterday from them there other villains that got out last night. She helped 'em, or I 'm a Dutchman!"

"What are you talking about, you old ass?"

"I mean, sheriff," for the leader was the deputy sheriff, "if that is n't the affectionate sister of that there mighty son of the Plutonian regions, then Jake Sniffens is a Dutchman; which he ain't, or he don't know himself."

"What is the fellow's name, Jake?" asked the man who had taken care of Linda.

"His name is Ben Wetherell," answered Jake, decidedly.

The sheriff turned to Linda and asked: "Are you Ben Wetherell's sister?"

"Yes, sir, I am," was her firm reply.

"Did you have anything to do with his friends escape last night?" he asked again.

"If she did n't, then I 'm a sold Dutchman," interrupted Jake.

"Hold your tongue, you chattering ape, until I speak to you," growled the sheriff, fiercely.

Turning to Linda, and apparently having forgotten his first question, "Do you know where your brother's friends are, who escaped from jail last night?"

Linda hesitated a moment, then answered: "No, sir, I do not," with a mental reservation, "I only know where one is."

The sheriff noticed her hesitation, and it exasperated him. He took her roughly by the arm and drew her toward him, saying roughly: "Perhaps we can refresh your memory. Jake, take her and put her where she will be safe for the present."

Linda's quick ear detected the sound of horses' hoofs upon the road. She screamed loudly for help. In a few seconds a horseman came dashing toward the group.

"Walter!" cried Linda, and he was by her side.

"What does this mean?" he asked.

"It means," said the sheriff, "through that girl's agency two of the most desperate fellows in jail escaped last night, and she refuses to tell where they are."

"Perhaps she does not know," said Walter.

"She says she don't," answered the sheriff, maliciously; "but I know better."

"What did you propose doing with her because she refused to tell what she did not know?" asked Walter.

"I propose to compel her, sir, or shut her up in their place until she would tell," was the cool rejoinder.

"You will do nothing of the kind," said Walter, resolutely. "Go about your business, you vulgar fool! When you do your work so badly as to be foiled and fooled by a girl, you must swallow your chagrin, until you can prove she was implicated. This is Miss Wetherell, my affianced wife, and by the right of my relationship I command you to go about your business."

The sheriff mounted his horse sullenly, and with his men rode off toward Nevada.

CHAPTER XXVI.

PLIGHTED LOVES.

WALTER led Linda to a fallen tree, and sitting down by her side, put his arm about her waist and drew the weary girl to his breast. Her face was so pale, her great brown eyes so wild and anxious, that he felt greatly alarmed about her. Not wishing to tax her with questions until she was rested, he said, as cheerfully as possible :

"I come with good news this morning to claim my wife. The long looked for letter from Belle Burton has at last arrived. Here it is, my darling; put it in your pocket, and read it at your leisure. She apologizes for her delay, by saying she had been very much occupied, owing to her approaching marriage—that her name will be Mrs. Colonel Wall before this letter reaches me. Now, is my particular, conscientious little pet satisfied ? "

"Walter, how can you love such a pitiable object as I am ? " asked Linda, with her great eyes full of unshed tears.

"Tell me first how I can help loving you," said Walter, tenderly, "then I will try to answer your question. But, Linda, do you love me as well as you once did ? "

"How can you ask such a question, Walter ? You surely cannot doubt it," and Linda's voice was choked with tears. "You know there are two persons in this world I think of always. One is poor Ben ; the other, and the chief, your noble self. Dear Walter, you are my idol. When I give you the devotion of my life, and all the love of my poor, blighted heart, I am not giving you half enough in return for your noble conduct toward me."

"It has been impossible for me to do anything for you, darling, and I would feel that your brave little self would more than repay me, if I had sacrificed half of my existence for you. Tell me, dear, how you happen to be out here so early in the morning, and in such trouble."

Linda repeated all the events of the previous night, and when she mentioned Bob Rivers, she spoke of him as her noble rescuer two months before.

"What happened to you two months ago?" asked Walter, eagerly, for the memory of that anonymous note flashed across his mind.

Linda related all the circumstances connected with her fruitless walk to Nevada and back again to see Ben — that by taking a by-path she had gone accidentally to Curly Smith's cabin. How noble and kind Bob Rivers had been to her, and finally of her mother and Major Warren dashing past just as she was bidding him good-by. She did not fail to repeat the conversation between the two men who had passed her during the night, that he might understand Bob Rivers had gone to prison through his kind act toward her.

Walter sat gazing into her truthful eyes, with worshipful admiration, for one so young, so brave and daring, yet so tender and womanly withal. She sat a few minutes, looking off into space, then said, thoughtfully:

"Walter, dear, I cannot tell you how thankful I am that Bob Rivers was one of the men who escaped last night. I felt under such deep obligations to him, but now his kindness to me is, in a measure, returned. I intended telling you all about it sometime, and thought perhaps you could do something for him."

"It will afford me great pleasure to serve him, for your sake, Linda; but first of all, from your desperate doings, my brave girl, you need some one to take care of you. One who dares so much for a wayward brother will surely prove a faithful wife, and I want to assume my prerogative at once."

"I will be as good a wife to you as I know how, Walter," answered Linda, in her innocent, girlish way.

"Then, dear, I shall have all the happiness I want in this world, and doubt if I will be anxious to try any other."

CHAPTER XXVII.

FOREBODINGS OF EVIL.

IT was near noon when Walter and Linda arrived at Mrs. Neal's. They found that good woman anxiously pacing up and down the little veranda. In meeting Linda she neither upbraided nor asked questions, but simply expressed great joy at her safe return.

Linda was greatly surprised by her mother's presence as she entered the cottage. She approached to welcome her, but Mrs. Wetherell disdainfully ignored all such familiarity, and, for Mrs. Neal's benefit, said:

"You are at your old tricks again, are you? Running away and staying all night, no one knows where, seems to be a favorite amusement of yours." Seeing Walter, she added, quickly, "Excuse me, Mr. French, I was not aware of your presence, or I would not have exposed my daughter's want of propriety."

Linda's cheeks were crimson at the taunt, and Walter only by a strong effort mastered his indignation.

"Madam, you misjudge your daughter. Her errands have been for humanity's sake."

"I have no doubt," said Mrs. Wetherell, coldly; "but her humanity is confined to one person, if I am not mistaken."

"Yes, madam," and Walter's eyes flashed. "To one person — your ill-raised and abandoned son. If he had a mother equal to his sister, he might now have been a free man, instead of a prisoner."

"You speak of my daughter rather familiarly, Mr. French," said Mrs. Wetherell, sarcastically, trying to conceal her chagrin at Walter's remarks.

"Yes, madam, I claim that right," answered Walter, with dignity. "As you have resigned all care over her, and denied her your protection, I have not felt it my duty to consult you in the matter. I am your daughter's affianced husband, madam."

"Yes," said Mrs. Wetherell, smiling wickedly, "I wish you joy of your choice. She has been a sweet daughter, and I have no doubt will prove as good a wife."

She did not wait for any reply, but swept out of the room.

"Oh, Walter," cried Linda, with tears in her eyes, "why did you tell her that?"

"She cannot interfere with us, darling. If she annoys you in the least, send for me."

"Yes, that is all very well, Walter; but you cannot imagine the depth of that woman's capacity for making those miserable whom she hates."

"She shall not have long to make you miserable, Linda. Next week Ben will be free, and then, without any unnecessary ceremony, we will be married."

"Next week is a long way off, Walter, and I shall live in dread until it comes."

"My little girl is tired and half sick," said Walter, tenderly; "that is what makes her so apprehensive. Lie down and rest all day, darling, and do not let any one disturb you. I must leave you now, for I promised to be home at eleven, and it is already past noon."

"Good-by, then, dear Walter," said Linda, fondly.

"Good-by, my darling. I will come to see you day after to-morrow, and shall expect to find you cheerful and well."

Linda went to her room and threw herself upon the snowy little bed. Mrs. Neal, entering soon after, found her weeping bitterly. When she attempted to account for her long absence, the good Mother Neal stroked her hot forehead, and said, soothingly:

"You are too tired to talk now, child; rest first. I know you have been doing what was right, and you shall not fret yourself now by talking. Sleep sweetly, dear; you shall not be disturbed."

"My precious, darling Mother Neal," said Linda, affectionately, returning her caresses.

CHAPTER XXVIII.

THE MARRIAGE.

"What I do thou knowest not now, but thou shalt know hereafter."
"Some bring libations to mammon, some to ambition, some to love."

WHILE Mrs. Neal was with Linda, a messenger came with a note addressed to Miss Wetherell. Mrs. Wetherell received it at the door. After reading the superscription, she tore it open, and, to her amazement, read:

Come immediately. We fear your father has been fatally injured in the mine this afternoon.

Your obedient servant,
JOHN MURPHY,
Boss workman.

"I will go with you at once instead of my daughter, who is ill," said Mrs. Wetherell to the messenger. She threw on her shawl and bonnet, telling Mrs. Neal she was called away on important business, and might possibly not return that night.

Linda saw her mother go away in the dilapidated old wagon that had driven up a few moments before, with a sense of relief at her departure. The note went with her, so Linda was left wholly ignorant of what was transpiring.

The mill was three miles from Nevada, the road very uneven and rough, and the ride slow and tiresome; still, Mrs. Wetherell did not deign to ask any questions of the stupid little driver by her side. She seemed lost in deep meditation. When the wagon stopped, she sprang out without assistance, and stepped quickly into the house.

"It's all over wid 'im, ma'am," said the faithful John Murphy, sadly.

An expression of satisfaction passed over Mrs. Wetherell's face, and her eyes were blacker and burned more fiercely than usual. She made no pretence at sorrow, but gazed upon the lifeless form of the man who had been her husband so many years as one would look at a dead dog.

"How long since he died?" she asked.

"It's about ten minutes agone since he brathed his last, ma'am," answered John.

"Did he leave any papers?" asked Mrs. Wetherell, looking searchingly into John's face.

"None, I think, ma'am; leastways, I hain't got none."

John gave a side glance at the old man to see if he really was dead, and if he approved of that sort of gabble.

Mrs. Wetherell gave a significant smile and walked to the door.

John remarked aside to the old man: "Begorra, I did that

14

foine.   If that she-divil thinks she can pull the wool o'er John Murphy's eyes, sure she 's wilcome.   Bedad, I 'll do as yez tould me, ould gintleman, for I 'm not afther wantin' yer un- aisy spirit to be hobgoblin afther me.   Yez fixed it foine wid 'er, but I 'm afther thinkin' the divil fixed 'er afore yez, and gave her a gizzard instead of a heart.''

"John,'' called Mrs. Wetherell.

"Yis, ma'am,'' and John was by her side.

"Dig a grave under that pine-tree to night, and make a rough coffin.   I want you to bury the Captain before daylight to-mor- row morning.''

"Begorra, and would ye no let a man get cowld afore yez put him under?'' asked John, in amazement.

"Yes, John,'' said Mrs. Wetherell, more mildly.   "It is unnecessary to explain my undue haste.   I am obliged to go away suddenly, and cannot delay for funeral services.''

"Be the stick, that bates the divil! for I do na think he 's got to the ould un yet,'' said John, meditatively.

"Will you obey my orders, John?'' asked Mrs. Wetherell.

"Ye, ye-ez, ma'am,'' said John, doubtfully.

"Then take this for your pains — get a keg of whiskey and have a wake over the Captain, if you like, to-night,'' and Mrs. Wetherell handed him some money.

"Thank yez, ma'am,'' said John, taking the gold.

Turning to the boy who had brought her there, she said: "Drive me back to Nevada as fast as possible.''

"Begorra, if she ain't a tough 'un!'' exclaimed John Murphy, as they drove off.

When they reached Nevada, she asked the boy to stop at the telegraph office, and leave his horse there until he was ready to return home.   Going inside she asked the operator if there was any dispatch for Mrs. Wetherell, and appeared very much disappointed when she was told there was none. She picked up a blank lying on the desk, and asked for pen and ink, remarking that she wished to make a memorandum. When she had finished, she asked, pleasantly:

"Will you please give me an envelope?"

"Certainly, madam," said the operator, who was busy writing, and had paid little attention to her.

She addressed the envelope, and saying, sweetly, "Good-evening, sir; I am obliged to you," went outside where the boy was waiting.

"I want you to remain here about half an hour, then bring this note up to the same house where you came after me, and take this for your pains," handing him some money.

The boy nodded stupidly, and she walked hurriedly away, with her imperious air.

It was almost dark when the boy arrived with the note. Mrs. Neal took it hastily to Linda's room.

"A telegraphic despatch for me?" asked Linda, alarmed. "What can it mean?" She read, hurriedly:

ORLEANS HOTEL, SACRAMENTO.

Come to me, daughter. I am very ill, I fear dying. Bring your mother, that we may part friends.

RICHARD WETHERELL.

Linda read the despatch aloud, and turned to Mrs. Neal for advice:

"Tell me, dear friend, what shall I do?"

"You must go, of course," said honest Mrs. Neal; "and, by all means, take your mother with you. It may result in once more uniting your whole family."

"You are always right, Mother Neal," said Linda, perfectly convinced. "Will you be so kind as to ask my mother to come to me?"

"Yes; but she is all ready to go home."

"How fortunate I received this despatch before she left," said Linda, rising and beginning to dress.

In a few minutes, Mrs. Wetherell entered Linda's room as cold and stately as ever. Linda handed her the despatch. She glanced over it hastily, threw it aside, and hiding her face in her hands, exclaimed:

"Great Heaven! What other calamity can befall me? At war with every one and myself, goaded by remorse, and now, at my time of life, left penniless!"

Linda's sympathies were deeply touched, and she used every possible means to comfort and console her.

"Will you go with me to see him, mother?" she asked.

"Yes, Linda," answered Mrs. Wetherell, more calmly. "Perhaps I have not been quite as good a wife to him as I should have been, and I will comply with his last request."

She kindly offered to assist Linda in preparing for her journey. The carriage was waiting to take her back to Grass Valley, and she thought Linda had better hasten to accompany her, that she might also have time to make some preparations for their departure in the morning. Her manner was so kind and affable, that Linda thought in her heart Mrs. Neal was surely right, and this misfortune would entirely change her mother.

They had a lonely ride in the dark, although the distance was only four miles. Linda's heart was full of conflicting thoughts and emotions over the events of the day. Her mother requested her not to mention the cause of their sudden departure to any one, to which she assented. There was no other conversation between them.

To Linda's great astonishment, on their arrival home, they were warmly welcomed, and assisted from the carriage, by Major Warren. She was unusually polite to him, but so soon

as possible passed on to her own room, leaving her mother to
entertain him.

"Have you forgotten, dear madam, this was to be my wedding day?" he asked, with an aggrieved air.

"No, indeed," said Mrs. Wetherell, earnestly. "But we
met with a misfortune, which delayed us so long. It must be
nine o'clock. I fear you will have to postpone it until to-morrow, dear Major, owing to our delay in getting here."

"Nine o'clock is only late in the country," pleaded the
Major. "I spoke to the magistrate, and he is in his office
every evening until ten. Besides — forgive the weakness, dear
madam — but I have a terrible feeling of superstition about
postponing marriages."

"Excuse me, then, a little while; perhaps I can still arrange
matters to suit you."

Mrs. Wetherell left the Major with a bewitching smile. In
a few moments she returned. The Major, all excitement,
sprang to meet her.

"Well, my dear madam, am I to be so happy as to claim my
bride?"

"Yes," was the calm reply. "My daughter says on two
conditions, owing to her brother's trouble. First, that you
permit her to go veiled during the ceremony; second, that you
will not claim her for one month."

"To obtain my long-sought prize I will agree to anything,"
warmly kissing Mrs. Wetherell's hand. "And you, dear
madam, I shall always bless you for your perseverance and great
kindness to me."

A few minutes later Major Warren left the house with a
closely veiled lady. The marriage ceremony was performed
by the justice of the peace, and two strangers were witnesses.

14 *   L

CHAPTER XXIX.

THE BRIDAL TRIP.

THE next morning, at daybreak, a carriage left Grass Valley containing Major Warren, Mrs. Wetherell, and Linda.

After travelling all day, they arrived at Sacramento as the street lamps were being lighted. The carriage passed leisurely up J Street, and, turning to the left, stopped before a genteel residence. It was a two-story brick, covered with running roses and honeysuckles, and so completely surrounded by fruit and fancy trees, it seemed to have dropped in the midst of a miniature forest. The bright lights streaming from every window, as tokens of welcome, gave it a cheerful, inviting appearance. As the carriage stopped, a middle-aged servant received them, and assisted with the many necessary travelling packages.

Linda had caught a severe cold the night she spent in the storm by the roadside awaiting Ben, from which she had been suffering severely. During their long ride she had acted in a strange manner, dozing almost constantly. When she did wake up, it was with a frightened look, only to fall asleep again.

Mrs. Wetherell told the Major her daughter had not been well for several days, owing, she thought, to the excitement attending her brother's misfortunes and her approaching marriage. With the additional cold she had caught, she feared she might be seriously ill.

The servant who received them led the way to a nicely furnished room up stairs, while the driver carried Linda in his arms and laid her upon the bed. She was perfectly helpless and passive to all that took place.

The Major said quietly to the servant: "Ann, Mrs. Warren is quite ill. I want you to sleep on the sofa here to-night and take care of her. The madam," pointing to Mrs. Wetherell, "can take the next room. In case of any alarming symptoms, call her. Give us our supper now, and serve Mrs. Warren something delicate."

Mrs. Wetherell began taking off Linda's wrappings, when the Major, who was standing by her side, said, "Mother."

Mrs. Wetherell turned suddenly and looked severely at him, then, as if suddenly comprehending his meaning, smiled sarcastically.

"I beg your pardon, madam," said the Major, somewhat confused, "but am I not your son now, and your daughter, my wife, is seriously ill? It befits us to take care of her tenderly and well, as mother and son should do. Shall I not send for the doctor?"

"I think it is unnecessary, dear Major," said Mrs. Wetherell, without the least concern. "Linda is quite ill, I admit, but I think, as she appears so drowsy, she may sleep off her sickness, and be quite herself again by morning."

"But she has a high fever," persisted the Major.

"Yes," said Mrs. Wetherell, feeling the burning brow. "Still, I think that is caused by the severe cold she has had for several days."

Mrs. Wetherell gained her point — the doctor was not sent for. They ate their supper agreeably and socially, and afterward sent Ann to wait upon Linda.

The next morning she was quite delirious from fever. The Major, greatly alarmed, went himself for the doctor, who pronounced the patient dangerously ill from pneumonia.

CHAPTER XXX.

" GUILTY."

A WEEK had passed since Linda bade Mrs. Neal good-by, promising to write her at once in regard to her father's condition, and, under all circumstances, to return to Nevada before Ben's trial. Yet not one line had been received from her, and the time of Ben's trial was at hand. Walter had been twice to inquire after her, but was not alarmed at her silence, thinking the extreme illness of her father, undoubtedly, occupied all her attention. Mrs. Neal also thought that was the case until Ben's trial took place, and still no word came; then she became greatly alarmed, and expressed her anxiety freely to Walter, who remained in Nevada during the entire trial, doing all in his power to save Ben, but to no purpose.

It was a simple case. The teamster had been robbed, and he swore Ben was the man who robbed him. Although Ben's friends were confident of his innocence, they could do nothing for him. The simple truth condemned him. He had been out hunting that afternoon, and, although it was his custom, he had remained out later than usual on that particular day, and was still away at the time the robbery had been committed.

He was found guilty of grand larceny, and sentenced to seven years in State's prison. Although he had expected that result, the sentence came like a death-blow. Seven years ! He sat motionless, looking vacantly over the curious throng, not seeing any one, nor anything, but a confused, misty expanse of seven bleak, weary years. His suffering was so intense, so deep, the crowd was awed and every heart was touched with pity.

In the farthest corner of the court-room sat a crouching figure that might be sixty years old. His hat was drawn closely over his forehead and eyes, and most of his face was concealed by a heavy moustache and full beard. What little could be seen was strangely at variance with the rest of the man, for the fresh, soft cheeks belonged only to youth. His eyes, like all the others, were riveted upon the doomed man. When the sentence was read, and the noble, manly prisoner, without a shudder or external sign of grief, sat looking blankly into space, the crouching figure shuddered — his hands grasped the seat convulsively, as from a sudden spasm of pain. Once he made a motion as if to rise, but dropped heavily back into his seat, and his black eyes darted quick, nervous glances from face to face. It was not an expression of fear, for he knew no one would ever recognize in that heavily-bearded, stooping, sluggish man, the smooth-faced, youthful, graceful figure of Bill Brown. But why should Bill Brown manifest such interest in Ben Wetherell's fate, and run the risk of detection and arrest in coming publicly to the very place where he was to have been arraigned for trial the following week?

Walter would not permit the sheriff to return Ben alone from the court-room. He put his arm within his, led him with brotherly affection back to his gloomy cell, and there talked hopefully, when he knew there was no hope, trying to cheer him, but it was useless. The broken pride and crushed feelings refused to rally. His bright, young life seemed shattered forever. He sat listening without hearing a word, and it was with great apprehensions for his mental faculties that Walter reluctantly left him, and returned to Mrs. Neal's, where Nellie was anxiously waiting to hear the result of the trial. It was

a solemn announcement, and sadly accepted.   They could not
think it possible there had been any mistake, yet they had
hoped for something better for Linda's sake.

Walter sat down wearily, and, taking up the day's paper,
glanced carelessly over its columns.   Suddenly he threw it
from him, and went hurriedly out of the room.

"What can be the matter?" said Nellie, anxiously, starting
to follow him.   "Is Walter sick?"

"I would not follow him," said Mrs. Neal, quietly, taking
up the discarded paper.   "He read something here that shocked
him.   I was looking at him when he first saw it.   Whatever
it was, it gave him great pain."

"What can it be?" and Nellie glanced over the paper with
Mrs. Neal.

"It is that!" said the widow, grasping the paper firmly
with one hand, and pointing with the other to a paragraph that
read:

"Married.   On the twentieth instant, in Grass Valley, Major William Warren to Linda, only daughter of Captain and
Mrs. Wetherell."

The two friends stood looking with astonishment at each
other.   Mrs. Neal was the first to recover herself, and said,
with a strangely fierce tone for her:

"Mrs. Gray, there has been foul play with the child."

"I did not think that of Linda," answered Nellie, with bitter disappointment in her voice.

"Linda is not to blame," insisted Mrs. Neal.

"I am not so sure," said Nellie, her confidence in Linda
evidently shaken.   "No matter how great the pressure brought
to bear by her mother, Linda could not have been forced into
marrying the Major, if she had had proper affection for Walter."

"You forget her father was dying when she left here, and this might have been his last request; and dying requests are hard to refuse."

"But why has she not written to you and explained her troubles?"

"That I cannot answer, Mrs. Gray; but my confidence in Linda is so implicit, I am positive only extreme necessity would compel her to do what she so strongly opposed, and then there would have to be a perfect conviction that in sacrificing her own feelings she was doing her duty."

"But Walter! has she no pity for him?"

Nellie's voice trembled, and tears of sympathy for her idolized brother streamed down her cheeks. She went quietly into the adjoining room, and going up to him, put her arms around his neck and caressed him fondly. He grasped her hand spasmodically, and his features worked convulsively as he hissed out:

"False! false! Never let her name be spoken in my presence." Then, as if ashamed of his weakness, he rose hurriedly, saying, quite like himself, "Nellie, it is time we were going home."

Mrs. Neal's heart ached for him, but she only pressed his hand warmly at parting, and whispered, "Never doubt her. She has been wronged."

Walter glanced quickly at the sweet, motherly face at his side. She had poured oil upon his burning wounds; they burned less fiercely; but they were still there, deep and bleeding. Then he thought, "Only one more dupe. She has deceived us all. It is better so than to discover it later."

On their arriving home, as George was assisting Nellie from the carriage, Walter joined them and said, abruptly:

"George, come down to my office right away. I want to see you on business."

"All right, I will come," said George, wondering what the sudden haste could mean.

Nellie put her arm in George's, and like a cooing dove related all the sad events of the day. She could not think Linda deliberately false, but, in her sympathy for Walter, felt she might have done otherwise.

When George arrived at the office, he found Walter restlessly pacing the floor. He turned suddenly at George's entrance, saying :

"George, Wheeler has offered me eighty thousand dollars for the mill, and I want to sell."

George was greatly surprised at the announcement, but after what Nellie had told him, he comprehended the cause perfectly. As Walter seemed waiting for an answer, he said :

"Well?" apparently waiting for further particulars.

"I am sick of this country," burst out Walter. "I will sell my interest. You can do as you like. I shall go East at once, and settle down South."

"If you sell," said George, in his characteristic, earnest way, "I will too, and go with you."

"Agreed!" said Walter, grasping his hand warmly. "It is a bargain, is it?"

"Yes, so far as I am concerned."

"Will you never regret it?" asked Walter, eagerly.

"No. I want to go East anyway. You know mother is failing fast, and wants to see us all once more."

"Yes," added Walter, thoughtfully, "and you are the only heir to all that estate."

"The only one." George put his arm through Walter's, and they walked in silence up to the cottage.

CHAPTER XXXI.

CONVALESCING.

THREE weeks had elapsed, and Linda was still confined to her bed. The disease was conquered, but the great prostration following such a severe attack required time and patience to recuperate. Convalescence, under pleasant circumstances, is tedious; but to one in Linda's situation it was doubly wearisome. She was continually harassed by anxiety for Ben, and her peculiar, incomprehensible situation in Major Warren's house, added to her separation from Mrs. Neal and Walter, weighed heavily upon her mind. They were all kind to her, but she did not dare ask questions. Once she ventured to inquire of her mother where her father was. She answered: "He recovered, and went home long ago."

Encouraged by that reply, she asked why the servants called her Mrs. Warren.

"Because you are Mrs. Warren, I suppose," answered Mrs. Wetherell, shortly, and withdrew apparently to avoid further questions.

Still another week had gone by, during which Linda had been sitting up part of each day, and was rapidly regaining her strength.

The Doctor came to pay one of his regular visits, and fearing they might cease altogether, without an opportunity of advising with him, she took advantage of the first occasion of their being alone.

"Doctor, you have been very kind, and I am so much in need of a friend. I feel I can take the liberty of saying to you what I cannot to any one else. You call me Mrs. Warren;

15

so do the servants; but by what right, I assure you I do not know."

"By the common right a wife has to her husband's name, no doubt," said the Doctor, eyeing her strangely.

· "But I do not know that I have a husband," said Linda, earnestly. "If I have been married, I assure you I was not in my right senses at the time."

"You astonish me!" said the Doctor, still regarding her intently. "You must be laboring under some mental excitement, my child, and need rest."

"No, Doctor," said Linda, firmly. "I am perfectly calm and collected, when I tell you I have no knowledge of my marriage, neither have I the slightest idea how I came here."

"Perhaps your illness has impaired your memory. When you regain your strength entirely, all will return fresh to your mind again," and the Doctor withdrew his searching gaze, apparently satisfied.

"No, Doctor. I think I will be firmer in my belief that I have been wronged in some way. My mother was so determined I should marry Major Warren, and I so positively opposed it, I assure you there has been foul play. I know her well, and no obstacle would prevent her gaining her object. That I was wholly unconscious the day I came here is certain. Sometimes I have thought I must have been drugged."

It was Linda's turn to look searchingly at the Doctor, and her quick eye detected the contraction of his firm mouth, and the lines on his brow grow deeper. When she had finished speaking, he sat thoughtfully a few seconds, then taking her hand in his, the good old man said, with much earnestness :

"My child, I am of the same opinion as yourself in regard to the drugging. The first morning I came to see you I immediately said you had pneumonia, but were also suffering from some narcotic poison. I asked your mother and the Major, but they both positively denied the use of any drugs. Still, they admitted you had been very stupid, and slept most of the previous day on your way from Grass Valley. They had been with you all the time, they said, and were sure you had not taken any medicine whatever. I still persisted firmly in my decision, although I said nothing more to them, excepting to ask the Major's permission to bring Dr. Moore, an old friend of mine, with me to see you, as I thought you were alarmingly ill. As he not only gave his consent, but asked me to spare no pains in having everything done for you at once that I possibly could, I immediately found my friend, and brought him around, my motive being entirely to have his opinion in regard to the narcotics you had taken. His decision coincided exactly with mine, that you had taken powerful narcotics, and he expressed great astonishment that you were alive, considering the inflamed condition of your lungs. If I had not given you antidotes at once, notwithstanding the assertions of your mother and the Major, in all probability you would not have been alive now. I tell you this in confidence, and hope you will not repeat it. However, if there is anything wrong in this matter, come to me and I will befriend you. You are getting along so nicely, I had intended to dispense with my daily visits, but now I will continue to come as your friend."

"Thank you, Doctor. You do not know how grateful I am for all you have told me. It will put me now on my guard. I am in constant fear of something, I scarcely know what. My mother is hard and ambitious, and I have opposed her wishes, which gives me cause to fear her. The Major I despise. I am greatly in need of friendly advice; although I am still so weak, I suppose I must sit here and wait until my strength returns before undertaking anything."

"Yes, you must keep moderately quiet. Be guarded in your conversations, and advise with me before taking any decided measures."

"As you are to be my friend, will you begin by doing me a favor?"

"With pleasure, my child," said the Doctor, kindly.

"Thank you. Will you please mail these letters? One is for my sister-in-law, as you will see by the superscription. I am anxious she should get it, for she must be very lonely. My brother, I expect, is away from home. His marriage is a secret from my mother, that is the reason I could not mail the letter through any one in the house. The other is for the dearest, best woman on earth, Mrs. Neal."

The Doctor put the letters carefully in his pocket, and rose to take his leave, saying:

"I will come to see you again to-morrow. Until then, good-by."

"Good-by, my good friend," said Linda, returning the friendly pressure of the hand.

From the window she watched him as he drove off, smiling a last adieu, as was his custom. She buried her face in her hands and wept bitterly. She was still so feeble from her long sickness, the slight effort of conversing with the Doctor completely unnerved her. With an impatient yearning, she cried aloud:

"Oh, what a tiresome, unreal month this has been. Not one tender, affectionate word during all my suffering. Only the Doctor was really kind. All my prayers for death have availed nothing. Still, I am not entirely forgotten, for in the midst of my desolation another friend comes to me. Blessings seem to spring from the very shadows of curses."

She threw herself wearily upon the sofa. Her thoughts wandered back to the dear old times with Walter and Nellie, and she chafed impatiently at the weeks that must elapse before those happy days would come again. Then came the overwhelming thought — perhaps she was really married to the Major. If so, what should she do — what could she do? Again, like the ever-varying kaleidoscope, old memories passed before her. She was happy with Walter or Mrs. Neal. Ben was in trouble again, and she was trying to liberate him. Then came the sad, sweet face of Lucy, as she had left her at her cabin door — until all became a confused mass, and she slept.

It was dusk when she was awakened by the entrance of her nurse, with a tray of tempting delicacies. While she was partaking sparingly of her evening meal, the nurse said:

"I am very sorry, Mrs. Warren, that I have to leave you to-night, but my time is up; and I should have gone this morning."

"Going away?" asked Linda, surprised. "Do not leave me, Margaret; you have been so kind and pleasant, I cannot get along without you."

"I am just as sorry to go as you are to have me," answered Margaret. "But Major Warren has paid me my wages, and told me I could go, for you were so well now you did not need my services any longer, and Ann could bring up your meals."

"Then I suppose you must go," said Linda; "but I will be very lonely without you. You have made many weary hours pass pleasantly, Margaret."

"Thank you, ma'am. If I have done you good service, I did only my duty, and was well paid for it."

"You have done more than you were paid for," said Linda, kindly. "And if I can ever do anything for you, come to me without hesitation."

"Thank you, ma'am," said Margaret, quite moved by Linda's disinterested kindness. "You are sweet and good, indeed, and I shall never forget your kindness to me. Oh, bless me! I almost forgot. Here are all those Nevada papers you wanted, for a whole month back, pinned up in my petticoat, and I liked to have gone away with them."

"Oh, thank you," said Linda, taking them, hurriedly.

She looked over each paper carefully until she came to the date of Ben's trial. During the long month of her sickness, as soon as consciousness returned, she had thought continually of him, yet did not dare ask questions. Now, after long and patient waiting, she had the whole truth before her. She thought she was prepared for anything, and had given up all hope, but when she read over the trial, and found it was just as Ben had said, her heart grew faint. The teamster swore Ben was the man who had robbed him. His partners could only say that he was absent from home that evening hunting, although that was his habit; he had remained out later than usual on that particular evening, and was still away at the time the teamster was robbed. Nothing could be done in Ben's favor. He had no evidence to offer, only his solemn oath that he was an innocent man. And what regard has a judge of justice for the oath of a highwayman? The trial was short, but decisive, and Ben Wetherell was sentenced to imprisonment, in the State's prison at San Quentin, for the term of seven years.

When Linda had finished reading, she leaned back as lifeless and hopeless as if every ray of sunshine had been forever shut out from her soul. She thought she was prepared for the worst, but all frail mortals will hope even when there is no hope. When Pandora let the miseries out over the earth, she kept back hope to cheer us, but so cunningly, that hope, when disappointed, proves only a misery in disguise.

Linda sat as if stupefied. She tried to arrange some plans for the future, but could not concentrate her ideas sufficiently to think of anything but her brother, in his lonely cell that night in State's prison.

CHAPTER XXXII.

DEMANDING THE PLEDGE.

THE little clock on the mantle struck ten : Linda started, surprised at the lateness of the hour. She had just risen to retire, when there was a gentle tap at the door, and Major Warren entered. Although Linda was alarmed at the unusual familiarity, she demanded, with dignity :

"What is your errand at this late hour, Major Warren ?"

The Major smiled, as he said, sarcastically : "That is a strange question for a wife to ask her husband, because he comes to her room unannounced, when they have been married a month."

"Sir," said Linda, defiantly, "I do not believe I am married to you at all, and never will, until you give me positive proofs."

"Girl," said the Major, furiously, "you will find no niggard fool in me. I promised your mother, at your request, not to claim you for one month after our marriage. Your sickness has kept us more apart than I desired, but your month is up to-day, and I claim the rights of a husband."

"Will you please tell me where and by whom we were married ?" asked Linda, with ill-feigned coolness.

"Your memory seems remarkably short," said the Major,

curtly. "We were married in Grass Valley, one month ago to-day, by the justice of the peace."

"Major Warren, there is something wrong about this." Linda trembled visibly. "I still do not believe I am your wife, and if I am, it shall only be in name — I will never be a wife to you!"

"Do you take me for a fool?" asked the enraged Major. "I will show you who is master in this house. As your husband, I will either bend or break you."

He made a motion as if to grasp her arm, but Linda, who was standing near a window, threw up the sash and sprang into it.

"Not one step nearer, sir, or I will throw myself from this window," almost shrieked the frightened girl.

"Fool!" hissed the Major. "Don't you know that would be instant death."

He took another step nearer.

"I tell you again, keep off. I know in all probability it would be death to fall from here, but death would be welcome, rather than life with you and that woman in the other room."

Linda's pale face and firm manner forced the Major to retreat a few steps.

"I cannot expect much from one who speaks so disrespectfully of her kind and worthy mother." He stopped a second, but receiving no answer, continued, in a more subdued manner, "I did not expect much love from you, but I certainly felt I could command your respect."

"Major Warren, I despise any man who would persevere, as you have, in marrying a young girl whom he knew did not love him, and never would. If we are so unfortunate as to be married, it is without my consent or knowledge, and there is no law that can compel me to live with you. Leave me."

"Leave you?" said the Major, fiercely. "I will not leave you, you scrap of a disgraced family. What your noble, generous, heart-grieved mother can endure, I may be able to bear in part."

"Major Warren!" said Linda, fiercely, "leave this room. I will not get down from this open window until you have gone."

"You are weak and sick, I know," said the Major, finding it was useless to parley with her. "I have still a little feeling of humanity left. Get down from that window. I will give you still another week to think this matter over; if you then persist in your stupid stubbornness, you shall bear the consequence of my just anger."

The door closed after him, and Linda hastened to draw the bolt, then she threw herself upon the lounge, where she lay a long time before she was able to undress and retire.

When the Doctor called the next day, she felt her good friend, after all, could be of little service. She could not confide to him the scene of the previous evening, lest he might condemn her conduct toward the Major; so the conversation was principally concerning her health. He told her all she required was a good tonic, gentle exercise, and nutritious food, and in a few weeks she would be as well as ever again. If the next day was pleasant, she could go out riding a little while, and he bade her a friendly good-morning.

He had only been gone a short time, when Mrs. Wetherell entered, dressed for a ride. She walked to the window, and looking out, said indifferently, "Your friends, the Grays, were at the Orleans Hotel yesterday on their way East. Why, the Major has returned already," and dashing out of the room, seemed perfectly contented, knowing she had said enough to make Linda very miserable all that afternoon.

M

An hour after the Major and Mrs. Wetherell had gone, Ann came to ask Linda's permission to visit her sister, who was very ill. "If Mrs. Warren would not be too lonesome, for the Major and Mrs. Wetherell would not be home until late."

"How far is it to your sister's?" asked Linda.

"It is about half a mile," said Ann; "but it won't take me a great while."

"I do not mind being alone, Ann," said Linda, thought-, fully. "You can go to see your sister, and remain as long as you like, if you are only back in time to receive the Major and mother."

"Thank you," said Ann, going away delighted.

"Now," thought Linda, "is my time; when will I have another opportunity like this? Great God, this must be providential! What a superstitious child I am getting to be. I honestly believe, if I keep on in my stupid course, and made up my mind to cut my throat, I could soon convince myself it was providential it should be done. Oh, Linda, I fear it is a very dim star that rules your destiny; it leaves you groping in the dark so much."

She sat by the window until Ann was quite out of sight, then, with a smile, she energetically addressed herself: "Now, invalid, you must work industriously." She sprang up with her old elastic, buoyant step, ready for anything, almost forgetting she had ever been ill.

There were two boys playing with marbles on the sidewalk below; she had been watching them for some time; now she called to them:

"Boys, if you will go very quickly, and bring me an express wagon to take a trunk to the express office, I will give you each a dollar."

"Yes, ma'am, I will," said one.

"So 'll I, ma'am," said the other.

"But," said Linda, "you must bring the wagon immediately, or you will not have performed your part of the bargain."

"Yes, ma'am," said one.

"Oh, we will," said the other, as he went tumbling down the steps, saying, "Oh, my! what lots of marbles we 'll have."

Not many of Linda's things had been unpacked during her sickness, so it was only the work of a few moments to gather them together; but with all her haste, the boys were back before she was ready for them. Breathless they rushed up the steps, saying:

"He 's come, ma'am. He 's here."

Linda hastily completed her work. The expressman strapped her trunk, and promised to send it at once to the address of Mrs. Neal. He was to engage a seat in the stage the next morning for Miss Forbes to Nevada, and return as soon as possible with the receipt for her trunk. Away went the wagon, trunk, and all.

Linda turned from the window with a sigh of relief, and there stood the boys looking earnestly at her.

"Oh, boys, I almost forgot you," said she, smiling at their anxious little faces. "You must not tell any one but your mothers how you got this money. Run along now and finish your game of marbles."

The expressman was so long in returning, Linda became nervous least Ann should come first; but, to her delight, he had delivered the receipt and just left when Ann's freckled face made its appearance around the corner.

CHAPTER XXXIII.

THE FLIGHT.

THE first pale light of morning had scarcely dawned over the horizon, when Linda arose, dressed herself, and with satchel in hand went stealthily down the stairs, that would give back an answer at every step, despite her caution, that made her heart beat violently. Out into the street she followed the direction the expressman had taken, and soon arrived at the Orleans Hotel. She asked the privilege of looking over the hotel register, but her search did not meet with the success she had expected. The names of Walter French, Mr. and Mrs. Gray, nurse, and two children, were there as her mother had said, but she could not find her father's name. The clerk came to her assistance, and every name was carefully read over for three months back, but no one by the name of Wetherell had been there.

After breakfast the stage drove up to the door. "All aboard!" shouted Cal Crippen, the driver. Linda took her place on the back seat.

"All aboard here for Rough and Ready, Grass Valley, Nevada, and Red Dog."

Crack went the long whip, and the four little mustangs gave a desperate plunge forward, to be pulled back instantly by the muscular Cal, giving the occupants a sound shaking.

It was a long, tiresome ride of thirteen hours to Nevada. When the stage stopped at Mrs. Neal's door, the good-hearted driver handed the reins to a passenger, and carefully assisted the exhausted Linda into the house.

"My dear child," exclaimed Mrs. Neal, "what is the matter?"

"I have been sick, Mother Neal, but am well again, and so glad to be at home with you."

"Well again, darling? Are you well again? You are only the shadow of your old self, child; but we will take good care of you, dear, and soon get back the roses."

The door opened, and Lucy entered, sad and pale. Seeing Linda, her face brightened; she put her arms about her and held her to her heart, as she said, with a soft wail:

"Oh, Linda, he has been sent away; and we thought you had forgotten us. But for Mrs. Neal, baby and I would have been desolate indeed."

"Forget you?" said Linda. "You do not know me, Lucy. I have a sad, broken heart for a young girl, but it is honest and true. Forget you and Mother Neal? Oh, no."

After a long night's rest, Linda arose refreshed, and the freedom of her soul seemed to bring back the light spirits of health. She related all that had happened since the evening she went away in company with her mother. Finally, when she came to the fact that her father's name was not on the register of the hotel at Sacramento, Mrs. Neal expressed her belief that the whole thing had been a plot to get her away.

Linda was too impatient to wait; so a carriage was sent for, and the young ladies drove out to Captain Wetherell's mill, as Mrs. Neal declined accompanying them.

They were met by John Murphy, who very laconically pointed to the mound under the great pine, when Lucy asked for Captain Wetherell. Seeing Linda's pale face, he explained in his rough way all about the accident in the mine, and her father's sudden death, Mrs. Wetherell's visit, and the Captain's

16

burial. Then he went into the house and brought out a large package of papers, which he handed to Linda, saying:

"He gave 'em to me, Miss, for you. The ould lady wanted 'em, but she did n't get 'em."

Making a note of her father's death and burial, Linda bade the faithful John good-by, telling him where he could find her at any time, and assuring him when the estate was settled he should not be forgotten.

Back in the cottage every detail was gone over to Mrs. Neal. That wise mother sat long in earnest thought, then insisting upon Linda's resting awhile, put on her bonnet and shawl, without any explanations, and drove at once to Grass Valley.

An examination of the records of marriage by the justice of the peace proved that on the same date of Captain Wetherell's death, and the same evening Linda had gone away with her mother, Major William Warren had married Laura Wetherell, instead of Linda. The joy that lighted up that sweet, motherly face, with its crown of snowy hair, seemed like a ray of glory from the very throne of heaven.

"Back home as fast as possible," she said to the driver, as she sprang into the carriage as lightly as a young girl.

The four miles seemed interminable. As she found Linda still sleeping, she took her old position by the bedside, patiently waiting to tell her the joyful tidings of her perfect freedom. Regarding the thin, pale face, so peacefully calm in its refreshing slumber, Zedlitz's lines to Mary came to her mind, and she repeated, softly:

> "Wie schläfst du so ruhig und träumest,
>   Du armer, verlassener Wurm,
>   Es donnert, die Tropfen fallen,
>   Die Bäume schüttelt der Sturm!

"Dein Vater hat dich vergessen,
   Dich und die Mutter dein;
Du bist, du arme Waise,
   Auf der weiten Erde allein!"

When Linda opened her eyes, Mrs. Neal put her arms affectionately about her neck and imprinted a fond kiss upon her brow.

"At your old post, Mother Neal. If you only knew how happy I am to be back under your loving care. Nothing can ever get me away again."

"No, darling, nothing," and Mrs. Neal stroked Linda's forehead caressingly. "Since you have been sleeping, I have been to Grass Valley to look over the marriage records of the justice of the peace; and, dear, they say that Major Warren was married to Laura Wetherell, not Linda."

"To my mother!" exclaimed Linda.

"Yes, to your mother; the evening of the day your father was killed. It must have been that night you went to Grass Valley from here."

"Oh, you darling, Mother Neal! what glorious news! Then I am the same old Linda, and not married; but —" The joy left her face, and she leaned wearily back upon the pillow, "Walter has gone forever."

"Perhaps not, child. You must not yield to despair so easily. Every morning begins a new chapter in our lives, and often the saddest openings are sometimes the most joyous endings. The workings of life are sadly irregular and hopelessly incomprehensible. Some of us do not live one life, nor two, but many. As long as the vital organs perform their functions, the mechanisms of life go on; but the senses or soul of man live and die and live again. Most of us, looking back, can remember when life was dead — every joy, every hope; and if the beating of our hearts could have stopped, how gladly the weary soul would have taken its flight. But the heart went on beating to its own funeral, until new hopes, new joys, new life were born out of the old one, wholly unlike, and seemingly in no way related to it."

"With your ideas, you cannot dread death, Mother Neal."

"Death, my child, only relates to these bodies, and surely there can be nothing to dread in the thought that we can one day leave these aching, tired, decaying tenements. Scientists may prate of nervous centres being all there is of life. It is false — for the paralytic has still his life, his soul, without sensibilities. I believe we have more than one soul — that every human being is possessed of two. Life is a perpetual warfare between right and wrong, duty and inclination, and there must be conflicting elements to make contention. One soul cannot fight itself. There is nothing in our bodies to fight. Without the souls they are, like other great and wonderful machines, harmless and useless until set in motion by the great life-giving power, steam. Very often a great soul enshrined in a feeble casket wears it out prematurely, with its perpetual fretting and longing for grander, nobler exploits. To my poor judgment, everything indicates two persons in one, two ruling spirits. We often start out under the dictation of one soul, and the other, under what we term circumstances, interferes, and we do exactly the reverse of our first intention. We have not a thought that cannot be opposed. When two spirits are of equal strength it leaves a vacillating condition of mind, never at rest, never satisfied. One must be superior to the other, for good or bad, to make a decided character, and even then the weaker cries ever for pre-eminence and power. We are fearfully weak and ignorant human beings to be made in the likeness of God himself; for His commonest attribute, creation, we can neither understand nor imitate. We all know we exist, yet we cannot define what it is. My dear child, when we can humbly accept our position, and bow reverently to the Great Power that controls us, whatever it may be — when we can lay aside our importance, and realize that we are mere atoms of a vast machine, run by an all-wise Creator, knowing no more of the use of our neighbor machine than the revolving spoke knows of the axle upon which it makes its revolutions, then we can realize that the Great Creator, who had use for us here in our infancy, can need us for something better after the purifying fires of His chastenings.''

'' But so many believe in annihilation after death, perpetual rest, eternal sleep,'' suggested Linda.

'' It is a very senseless theory to me, '*Ex nihilo nihil fit*,' out of nothing, nothing is made. Nature has no such word as *nothing* in her vocabulary. She does everything for something. It has always been a mystery to me why we should have been created for so much rest, when there is so much in the world to be done, and so short a time to accomplish it. Surely if there was nothing but sleep hereafter, there would be less of it here; for man sleeps away more than one-third of his life.''

'' Just think of a man sixty years old, having slept over twenty years. I never thought of it before,'' said Linda. '' Surely one should have a very comfortable bed, when so much more time is passed there than anywhere else during life.''

'' Yes, it is all-important, for the bodies require much rest; and yet every organ performs its duty whether sleeping or waking, though in sleep more sluggishly. The spirits never rest. They go out while we sleep. We often meet people whom we feel we have met before, and so we have in spirit. When we swoon, life goes out. There may not be the

16 *

slightest defect in the human organization, yet a sudden shock may lay it apparently lifeless. Everything is there — nerves, brains, and all, in perfect working order — yet stopped because the appalled spirits have fled. Sometimes, when you sleep, dear, your longing, unsatisfied soul will go out to that of Walter, and you will meet again.''

" How hopefully you talk," said Linda, encouraged.

" I feel what I say, dear, for I have some place a daughter, a little older than yourself; and I am sure I have been with her sometimes, for I awake refreshed in body and satisfied in mind.''

"You promised long ago to tell me about her, Mother Neal.''

" Yes, child, if you can listen to such a sad story, I will tell you how I lost my babies," and Mrs. Neal related, with the pathos of a broken-hearted mother, all the terrors of that dark, stormy night, and the darker dawn for her.

Linda sat as if spell-bound, listening to every word. Then turning her great brown eyes upon Mrs. Neal, exclaimed:

" Why, Mother Neal, I have heard that story before."

Mrs. Neal started nervously. " Heard that? How could you have heard it?''

" Mr. Warren told me, in relating the history of his adopted daughter, Alice. It was he who lived opposite to you. It was his wife you watched so tenderly, and he has still that little girl that was left with you."

" Yes, it was Mrs. Warren I was with; but Warren is not a remarkable name, and I never expected to hear of them again. Besides, you never mentioned his adopted daughter. Poor child," she said, thoughtfully, "I wonder if that dark mystery will ever be solved?''

" I hope so, with all my heart," said Linda, earnestly.

"My child, I must hold my daughter to my heart as I hold you now, or I could not die contentedly." And the tears that came to the longing mother's eyes, might have been drops of life-blood wrung from her heart.

CHAPTER XXXIV.

THE FATAL SECRET.

MAJOR WARREN and Mrs. Wetherell were greatly alarmed at Linda's mysterious disappearance. All possible search was made to no purpose — not the slightest trace could be found. They supposed she had gone back to Nevada, but her registering as Miss Forbes quite misled them.

"I will write to a friend of mine in Nevada, upon whom I can rely, without creating any suspicions," said the Major, one evening, as he unfolded the paper and began reading.

"It would be shocking to have a disgraceful scandal about your runaway wife," said Mrs. Wetherell. "I feel convinced she is in Nevada, and as soon as you can ascertain to a certainty, I will quietly go and bring her back."

"Halloo! what is this?" The Major dropped his paper, and stared at Mrs. Wetherell.

"Why, Major, have you seen a ghost?" asked Mrs. Wetherell, smiling.

"A ghost!" ejaculated the Major. "Almost, madam," and he lowered his voice almost to a whisper. "Did you know your husband was dead?"

"My husband dead! Major, you joke," said Mrs. Wetherell, with a forced smile, and a shade paler than usual.

"Read this." The Major thrust the paper into her hand.
"The will of Richard Wetherell, of Grass Valley, was filed
in the probate court on Monday last."   ·

"Merciful heaven!" exclaimed Mrs. Wetherell, dropping
her head upon her hands. Her whole frame shook convulsively. It was well done; that woman, whose every act in life
was a lie, played her part to the end. There were no particulars, only the simple statement.

The Major, really quite affected, led her to her room, earnestly entreating her to bear patiently the cross common to all.
He sat down at once and wrote to an attorney in behalf of Mrs.
Wetherell's interest in her husband's estate, and also to ascertain if the daughter was at Mrs. Neal's.

A few days later, Mrs. Wetherell, robed in deep mourning,
with a very becoming widow's cap, sat awaiting the Major's
return to dinner. The door opened, and the usually benign,
amiable Major stalked into the room, his face livid, and his
eyes bloodshot.

"My dear Major, what has happened?" asked Mrs. Wetherell, going toward him.

He waved her back with his hand, looking her steadily in
the face with a hard expression hitherto wholly unknown to
him, and handing her a letter, he growled savagely: "Read
that!"

Mrs. Wetherell took the paper, and, as she read, her face
blanched.

MAJOR WARREN.

DEAR SIR:—You have requested me to look after Mrs. Wetherell's interest in her husband's estate, whose real name, by the
way, was Richard Neal, instead of Wetherell. The will gives
her one-third in case she never marries again; in that event,
nothing. As she was married in Grass Valley the day of her

husband's death, to William Warren, she has forfeited all claim.

Your obedient servant,
MARK WINTERS,
Attorney-at-Law.

As her face blanched, the Major· grew more livid. There was a demoniac glare from his gray eyes. .His breathing was heavy and irregular. He grasped her by the arm and screamed into her ear, "Tell me, woman, is that true or false?"

For once, the woman who had moulded all obstacles to her will was awe-stricken. She dropped the paper; her chin fell upon her breast. She tried several times to articulate, but seemed incapable.

"Tell me, woman!" and the iron grasp of the Major's hand sent a sharp cry of pain from the statue-like figure before him.

"It is —" she began.

"Don't you dare to lie to me!" hissed the Major between his teeth, and the iron grasp tightened; "speak, or I'll kill you!"

The miserable woman gasped, rather than spoke, "It—is—true."

With one effort of his strong arm he flung her from him across the room. Regarding her senseless form with a fiendish grin, he paced the floor like a wild beast. The form before him moved, gradually raised herself upon her hand, and with the other felt her head, while she stared about vacantly.

The Major, with his arms crossed over his breast, stood regarding her with bitter defiance:

"Do not muss your widow's cap, Mrs. Wetherell. I forgot — you are — no! I swear — you never shall be called Mrs. Warren. Such a devil my wife! It must have been a sacred rite that bound your cursed, lying self to me. You, monster, are the mother of a lovely, artless girl, whom I condemned because you did — whom you would have vilely prostituted, under sacred garbs, and for what, God only knows."

"For money!" gasped Mrs. Wetherell.

"For money! There are women who sell their own souls for money; but a mother who could sell her innocent child is too vile a thing for hell!"

"Hell!" moaned Mrs. Wetherell. "Hell! I've had it all my life."

"And if you have it through all eternity, too, the devil will not get even with you."

Where was the affable, courteous Major Warren? There was not a shadow of the old Major left. His very features seemed to have changed, as he stood with outstretched hand pointing toward the door, and, with voice hoarse and discordant, commanded:

"Go to your room, madam!"

The frightened woman tried to obey, but fell back exhausted.

"Go to your room, I say!" thundered the Major.

She made another desperate effort, and by the aid of a chair and the wall reached the foot of the stairs, when she sank helpless.

The merciless Major following, still with outstretched hand pointing the way, said again, "Go!"

She turned her great black eyes upon him — so strangely glaring and cowed—and slowly climbed on her hands and knees, step by step, until she reached the top, then fell prostrate.

That night was a busy one in the Major's house, which the still, balmy morning seemed to smile at. In the rear of the house, back of the twining roses, was a window, on the inside of which were great iron bars, and the door was heavily bolted. On the bed lay a pale woman with staring eyes, that seemed the loopholes of a sepulchre, and the room was a living tomb.

CHAPTER XXXV.

UNDERCURRENTS IN PRISON.

ROSE-TINTS of morning were playing on the rippling waves, as the waters of the San Francisco Bay swept the sands and bore them away—wailing a low refrain over the dead night, and sighing at the dawning day. Afar off was Mount Tamelpais, capped with floating clouds, that in their fleecy rose-tints seemed stray blushes from the mist maiden's cheeks.

On the bleak and barren promontory, with its great stone walls, under the very smile of the soft-tinted Tamelpais, was the prison of San Quentin. Click, click, click. In quick succession the iron doors swung back, and the hundreds of doomed mortals, expiating their sins, came out in their striped felon's clothes, passed over to the eating-hall, where they partook of the plain prison fare, then out into God's sunshine, that will smile upon the good and the bad alike. It was Sunday, an idle day. Some collected in groups, and in loud bravado boasted of their exploits in the crimes that brought them there, while others, less inured to vice, drank in the unwholesome lesson for future use. Some in silence and alone walked up and down, while their hungry souls went out in search of happiness, or were turned inward, seeking peace in memory's granary —away back—before temptations came and the iron hand of fate ground their souls to the dust.

Apart sat Ben Wetherell, with his hand full of letters. A letter was part of Ben's every-day existence. Twice a week the three faithful women wrote. So he received a letter every day, excepting Sunday, and on that day, when he had more leisure, he read them all over. This Sunday his eyes were moist, as he sat intently gazing at a photograph — his baby's likeness. An old, gray-headed man came up and accosted him. Ben startled in surprise at the sound of the well-known voice.

"Why, Walker, are you back here?"

"Yes, and glad to get back," was the hopeless reply.

"You cannot mean what you say?" said Ben, in astonishment.

"Yes, Wetherell, I mean what I say. You know I had been here ten years—that is, prison years, for I always got my credits for good behavior, — and when I went into the world again I was like a cat in a strange garret. Nobody knew me, or wanted to — nobody wanted a felon to work for him. I got hungry, and stole to get back here. I have no relations with the world any more, Wetherell, and before my next ten years are up, it will all be up with me, too, and it will be best so."

"My dear fellow," said Ben, in deepest pity, "have you no friends?"

"Friends? A State's-prison bird have friends? ha, ha," and Walker laughed a hard, hollow laugh.

Catching a glimpse of the baby's picture and the pile of letters, a softer expression passed over his face, and he said, politely:

"I beg your pardon, Wetherell. I forgot you are one of the few lucky dogs who has friends. For my part, I agree with the minstrel who said, 'Every dog must have his day;' but he had come to the conclusion there were more dogs than days. But, Wetherell," and Walker's voice grew soft and musical, "I had friends once.

" ' My hair is gray, but not with years;
　　Nor grew it white
　　In a single night,
As men's have grown, from sudden fears;
My limbs are bow'd, though not with toil,
　　But rusted with a vile repose,
For they have been a dungeon's spoil.
　　And mine has been the fate of those
　　To whom the goodly earth and air
　　Are bann'd and barr'd — forbidden fare.'

" Twelve years ago I came to California with my family — a wife so sweet and fondly true, that she seemed a waif from heaven's throne. We had been married ten years, and ten such years of happiness are not often allotted to man. Young, earnest, and full of health, we walked the path of life hand in hand, sharing every joy and sorrow, every thought and care— at least, I thought so then; but since I have often fancied Mary kept many weary, anxious thoughts from me. We had three children the oldest a girl nine years of age. The other two were boys, seven and five years old. When I look back, I remember my Mary never complained, never fretted; and yet I know there were times when she would come and rest her head on my shoulder, with a faint, weary sigh, that comes to me after all these years, and tells me what I could not see then, that her life was going away — but I weary you."

" No, indeed, Walker; talk on. It does one good sometimes."

" Well, we came to California, the land of gold and promise; brought with us all our possessions, which were not very much, and rented a little house, but, with the best of recommendations, it was two months before I obtained a clerkship in a bank. I had been employed six months when I was taken ill with

17　　　　　　　　　　N

typhoid fever, which confined me to the house for weeks. As soon as I was able, I went to the bank, but, to my horror, I had been superseded, and there was no vacancy. Our resources were almost gone, and my wife was expecting soon to add a little member to our household. Day after day I searched for work, but without success. Finally my wife became sick, and on me devolved the care of the other children. Wetherell, can you imagine how I felt, when I discovered what my wife had hidden from me? The last morsel of food had been eaten, and we were positively destitute. The dear, pale wife had almost starved herself to keep the shocking truth from me. To be a man, with all the pride of manhood, enfeebled from sickness, and stand by helpless, while those we love suffer for the necessaries of life — great God! what torture. So the tempter came. The man I had served, though a man of family, had a mistress, to whom he gave monthly the generous check of two thousand dollars. I had blanks, and knew his signature fatally well. I had always been an adept with my pen. I wrote the check; it was cashed. Then I laughed in my heart to think I had so cunningly fooled the harlot out of her ill-gotten gains, and my good, suffering wife could have the comforts of life. I must have been mad to have hoped for success. My gift at imitation was well known, and betrayed me. I was lodged in jail, and my sick wife and starving children left. My God! man, that thought maddens me to this hour. For months I languished in a crowded jail, then was sentenced to ten years here. My Mary faded like a flower, and died before I came, and the baby went with her. The other children were sent to an orphan asylum. The years went by, and I was released, with still some of the hopes of a man, to find my sons had both died, and my daughter was an outcast.''

The man's head fell lower between his stooping shoulders,

and the two sat long in silence. Ben could understand how it was he had no relations with the world.

He handed him a letter from Mrs. Neal, saying, "Read that." Walker took it mechanically, and read:

NEVADA, June 20.

MY DEAR YOUNG FRIEND : — The melancholy tenor of your letters grieves me. Be not so oppressed by your bondage, for, after all, Ben, we are all prisoners. Every heart is a prison-house bound by fetters, invisible to the human eye, but surely bound. There is not one soul upon the face of the earth entirely satisfied, and, unfortunately, the more refined the feelings and cultivated the intellect, the more perplexing and unreal becomes this ever-revolving treadmill called life.

It has been wisely said, "there is nothing new under the sun." Your experience is an old story of life, only differently worded. The inevitable is submission to fate, and inevitable fate is sorrow. The youngest heart has the germ that will bind it sooner or later. Deck it in gorgeous apparel, link it with jewels, the chain of sorrow ever so deep is surely hidden in the human heart. Perfect happiness has been and is, but no one dare say it is his, for it is turned to ashes by a breath from heaven, and fades like the rose-tints of morning. Each thinks his lot the hardest, and we are given to envying our neighbor's peace and contentment, but when the veil is raised there is neither peace nor contentment there, because man is ever longing for what he does not possess, and craves what he cannot attain. Labor as he will, the summit of his ambitions is never attained, because every success opens a new vista of glory, and after a life of toil, in the very zenith of his power, like Moses, he dies on the threshold of success. Another takes up the burden where he left off, but it is incomprehensible and beyond him. He, too, must take the first step on the ladder, and each round at a time, and possibly reach a few degrees higher than his predecessor, but the result is quite as unsatisfactory and incomplete. So man, in his self-righteousness, goes on working over and over the old clay that composed the earth centuries ago, pulling down and building up — like the sweeping waves of ocean, washing away the sands on one shore to strand them on another.

It impresses me rather strangely, that in your physical bondage, your soul should yearn so for the material instead of the spiritual, and you avoid using the name of God, my dear, which grieves me. I would have you bow submissively and reverently before the Great Power that controls us; whose mandate is supreme, divine; in whom we live and have our being; whose laws of discipline are for the perfection of our souls. Regard it in that light, if possible, Ben. Remember you are no exception — every soul is a prisoner — free agency is a fallacy. There is no perfect freedom for mortals. According to worldly interpretation, I am free, and yet if my longing soul could escape from the body that holds it, and go out into the world in search of my long lost beloved, I would be free. As it is, I am a pitiable prisoner to the decrees of fate. While your body is in bondage your soul is freer than mine, for it has its loved ones, and your mind no man can control. No one is entirely free, body and soul. We are all free prisoners, serving out the penalty of fallen humanity. It is the curse of mortality. When our race is run, our time is served, then we will be free to accept the reward of our long-suffering penance.

' God bless you, dear Ben, in your affliction, and always be comforted by the sweet assurance that faithful love awaits impatiently your release.

Your friend, most sincerely,
AGNES NEAL.

CHAPTER XXXVI.

JACK HUNTER'S UNFINISHED STORY.

A THIRD prisoner had joined them quietly and sat down by Ben, listening to Walker. After a long silence, he said:

"Boys, maybe my story might interest you, if you would like to hear it."

Ben and Walker inclined their heads affirmatively, and the speaker began.

"Twenty-five years ago I fell in love with a minister's daughter. Her name was Agnes White. I was a poor country school-teacher, scarcely making a living for myself, let alone a wife, who was as poor as I was. A young heart can love as ardently with an empty purse as a full one; but hearts are not so easily kindled into passion without the blaze of gold — at least I thought so then, now I see I might have been mistaken. We cannot force the fruit before the blossom, and in my hot impetuosity I thought her heart must respond to mine, no matter what its feelings were.

"It happened at that time there was a steamboat accident on the Mississippi. Many were killed, and as many more wounded. Among the latter was the captain, who was taken to Parson White's, and for weeks lay ill, attended by the parson's wife and daughter, Agnes, their only child. Agnes read to him and talked to him, in fact was his constant companion. I went sometimes to relieve her, but soon found she drooped her eyes and blushed when I spoke of the captain, and he was not content when she was out of his sight. I became a jealous monster, continually watching and scheming to get rid of him ; then imagine my despair when I heard, one day, Agnes had been quietly married to the captain, who was to return on duty at once. He did not take her with him, but came every Saturday to spend Sunday with her.

"I wandered about for years, and returned to find Agnes the happy mother of a son and daughter. All my old love for her came back, and my jealous hatred for her husband preyed upon me so I was compelled to leave that part of the world, for in my innermost soul I nursed a demon of revenge, before whom I sometimes quailed myself.

"I went to New Orleans, obtained employment, and strove manfully to tear the past from my heart; but the hand of fate

17 *

was upon me. I was a doomed mortal.   While I was thus trying to bridge over the past, imagine my astonishment, one day,
in seeing the captain, Agnes's husband, seated in an open carriage with a dashing beauty by his side. It was evidently a
private carriage, and I followed it. It drove into the grounds
and stopped before the door of a princely mansion. The occupants alighted, entered the house, and the carriage was driven
around to the stable. 'So,' I thought, 'my enemy on such
intimate terms here. What can it mean?' I inquired of a
policeman who lived in that elegant house. He answered,
'Captain Wetherell.'"

Ben started at the name, and the speaker looked at him
strangely.

"His name is Wetherell, you know, Jack?" explained
Walker.

"And my father was captain of a Mississippi steamboat,
once," added Ben. "It is a strange coincidence."

"It is strange," said Jack, stupidly, as if he could not comprehend. "May I ask what your father's first name is?"

"My father is dead. His name was Richard."

Jack's thin lips were firmly compressed an instant. He drew
his fists tight together, and whispered faintly, as if it had been
the refrain of a sigh, "At last!"

Ben regarded him in surprise, but there was nothing to be
read in the man's face, as he asked: "May I also ask your
mother's name?"

"Yes; her name is Laura."

"Is Laura—" Jack sat silently a long time, as if lost in
thought, when the stillness was broken by Walker.

"Well, Jack, you began to tell us something very interesting, and stopped rather queer. Do those names fit in your
story?"

"What names?" asked Jack.

"What is the matter with you, man?" asked Walker.

Jack's eyes came back from their far-off journey, as he continued:

"Oh, yes, I remember. I spoke of Captain Wetherell, and this young man's name is Wetherell, and you thought it queer. Yes, it is queer. Well, will you believe it, that wretch I was talking about was married to that dashing creature, living like a prince in New Orleans, and he had brought the sweet woman I loved there too, and she was living in a cottage not half a mile away.

"I lost no time, and soon found out Agnes was the real wife, and the other was not. If it had been the other way, and my Agnes been deceived, I would have taken her with her guiltless soul away from the wretch who betrayed her; but, as it was, my case was hopeless.

"I opened a correspondence with the second wife—told her she had been betrayed, and I could prove it. It was some time before I could induce her to make any response. Finally, when I had almost despaired, a summons came to be at her house at a certain hour on a day named. I was ascending the marble steps, at the appointed time, when the door was opened by the lady herself, who was evidently awaiting me. I was shown into a reception room, with gold and brown hangings. Across the hall I could just catch a glimpse, in the soft light, of gold and silver and crimson. It was regal paradise, where even the delicate-tinted flowers under my feet seemed capable of sending forth perfumes in their artistic perfection. I had never seen such luxury before.

"The lady closed the door, and asked at once:

"'Are you the person who has been annoying me with anonymous letters?'

"I answered quite as coldly, 'Yes, madam, I am.'

"'What your object may be, I have been unable to understand. You have never threatened, or attempted any extortions. You utterly ignore my silence, and persistently write. Your letters annoy me, and I demand an explanation.'

"There was a dangerous flash from her black eyes, and she paced the floor without looking toward me. I had tracked a lion to its den, and had scarcely the courage to give the blow that would make it spring in self-defence. For one moment I had not the courage,— one moment, only one, in which I thought of my desolate fate, and all the bitterness of my soul came back.

"'Madam, I have written you nothing but the truth, for which I ignore return.'

"'Sir, do you dare to tell me to my face I am not the wife of the man whose name I bear, and my children are bastards?'

"That livid face, those burning eyes, and that stately woman, who stood looking fiercely into my face, as if she could annihilate me — I see them now. I had never been a bad man. My life had been a simple country life — a poor orphan, brought up here and there, without home or friends. Parson White was all the father I ever knew, and Agnes was my life, my all, and I had lost her. So you can understand I quailed before the appalling work I was doing. I had not counted on such a fury as I met.

"My silence and irresolution exasperated her. She stamped her foot, and the one word, 'Answer!' made me turn pale and tremble. She stood with her fierce eyes riveted on mine, and, as a snake charms its prey, drew forth the truth — drew it from me. Ay, I stood there like a tool at her command. I told her of her husband's double marriage and my lost love — that Agnes was his wife and the mother of two children, while she, the beautiful fiend before me, was the mistress of the man she lived with, and her children were bastards.

"She paced the floor with clinched hands. A deep shadow had fallen over her handsome face. She was thinking, darkly thinking, and she took long, sweeping strides to keep pace with her thoughts. An hour must have passed, when she turned suddenly to me.

"'You have been wronged, too. You hate them both. I will investigate this matter, and if it is as you say, may I trust to your aid for revenge?'

"'You can,' I answered, with all my heart.

"'I believe you,' she gasped, almost breathless, as she firmly grasped my hand. 'Come at this same hour one week from to-day, and we will see what can be done.'

"She opened the door, and I went silently out into the dark night.

"I went again in one week. As I ascended the steps the door was opened, as on my previous visit, by the lady herself, and I was silently motioned into the reception room. To my amazement, there sat the Captain.

"The madam had examined the marriage register and found Captain Richard Neal had married Agnes White, and that Captain Wetherell's name was Neal she was perfectly convinced, for all his property was in that name. His second marriage was registered R. Wetherell. There was no mistake. The little country girl, whose sweet devotion had won the Captain, he thought harmless, and he was determined to possess the beautiful woman who had completely fascinated him.

"She did not hesitate an instant. The inquisition began.

"'Captain Wetherell, look at this young man.'

"The Captain raised his eyes to mine, and turned deathly pale.

"'You know him,' she continued. 'You married the woman he loved. She has two children bearing your name. You
married me, Captain Wetherell, and I have two children — two
illegitimate children — you parade before the world in this
princely home, where you keep your mistress. The others, who
bear your name, and are the heirs to your estate, are hidden in
an obscure cottage.'

"She sprang in front of the silent, cowering man, and hissed :

"'If I had a dagger that could cut but never kill, never
cease its exquisite torture, how I could plunge it into your false
heart. Captain Wetherell, I am from this hour my own mistress, not yours. You are my tool. You shall obey my slightest command. Make over this day your estate to me, and leave
this country. Do you hear? You are a felon, if I speak but
the word. You dare not disobey. I choose to remain Mrs.
Wetherell. The little country girl need never know. She will
never take the pains to find out. You had an offer to go to
India. Go, and never come back. If you dare to oppose my
command, I will throw aside my pride, and you shall meet what
you deserve — a felon's doom.'

"Every word came like a curse, and the woman who uttered
them looked a superb fiend.

"The Captain, with his head drooping on his breast, rose to
leave the room. She stepped in front of him. He shuddered,
as if she had been a viper.

"'I give you forty-eight hours to leave this place,' she said.
'Will you go?'

"The bowed head dropped lower in acquiescence, and he
passed out.

"The woman approached me. 'Sir,' she whispered, hoarsely,
'you will never relent; never repent? You swear it?'

"I answered, scarcely audible, 'I swear.'

"Again the ashen lips parted, her dark eyes scanned the room nervously, as she grasped my arm:

" ' I married that dotard for money. I hate him, but I must have his wealth. The other two children are his heirs; mine,' she trembled like an aspen, 'are nothing. You hate that other woman. So do I. She has robbed me. He is an arrant coward ; he will leave in two days. You tell me that woman spends a great deal of her time at a neighbor's. Watch the cottage closely. The first time she is absent after dark, meet me here with a carriage. No matter when, I will be ready. Be your own driver, for no other human being but you and I can ever know what is done. Drive to the rear of the cottage. Take her children and leave mine ; then we will get the property.'

"I shuddered at the thought of taking Agnes's children. It was horrible. But the still, small voice of revenge said, 'Agnes took your heart.'

"I answered promptly : 'I will do your bidding, madam ; but after that, we part forever.'

" ' It will be best,' she answered."

The man ceased talking. Presently he began again in a low whisper :

"I went like a thief, that I was, in the darkness of night; lightning flashed angrily from heaven ; thunder rolled over my head in awful threatening, but I took Agnes's children and left the bastards in their place. I left the city that night, and wandered over the earth like an evil spirit for rest, but there was none for me ; never any more. Sleeping or waking, I could not rest. Finally, I went back to confess my guilt, and restore the children, for whom I knew the mother's heart was breaking. They were gone — all gone. The cottage was for rent, and strangers occupied the mansion. What I have endured, wandering this wide world over, in search of the woman I wronged, no human tongue could ever tell. Poor, starving, haunted wretch that I am — if I could only redeem the past."

His eyes rested upon the open letter in Walker's hand, and on it was written "Agnes Neal." The man shrank back as if shot, and his face was convulsed with pain. He grasped Walker's arm with one hand and with the other pointed to the letter. His white lips parted, but for an instant no sound came. Finally, recovering himself, he whispered, "Where did you get that?"

"It is his," said Walker, pointing to Ben.

Jack picked up the envelope, read the post-mark, arose, staggered off, and was seen no more.

Ben's attention had been attracted in another direction, and he had not seen the strange pantomime. He turned toward Walker, saying:

"That is a strange specimen of humanity. I think his mind is affected. He started in to tell us how he came here, and never mentioned it after all."

Walker made no reply. He had read more in the man's face than Ben, and was strongly convinced that he was in some way connected with the story.

Poor Jack Hunter had been so long in the prison, and had never received any message from the outside world, that it had quite escaped the minds of others that he had ever been a part of it. For several years he had been a "trusty," never failing, never wavering in his duty. The day after the above conversation, he was sent with a guard on an errand. When they were about a mile away from the prison, where there were many curves in the road, and the hills were covered with underbrush, Jack suddenly discovered the linch-pin in the cart was missing.

"I think I know just where we lost it," he said. "I thought I heard something drop. I will run back and get it."

The guard waited, but Jack did not return. The guard went in search, but he was not to be found, and the prison walls were never to hold him any more.

CHAPTER XXXVII.

THE FATAL SHOT — A YEAR AND A HALF LATER.

WHO is that fellow?" asked Bill Brown of Blaize, the proprietor of the most extensive drinking and gambling saloon in Nevada, as Jack Hunter hobbled out by the aid of his cane.

"I don't know," answered Blaize. "We call him Jack. He came here over a year ago, so doubled up with rheumatism he could hardly move. He told me he had been a long time in a hospital somewhere. He wanted work, and I pitied the poor devil, for he was almost naked and half starved. The old darkey who used to take care of the saloon had just died, so I let him work around for his board and clothes. He's the most reliable fellow I ever saw, and the willingest dog alive. I pay him wages now, and he's worth a dozen ordinary sound men."

"He's a little crazy, I think," said Bill. "He's been talking about some mission he has to perform, and says I remind him of some one he used to know — asks me every time he sees me if I ever knew Captain Wetherell. It's blamed queer; almost every day I meet somebody who has known somebody else that I look like. I can't get rid of this fellow.

18

He wants me to walk a little way down the street with him this evening just after dark, to show me somebody, and ask my advice."

"Well, go with him," said Blaize. "If there is anything you can do for the poor devil, do it. I will consider it as a favor to me. Come, take a drink."

Presently Jack came limping in a great deal spryer than usual. Several people had congregated in the saloon in the meantime. In his usual quiet way he went up to Bill, and reminded him of the walk he had asked him to take an hour or two before.

"I was just going to have a game of cards with these friends of mine," answered Bill; but seeing Jack's disappointed face, he turned to his friends and said: "Gentlemen, excuse me a few minutes, I have to go up street a little ways with Jack, but will be back presently."

"I guess Jack can wait," said one, roughly.

"Well, we'll excuse you, but don't stay long," said another.

Bill and Jack walked silently along until they approached Mrs. Neal's cottage, when Jack, as if suddenly awakened from a reverie, said:

"You must go softly, so as not to disturb them."

"Disturb who? Who are you talking about?" asked Bill.

"Why, the two ladies."

"Are you bringing me away out here to see two ladies, you old fool, as though ladies were a curiosity about these diggins." Bill stopped short, as if to turn around and go back.

"Oh, sir, please come and look in at the window; just one moment, and see how happy they are," pleaded Jack.

"What do I want to look into people's windows for to see how happy they are?" growled Bill, sullenly.

"But I want you to; I want your advice," insisted Jack. "I stole her boy and girl from her eighteen years ago, and left two bastards in their place. For more than a year I have come here daily, watching her with that strange girl. They are so happy and contented, I have not had the courage to tell her how it happened, although I would give my life to redeem the past by restoring them to her."

"What are you talking about, Jack? I believe you are crazy," said Bill, impatiently.

"Crazy! I wish to God I was, for then this consuming remorse would be ended. No, I am worse than crazy — I'm a villain!"

They had reached the cottage, Jack had noiselessly approached a window, and motioned to Bill, who reluctantly followed, and looked in through the half-closed blinds where Jack indicated. He gave a sudden start, grasped Jack's arm, and said, excitedly :

"What did you bring me here for?"

Jack was terrified lest Mrs. Neal, who sat sewing, with Linda reading by her side, should hear the noise and become alarmed. He took Bill by the arm to lead him away, but his mute entreaties were of no avail. Bill stood persistently leaning against the window, looking intently at the little group, as if spellbound.

Finally, in terror, Jack whispered, "They are coming to close the blinds ; you must go."

Bill permitted himself to be led some distance from the cottage, when he stopped short, and facing Jack, demanded :

"Are you the devil who broke that woman's heart?"

"I am," whispered Jack, hoarsely.

"You ought to be killed," said Bill, fiercely clinching his arm.

"Will you be merciful enough to kill me?" asked Jack, with the most pitiful appeal.

Bill regarded him an instant with amazement, then, letting go his hold, said contemptuously, "It is greater punishment to let you live."

"Ay, my life is hell," said Jack, desperately. "But what do you know of *her?*"

"What do I know of her?" asked Bill, thoughtfully. "I know the whole story from her own lips. I was the boy who was left in the place of her lost one."

"You!" exclaimed Jack, staggering, as if from a blow, and he would have fallen had not Bill caught him. "Then you are that *woman's* child, and the boy in prison is Agnes Neal's son."

"What boy in prison, Jack?" It was Bill's turn to be astonished.

"Ben Wetherell," was the answer.

"What do you know of him?" asked Bill, nervously.

"I was in prison, too. I saw him there."

"How does the poor fellow bear it?" asked Bill, evincing great sympathy.

"Like a man," answered Jack.

"Poor fellow!" said Bill, more to himself than to Jack.

They were retracing their steps in silence, as they had come. Bill, with his slight, graceful figure, taking long, sweeping strides, while the stooped cripple by his side hobbled along, scarcely able to keep up with his young companion. Bill soon discovered the discomfort of his escort, and regarding him attentively, slackened his pace, as he said:

"Jack, if you stole me, you must know who I am, and where I belong. It would be some satisfaction to a fellow to know."

"All I could tell you would be very unsatisfactory," answered Jack, hesitatingly. "But you misunderstood me. I did not steal you. It was Agnes Neal's children I took, and left you and your sister in their place. It was all done at your mother's command.''

"At my mother's command?" asked Bill, in amazement. "Did my mother give her children about in that style?"

"Yes, sir; your mother had been betrayed. Your father was Mrs. Neal's husband, but under the name of Wetherell married your mother.''

"Under the name of Wetherell?" asked Bill, in breathless haste.

"Yes, your father always went by that name, although his real name was Richard Neal. Your mother married him for his wealth, and when she discovered how he had wronged her, and she had no claim or title to his estate, she conceived the hellish plot of taking Agnes Neal's children, who were his heirs, and leaving her illegitimate ones in their place. It was a horrible thing to do, but the woman hated the man so intensely for his perfidy, that I believe her hatred extended to the children she had borne him. I loved Agnes Neal, and she had preferred another. So I became your mother's accomplice, to avenge my own supposed wrong as well as her real one.''

"Where is that Wetherell now, my most honorable father?" asked Bill, in bitter irony.

"Captain Wetherell is dead," answered Jack.

"What! the old Captain, who was killed not far from here in a mine a year and a half ago. Ben's father — was he my father, too?"

"Yes, he was your father and Ben's.''

"That accounts for our wonderful resemblance," said Bill.

"Yes, you both look like your father. That's how I came to be around so much where you were. I thought I could not be mistaken. I knew you by your resemblance to Ben.''

18 *　　　　　　O

"Then the haughty Mrs. Wetherell, down in Sacramento, is my mother, is she?" asked Bill.

"Mrs. Wetherell in Sacramento. Where in Sacramento?" asked Jack, nervously.

"I don't exactly know — she went down there with a Mr. Warren. There was some talk about his marrying Ben's sister, but I think there is more probability of his marrying the old lady, for the sister lives here."

"Where does she live?" asked Jack, hurriedly.

"That was she we saw this evening in the cottage with Mrs. Neal."

"That! Is it possible? Agnes' own child happy with her mother? The fates are kinder than God's creatures."

"Yes, so it seems," added Bill, thoughtfully. "I took a deep interest in young Wetherell's case, knew all the parties connected with it by sight, and have kept track of them pretty well ever since. I see Miss Wetherell on the street quite often with Ben's wife, but I have never seen Mrs. Neal here before. You can readily imagine my surprise to find you were taking me to see the good woman who reared me until I was sixteen years old. Then I became restless and started westward. I wrote her regularly for several years, until her mother died and left her all alone in the world, and she wanted to join me out here. Then I ceased all correspondence, hoping she would think me dead. I had fallen into wild company, and led a reckless life, which would have been a new source of sorrow to her. But with all, Jack, I wish I was worthy to go to her, for I love her devotedly."

They had reached the saloon door. Bill's friends at once motioned for him to join them. He bade Jack good-night. Telling him they would have a long talk to-morrow, he joined his reckless companions. Jack, cuddled up in an easy chair, in one corner of the saloon, was so busy with his own wild thoughts, he heard nothing, although the talking grew louder and more desperate after every drink, and the stakes ran higher and higher.

Bill Brown was winning at every hand. It was a desperate stake. The last dollar of his antagonist was on the table, and Bill won.

The man, in despairing frenzy, grabbed the money, and hissed in Bill's ear, "It was foul! You're a thief!"

"You're a liar!" thundered Bill.

The discharge of a pistol rang through the saloon. A single shot, and every man sprang to his feet, as Bill Brown fell to the floor in a pool of blood. Jack was the first by his side.

Bill raised his eyes to the thin, searching face before him, and with effort said: "We won't have that 'long talk to-morrow,' Jack. It's all over with me."

"Oh, no, my boy. It's not so bad as you think," answered Jack, encouragingly.

A surgeon was found, who carefully dressed the wound, and had him removed to comfortable quarters. He pronounced his patient in a dangerous condition, but not necessarily fatal.

When Bill was comfortably in his own room, he whispered to Jack:

"I would like to see that good woman once more. Do you think she would come to me if you would ask her?"

"Why, of course she would," answered Jack, promptly, thinking only of the kind, thoughtful Agnes of many years ago. "I'll go at once and fetch her," and he limped off with wonderful alacrity.

CHAPTER XXXVIII.

MRS. NEAL FINDS HER DAUGHTER.

IT was midnight. The cottage was dark; the occupants all slept. The repeated knocking at the door awakened Mrs. Neal, and to her inquiry, "Who is there?" Jack Hunter, trembling in every limb, answered: "A person on urgent business."

"What business can you possibly have with me that should bring you at such a late hour?" asked Mrs. Neal, hurriedly dressing

"Madam, your son has met with an accident."

"My son?" asked Mrs. Neal, in amazement.

"Yes, madam, your son."

"You mean my adopted son, William Neal?"

Jack had only known him as Bill Brown, but at once understood his motive in having changed his name. He answered promptly, "Yes, madam, William Neal."

"Where, and how did it happen?" asked Mrs. Neal, anxiously, as she opened the door.

Jack had watched her face so often, it was perfectly familiar to him; but her voice — that same sweet, sympathetic voice, he had not heard for years — awakened every memory of the bitter past. He limped into the room, and fell heavily into a chair.

"You are tired, poor man. You came too rapidly. Rest a moment, then you can tell me better."

"He was shot by accident, madam," stammered Jack, as if he was suffocating. Suddenly, forgetting his infirmities, he rose to his feet, and looking eagerly into Mrs. Neal's face, asked, abruptly, "Do you know me?"

"No," she answered, quietly.

"Is there nothing about me you have ever seen before?"

Mrs. Neal scrutinized him earnestly, and answered deliberately, "Nothing that I recognize."

"Great God, Agnes, have I gone from your memory entirely?"

"Who are you, that you call me Agnes?"

"Who am I? You may well ask," cried the poor, wretched mortal. "I am the man who stole your children."

"You — you — and you dare to come and tell me?"

"Oh, Agnes, will you not forgive me?" and Jack Hunter knelt at her feet.

"No, never!" cried she, fiercely.

"Oh, Agnes, if the doors of the past could be opened, and you could see the path I have trodden step by step, the burning hell I have lived in year after year, searching this wide world over for you, you could forgive me. The letter I wrote and left on your chamber-floor in the cottage in New Orleans the night I took your children and left *hers*, explained my motive. I went away that night, but I soon came back, the victim of remorse, to confess my crime, to restore your children, but you had gone, and *she* had gone."

"*She* — who is *she?*"

"The illegal wife of Captain Wetherell. In my bitterness toward you, I lied in that note. You were his legal wife. His real name was Richard Neal, and the dashing beauty was his mistress. You each had two children, a son and a daughter; and that woman, to gain the Captain's property, induced me to steal your children and leave hers, for yours were the heirs to his estate."

"Then that woman has had my children all these years?" whispered the excited mother, hoarsely. Her very breathing was suspended, as if the next respiration depended upon the answer.

"Yes," whispered Jack, in terror, as if he thought the word would kill her.

"Linda — my child — my child — at last!" cried the over-joyed mother, and sank senseless to the floor.

Linda ran from her room at the piercing call, to find Mrs. Neal senseless upon the floor and Jack Hunter bending over her.

"What have you done to her?" she demanded, wildly. "Oh, Mother Neal, are you forever to be persecuted? Wake up, my darling, angel mother. There, that does her good," she said, as Jack bathed her face with cold water.

Mrs. Neal opened her eyes, and, seeing Jack bending over her, closed them again quickly. Shuddering, she turned to Linda, and said:

"Send him away, Linda; send him away. The very sight of him is horrible."

"Horrible!" cried poor Jack, rocking his body to and fro, weeping like a child. "Yes, horrible! I should be revolting to the sight of every human creature, and no one has a better right to tell me so than you."

Mrs. Neal seemed suddenly to have awakened to a full reali-zation of what had happened. Going to the cowering, weep-ing creature, with all the mildness of her old self, she said, earnestly:

"Jack Hunter, do you swear before God you have spoken the truth this night?"

Jack raised his two hands heavenward, and with great tears streaming from his uplifted eyes, that were wonderfully large and luminous in his emaciated face, said, solemnly:

"Agnes Neal, before God, I do most solemnly swear. Every

word I have spoken this night was the truth, the whole truth, and nothing but the truth. That is the daughter I stole from you," pointing toward Linda, "and Ben Wetherell, in San Quentin, is your son."

Linda stood in amazement, regarding first one, then the other.

"At last," exclaimed Mrs. Neal, "I live again. Linda, darling, you are my own, my long lost child."

"Oh, Mother Neal, what happiness!" and Linda was folded to her heart; "and Ben, what joyful news for him. How has it all come about, that we at last have a tender, loving mother? We could not love that woman, she was so hard and cold. I often asked myself, if it was possible for a mother to hate her own children as she evidently did us. But how strange that she should bring us together, to love one another, before we knew what a claim we had upon each other's affections."

They quite forgot Jack in their mutual happiness, and he in turn had forgotten the errand that brought him there, and was quietly moving toward the door, when Linda exclaimed:

"But this good man, who has brought us so much happiness, surely is not going without a word of thanks?"

Jack turned and looked at Linda, with his great eyes beaming with gratitude. He was so unaccustomed to consideration, it seemed like the dawning of a new life.

Her words awakened a cord of sympathy in Mrs. Neal's heart. She went to Jack, took his thin, bony hand in hers, and with deep feeling said:

"The agony I have suffered, through you, no words could adequately portray; but one need only look at you, to know how you have expiated your wrong. I forgive you."

"I don't deserve it, Agnes. I had no right to expect it," said poor Jack, quite overcome; "you are too good to me."

"But wait," said Mrs. Neal, "I must go with you to poor William, and you must tell me all about him on the way."

Mrs. Neal hurriedly explained that an accident had befallen her adopted son, for whom she had so long been searching in vain, and Jack had come to conduct her to him.

The unusual noise at that hour of the night awakened Lucy, who made her appearance, looking exceedingly sleepy, but she was suddenly thoroughly awakened by Linda springing toward her with the incomprehensible announcement:

"The world has turned upside down and inside out in the short space of an hour. Lucy, you are Mrs. Neal's daughter-in-law instead of Mrs. Wetherell's, and your name is not Wetherell at all."

Lucy rubbed her eyes, as if upon a clear vision depended a clear comprehension of such an enigmatical statement.

Mrs. Neal left them, with a request that they should retire and talk everything over in the morning. So it came to pass that Jack Hunter escorted the old sweetheart of his boyish days to the bedside of Richard Wetherell's illegitimate son.

As the physician said nothing but the best of care could save him, and even then there was little hope of his life being spared, Mrs. Neal had Bill Brown, who shall henceforth be known as William Neal — the name he had borne since the night he had been left in the cottage at New Orleans — removed to her own house, where he could be under her constant care.

CHAPTER XXXIX.

VENGEANCE.

AFTER William Neal was removed to the cottage, Jack Hunter grew restless and absent-minded. A cough that had been annoying him for a long time, became alarming. He grew daily more like a spectre than a man. Still, he mechanically performed his duties, until duty seemed to become insupportable. He asked for a leave of absence for a few weeks, under the pretence of ill health, and it was at once granted. Without saying a word to any one of his intentions, he took the midnight stage for Sacramento. There was a strange light in his large, searching eyes, that was attributed to the ravishings of consumption; but the approach of the end came with a new light in Jack's soul — that thirsting soul panting for revenge, and seeing it, at last, within its grasp.

On his arrival, he soon ascertained the residence of Major Warren. He took his post every evening among the shrubbery in the garden, where he could readily see all who came and went, and sometimes catch glimpses of the interior of the house. Night after night, for two weeks, he had watched, until every light in the house was extinguished, excepting one, that evidently burned all night, and often in the still hours a shadow passed between it and the barred window. It was the shadow of a woman.

Jack's curiosity was greatly excited over that lonely watcher, all the more because he could never see anything distinctly behind the thick vines, yet the blind seemed never down. A young lady came sometimes and walked in the garden — a tall, slight, graceful girl. Jack knew it was the discarded daughter of Mrs. Wetherell, and mentally asked, what the young girl had often asked herself : "Your mother, where is she?"

The still night gave back no answer — "The mills of the gods" grind noiselessly.

The next afternoon Jack came strolling lazily along and engaged the gardener in conversation, carefully leading him to talk of the family with whom he lived. The man was not inclined to be communicative, until after Jack had rendered him a slight service. Then he thanked him, and added :

"They do say 'the greather the haste the liss spade,' and I'm after doin' iverything wrong to-day, becase I'm in sich a divil o' a hurry. Miss Alice is to be married to-morrow, and there 's a hape to be done."

"Who is Miss Alice?" asked Jack, carelessly.

"Sure, she 's the Major's darter." The gardener stuck his spade deep in the ground, and turning to Jack, said, stupidly, as if the idea had just occurred to him : "Will, no, she beant the Major's darter, aither. They do say, as how he dun know whose darter she be; and I belave it, for he niver tould me she was his darter. Sure the Major is a little quare entirely, and do say quare things. He cum out here one day, whin I was a worken, and says he to me, says he, 'Mike.' Says I to him, says I, 'Sur!' Says he to me, says he, 'Mike, why don't yez be after gittin' married?' Says I to him, says I, 'What fur?' Says he to me, says he, 'It 's a dacent thing to be doin'.' Says I to him, says I, 'Major, if it 's a dacent thing entirely, why don't yez be after marryin' yerself,' says I, 'fur ye're hale and hearty, and younger than hapes o' the spry dogs around,' says I. Will, now, will ye blave it? He flew in a rage, and says, says he, 'Mike, ye're an impertant dog,' says he. Says I to him, says I, 'Axin' yer honor's pardon, it was yerself that first talked o'marryin'; and they do say, what 's sauce for the goose is sauce for the gander. Faith, I'm a goose entirely.' 'I belave ye're right,' says he. 'I did begin it,' says he, 'but it's a subject I don't care to be talkin' about,' says he, and divil a word could I git out o'im after that. Says I to myself, says I, 'The Major has had it rough,' says I; 'and niver a word did I say from that day to this; and there's Mag now, begorra I can't worry a word out o' her. There's something mysterious somewhere,'' and Mike gave Jack a knowing look, then silently went on with his work.

Jack bade him good afternoon, and went on his way, thinking of the barred window, with the light in it every night, and wondering who the human being was who occupied that chamber, and peered out so eagerly behind the vines; Mag, who could not be worried into telling anything, and what Mike's significant assurance of mystery was.

Twilight found Jack at his post in the shrubbery; the graceful form of Alice gliding to and fro on the veranda, and the eager eyes behind the vines at the barred window. That indistinct figure at its post every evening acted like a magnet upon Jack. His eyes scarcely left it, even to watch Alice's sweeping, graceful figure as it came and went.

Familiar footsteps were heard upon the walk, and the young girl hastened to meet her lover. Still, Jack watched those straining eyes at the barred window. If he could only get a glimpse of the face. There was nothing to be seen between the thick vines but two eyes—such strange, wild eyes, they could scarcely belong to a human being.

The lights came streaming from the lower windows. Soft strains of music filled the air, then two voices, fresh and musical, blended in sweetest harmony. Jack sat entranced, his eyes never leaving the mysterious window, that was dark, for the first time after twilight. But his thoughts were of those voices that filled the night with music — that woman's daughter, with her lover, and the morrow, when she would be his wife. He asked himself, "If I should rend the veil, and tell her birth, would he love her then, or would their happiness be dead? Happiness and contentment," murmured the shivering skeleton of unrest, "they are the only fragments left us of the wreck of Paradise, and rare as they are priceless."

At six o'clock, as usual, the door of Mrs. Wetherell's room, or rather Mrs. Warren's, was opened, and a dark figure entered with a tray of dinner. It was the nurse, who had for a year and a half waited upon the lonely inmate of that chamber, and no other human being had crossed the threshold. The room had, originally, a small hall connecting it with a larger one, but it had been boarded up and a private entrance made — so adroitly, that the house might be full of inmates and not one suspect there was such a tomb there.

The great masculine creature who waited upon Mrs. Wetherell seldom ever spoke — she obeyed orders and requests, but never volunteered a word. That night she seemed more affable than usual. As she lighted the lamp, she regarded Mrs. Wetherell with a strange, empty smile, that remained on the countenance long after the mind had ceased smiling. That slight indication of amiability encouraged Mrs. Wetherell wonderfully. It was an event, where there had not been a smile for a year and a half. She asked :

"Mag, what is the meaning of those three taps of the bell at intervals of three, at the convent, morning, noon, and night? I hear them so regularly, and they sound so free and clear, they have become quite like friends to me."

Other nights Mag would have arranged the tray, let her lower jaw drop an inch, as if to speak, but make no further indication of sociability, and pass out. To-night was Christmas eve, and her heart, or the tough substance that served in that capacity in her bony frame, was softened, and she answered in a rough, discordant voice:

"Thim bells? why, thim's the Angelis."

"What is the Angelis?" asked Mrs. Wetherell.

"Why, all thim as hares it drops on their knase, and says three Hail Marys."

"And what are Hail Marys?" asked Mrs. Wetherell, anxious to prolong the conversation.

"Lord luv ye, but ye're stupid," burst out Mag, impatiently. "Jist as he said — her head is gone entirely, all gone. Dun know what a Hail Mary is, and he tould me she was a gude Catholic. It's thankful I am, entirely, my head was niver turned upside down wi' book larnin'."

The door closed after her, and Mrs. Wetherell sank back in her chair tired, so tired. Never could she get any satisfaction out of that woman, and it seemed as if she would forget the English language, if she did not persist

"Three Hail Marys," she said, aloud. "How strange. For a year and a half I have heard those bells calling to prayer several times a day, and it never once occurred to me to pray. Why should I? What have I to pray for? My health? Surely that is no blessing, for death were preferable to this living tomb — but I will not die. Mag was a little better to-night. For a whole year she never spoke at all. Lately she is relenting. I will work upon her feelings, and surely I can get out of this wretched prison."

Mrs. Wetherell ate sparingly, and set the tray to one side. She went to a mirror and regarded herself attentively.

"This year and a half has not altered me much — ever so little older. How white my hair is getting, but it brings out my black eyes, and makes my complexion clearer. Thinner,

19*

yes, much thinner; pale, rather too pale, but erect; and altogether I am a handsome middle-aged woman.   There is a deal
of satisfaction in that, for I think this Christmas Major Warren will surely come, and I will use all the eloquence of looks
and words I used to command so well."

She sat rocking and waiting, as she had waited so often, but
no one came save Mag, with her heavy tread, to remove the
tray.

" Mag, please ask Major Warren to come to me," said Mrs.
Wetherell, pleadingly.

" It 's no use, ma'am," answered Mag, shaking her head.
" This is Christmas ave, and Miss Alice do be gettin' married
to-morrow avenin' to the rich banker, and there 'll be great
goins on altogither," and as Mag passed out her lower jaw dropped to express the reverse of what it indicated—that her mouth
was closed.

" Miss Alice to be married to-morrow," said Mrs. Wetherell,
who had a habit of talking aloud to herself, as if to hear a
human voice, even if it was her own.   " That sweet, pretty girl
I have seen through the vines, Miss Alice, his adopted daughter.
Old stupid, to adopt a daughter.   I tried that.   I wonder where
my daughter is?   *My* daughter — it seems like a dream that I
ever had one."

The light was turned very low, and she sat softly rocking,
with her arms crossed over her chest, thinking, thinking,
ever thinking; and her face changed continually under the vary-
ing brain flashes.   Soft strains of music came from below.   It
was the voice of her long lost daughter blended with that of
her lover — that long lost daughter under the same roof with
her, but lost to her forever.   The music died away and night
was still again.

Jack shivered.   It was damp and chilly.   He was feeling

worse than usual, and was just going to leave his hiding-place, when he heard voices approaching. One he recognized as Mike, the gardener, the other was a woman. They came near his place of concealment and stopped, when Mike said: _

"Mag, ye're too hard on a fellow intirely. A whole yare and a half ago, says ye to me, says ye, 'Mike, if ye'll only consint to me nussin' that woman, and yez be gardner yersilf, and lay up yer arnens a yare, I'll marry ye, says ye.' Now, it's a yare and a half, and ye says, says ye, 'Mike, it's well we're doin'; we'll wait a little longer.' It's nussin' a sick woman yez be; but nobody iver sane 'er or heard o'er but yersilf, and divil a whimper will yez tell a fellow."

"Mike, it's will paid I am for holdin' me tongue."

"Mag, I don't want to be hard on ye, but, by Saint Patrick, I'm after thinkin' it's fur sumthing ilse ye're paid."

"Mike, what the divil do ye mane?" burst out Mag, in a rage.

"Be aisy, Mag; be aisy, now. Sure, it's a bouncin', foine lass ye are now, Mag; and begorra, Mag, I've me eye on the foine Major, he pays ye so divilish well."

Mag drew her great, ungainly, bony figure more erect, with an air of conscious pride, and it was well for Mike that he could not see the flash of her cold gray eyes.

"Mike, it's a fool ye are. Do ye think I've lived these five and thirty years to be givin' meself to the loike o' the Major?"

Mike put his arm about her cautiously, as he said: "No, darlant, no; not whin I'm around. But begorra, Mag, it's divilish quare, so it is."

"Do ye sae yon window?" asked Mag, suddenly, pointing to the mysterious window.

Jack's eyes and ears were all attention.

"Begorra, I do," answered Mike, stupidly.

"Whist, thin. If iver yez brathe a word, I'll niver marry yez at all. Do yez moind that, now?"

"May the divil burn me if iver I do, Mag, ye swate crathur, ye."

"Will, thin, Mike, in that room is a woman. Will yez belave it, she's bin there a year and a half, and niver been out o' the door?"

"The divil!" exclaimed Mike.

"Yes, and it's there she'll stay; for the divil himsilf could n't hate a craythur like the Major do hate her. It's mad he says she is; but, Mike, take my word for 't, she's no madder than yez or me."

"Now, Mag, yez don't mane it?"

"Faith, an' I do mane ivery word o' it. That's what I'm here fur, moind; and the Major will double me wages sooner than let me go, becase I hould me tongue, and yez know I do, Mike."

"Hould yer tongue. I niver saw the bate o' ye for that now; but if the Major is nadin' ye so, sure he'd consint to our marryin' iny way, and stayin' on just the same."

"What's the use, Mike? Sure it's all nonsince. We're young and harty, and there's plenty o' time to be marryin' whin there's nothin' ilse to be done."

"Young, is it ye say? Now, Mag, I've known ye these twinty yares, darlant, and always wundered how ould ye were, for faith an' ye've looked loike a pache blossum iver since I furst sane ye. Now it's thirty-foive yares ould ye say ye are, an' ye call that young?"

"Mike, what's the matter wid ye? Who said I was thirty-foive years ould?"

"Ye did, yersilf."

"Ye're a loiar! How could I iver say sich a thing?"

"Begorra, Mag, I wundered mesilf. Sure, it's only afther tasin' ye, I am, ye swate little buttercup, ye daisy. Sure there's not a flower in the garden so swate and purty as yersilf," and Mike gave her a desperate hug.

"Will ye lave off yer foolin', now," said Mag, without attempting to resist.

"Say, Mag."

"Say it yersilf."

"Ax the Major to-morrow."

"Ax the Major what?"

"What I tould ye."

"Ax 'im yersilf."

"Lord luv ye. Thin ye're willin', are ye?"

"No, I ain't."

"Now, Mag."

"Mike, ye're a fool."

"Did iver ye hare tell o' the birds o' a feather? Sure, it's divilish fond ye are o' a fool, Mag."

"Now is n't it ashamed ye are o' yersilf?"

"Divil a bit, Mag. Shame and me parted company long ago."

"Faith an' yez spake the truth. Sure, yez might a' bin married, for the kinship's run out entirely. Jist look at the imperdense o' the spalpeen, now, wi his arrums both around me."

"It's jintle as a dove ye are, Mag. Sure, ye don't moind me arrums. Faith, ye're swater ivery day, darlant. If I was only a bae, sure I'd have swates fur the rist o' me loife."

"Mike, ye're a fool!"

"Now, Mag, how can yez call yer dare, ould gardner a fool? But ye're always right, darlant; faith, an' I have a lanin' fur grane things."

"Do ye mane me, now, Mike?"

P

"Mane ye? Now, Mag, ye know viry well there's nuthin' grane about ye, with yer beautiful brown frickles. I do think frickles is the beautifullest thing at all. One day I heard the Major say, says he, 'Miss Alice do have a beautiful nose,' says he. Now, Mag, it's too long and strait intirely fur my loikin'. If anything do plase me on arth, it be a nose jist loike yourn— short and round, and turnin' sort o' worshipful loike to hivin all the time."

"Oh, Mike, lave off yer blarneyin'. I'm frazin' cowld."

"Cowld in me arrums? Sure, Mag, the foire in me heart should kape ye warrum."

"Foire, do ye call it — foire? Sure, it's nuthin' but smoke wid yez, Mike."

"Smoke? Where the divil do the smoke cum from, if there beant no fire? It's yer own fault, Mag, that it has n't ben a blazin' these foive yares. Sure, I've kept the foire down, an' if I did n't take me poipe now an' thin, to show the smoke the way out, sure it would 'a choked me intirely."

"Faith, an' ye've let off enough stame to-night; an' I'm goin' in."

"Jist one more word, Mag. Will ye ax the Major?"

"Whin?"

"To-morrow."

"I'll sae."

"Ah, darlant, say yis."

"Wall — yis — Mike."

"Lord luve ye now, ye're an angel. One kiss, Mag, just one, Mag. Sure, ye're too savin' o' thim, intirely."

"It's savin' thim I am for ye, Mike."

"It's too gud ye are intirely to the loike o' me. But don't be after savin' 'em iny more. Sure, I'd be better plased if ye'd waste 'em on me."

CHAPTER XL.

ABSENT FRIENDS.

"La philosophie qui nous promet de nous rendre heureux, nous trompe."

WHEN Mr. and Mrs. Gray and Walter arrived in New York, they found the old lady Gray in declining health.

Her bachelor brother, who had always lived with her, and superintended her affairs, had suddenly died. The old lady, never very robust, was so overcome by the sudden calamity, she declined rapidly, only living a few weeks after their return. The estate had been judiciously managed; everything was under the most perfect system, and George found himself much better off than he had expected. Without anything in particular to do, he and Walter were quite out of their element, and the uncongenial winter offered no inducements to enter into business.

To Californians, accustomed to a mild climate, never excessively warm nor cold, the biting frosts and snow of New York were a poor substitute. They soon tired of their inactive indoor life,

And " folded their tents like the Arabs,
And as silently stole away "

over the boisterous Atlantic, and the letter Nellie wrote Mrs. Neal relating to all their movements, by some mischance, never reached its destination.

The little party wandered over the European world, among the beauties of gay, thoughtless, fascinating Paris, and up the Rhine with its picturesque relics of feudal times, and amid the ruins of the once glorious Roman empire, and to their anxious friends in California were lost entirely.

To Americans, born in the new world of energy and progress, travelling over the lethargic cities of Europe, moss-covered and gray from the dust of centuries, with their human beings for ever in the same place, forever repeating the same things, liv ing in an atmosphere of arts and sciences, yet in a lethiferous condition of inactivity, soon brings with it a feeling of empti- ness, a longing for the busy stir and bustle of progress.

For more than a year they travelled continually, seeing and studying life among the dead. Then came a yearning for home, a longing for rest, after the satiety of sightseeing, and they turned their faces homeward. But when they arrived there, New York had lost its charms.. The connecting links of maternal love and old friendships were gone — the cottage in Grass Valley, among the Sierra Nevada Mountains, only an- swered to the word "home." Finally, they decided to return to San Francisco, and make a new home in that city of many hills, with its invigorating sea breezes.

During their foreign travels they had formed the acquaint- ance of a Mr. Carlton of New York, who, upon learning their intentions of returning to California, insisted upon their becom- ing acquainted with his brother, R. R. Carlton, of Sacramento, and accordingly gave Walter letters to him, at the same time writing to his brother of his new friends.

CHAPTER XLI.

THE GHOSTLY APPARITION.

IT was Christmas night. Mr. Warren's house was a scene of festivity and mirth. The *élite* of Sacramento were in attendance at the marriage of his adopted daughter with Mr. Carlton, the junior partner of a large banking firm of that city. Neither of them had been long in California. The young lady had come from New York, under the care of a gentleman connected with the bank, at the same time Mr. Carlton had come to assume his duties as partner. It was a perfect love match, with a shade of romance that made it interesting. Everybody seemed delighted and satisfied.

Major Warren quite renewed his youth on the occasion, by being the gayest of the gay. He was lavish in his generosity toward his adopted daughter — presented her with an elegant home, furnished with all the requirements of comfort and luxury, and made her wedding night a *fête* long to be remembered by the gay and thoughtless as one of unbroken pleasure. But it was a night of tragedy to two accursed souls.

Carriages were coming and going; joyous music rang through the night air; the murmuring of distant voices and merry peals of laughter could be heard below stairs, while Mrs. Wetherell sat rocking, rocking, looking out into the dark night, toward the starry heavens, wistfully, longingly through the iron bars. There was no light in the room save the uncertain flicker from the fire, which made her pale face look ghastly, in its spasms of agony, at every strain of merry music and sound of joyous laughter. Never had she been so utterly

20

wretched. She who should be the mistress of the house, the bright particular star there to-night, was barred in like a wild beast. The very thought almost maddened her.

Christmas! Oh, the weary years since Christmas had been a festival to her. When in the humble home of Mrs. Graham, she and Henry had their joyous holidays — before the graves were dug in the old churchyard, and her soul stained with blood. All those hidden memories came back horribly fresh to her mind. She could not drive them away. Remorseless thought would not be conquered, but ran on and on to that stormy night in New Orleans, to which there had been no dawn in her life. She rose and paced the floor nervously, as her unbridled thoughts flew on. She wrung her clinched hands, and with all the agonizing despair of a lost soul, cried: "With such a dark past, what can there be in the future?"

She stopped suddenly before a piece of folded paper on the floor. A shudder ran through her frame. For an instant she dare not pick it up. Her eyes searched every corner of the small room with the terror of a hunted deer. She was all alone, and nothing was changed. The window was lowered at the top as usual, the vines were stirred by the night winds. That was all, and yet that scrap of paper had not been on the floor a moment before. As if ashamed of her weakness, she picked it up hastily, tore it open, and read by the uncertain light of the fire:

MRS. LAURA WETHERELL:

It is your daughter's marriage they are celebrating to-night beneath your living tomb — the little girl I left with Agnes Neal the night I stole her children for you. Mr. Warren adopted her because Mrs. Neal would not keep her.

Your son is now lying in Agnes Neal's house, in Nevada, dying from an assassin's blow, while you, more fiend than woman, are, as you justly deserve, suffering the penalty of your infamy.

Watch your window at midnight to-night.

JACK HUNTER.

At every word the woman grew more livid. Her thin lips parted; her breathing was hard and irregular, as if laboring under a death-blow.

"Merciful heaven!" she groaned, and fell heavily into a chair, overcome with horror. "Has that man come back at last to complete my torture?" she gasped, in despair. "A terror of eighteen years should cease to be a terror. Every day of my life, during those wretched years, I have lived in dread of meeting him, and at last he finds me here — here — to tell me Alice, the graceful, lovely girl I have watched so often from my window, is mine, *mine*, to fill my empty life, to bless my future."

She spoke hurriedly, as if fearful of losing that one faint ray of sunshine amid the darkness. "But what will she say? What?" All hope vanished at the dread question. She leaned back wearier and more desolate than ever, as she whispered hoarsely: "That I am a stranger, whom she does not know, and cannot love, and my empty life will be emptier than ever. They will tell her how infamously I deserted her, and she will loathe and hate me, so that my very life-blood will turn to venom. My son dying in *her* house, under *her* care — Agnes Neal, the woman to whom I took Linda! I wonder I did not drop dead at the sight of her. To think that white-haired woman should be Linda's mother, and I the means of bringing them together again, to be happy — to be happy!"

The woman gave a low, demoniac laugh. "Her son is in prison. A nice place to find him, surely. At least, her cup of happiness will not overflow. How quiet everything has become down-stairs. The music has stopped, yet I hear the hum of many voices. It must be the hour for supper, when the wine is poured in to let wit out — to make the nothingness of the merry festival charming. The bride will soon go to her new home, without a mother's blessing, and the man who loves her would hate her if he could see into her mother's dark past. I could almost crush their young lives for daring to be happy under the same roof with my misery."

There was a tap on the window. She sprang to her feet and raised her eyes, full of fiendish light, to behold the ghostly apparition of Jack Hunter, by the single gleam of a night-lantern. His lean, white face, with its eyes illumined by the flickering light of consumption, looking unnaturally large and wild in their hollow sockets, made indeed a ghostly thing of the handsome young man of eighteen years before. She stood appalled, staring in breathless terror.

As the music rang out again on the night air, she gave one heart-rending, piercing cry, and fell senseless to the floor, in the little room almost over the revellers' heads.

CHAPTER XLII.

THE LIVING TOMB.

"I'm like the dead ere death comes to o'erwhelm."

MAG found a sadly changed woman when she came with the breakfast the next morning. Pale and almost lifeless, Mrs. Wetherell lay upon the bed staring at the window. Mag was not a very discerning creature, and did not seem to notice; for she too had been up most of the preceding night. Mrs. Wetherell neither ate nor spoke; she lay still and white.

The Angelus pealed out at twelve o'clock. "Three hail Marys. I wish I knew what a 'hail Mary' was; but I can say something," and the cowed, broken woman fell on her knees on the floor, with uplifted hands, and cried: "God have mercy on me! God have mercy on me! God have mercy on me!" Overcome by the effort, she crawled back to bed, desolate, wretched.

That night again, at midnight, she lay staring in horror at the window, when the ghostly spectre came again, with the flash of light from his night-lantern gleaming upon his face. The terrified woman tried to scream, but voice failed her. She mechanically raised herself upon her arm, her eyes riveted upon the ghostly thing before her, and the man stared wildly back. So a fortnight passed, and every night at midnight that same dread spectre came.

The woman went to the glass, and shrank in terror at the answer it gave back.

"Two weeks!" she gasped; "two weeks, and my hair is white. No more streaks of black — snowy white. My face is gaunt, my eyes sunken, with great black circles around them. I am a shattered thing; a wreck! That spectre at the window has done in two weeks what a year and a half could not do before."

The Angelus pealed out in the still air, and the woman fell upon her knees, as she did regularly three times a day, and in wild despair cried: "God have mercy on me! God have mercy on me! God have mercy on me!"

When Mag came with the tray of dinner, she grasped her great bony hand tightly, turned her burning black eyes to her cold, stony orbs, and with the entreaty of a longing child begged:

"Mag, if you are human; if there is anything in you that
20 *

answers to the name of woman, for God's sake hear me. Look at me, Mag!"

Mag looked at the trembling woman before her with parted lips, suspended breath, and staring eyes, awaiting her answer; but the cold, gray eyes gave no token. There was no soul behind them.

The woman grasped her two shoulders, and, with the desperation of despair, shrieked, "Mag! Mag! are you a thing of stone? Do you not see that I am being tortured to death; that I am dying? For heaven's sake, take this note to Major Warren. Tell him what a ghostly thing I am. Oh, tell him to come and strike the blow that will end my misery. To live in death, is hell! Go, Mag, go; bring the answer soon, or I shall die waiting."

Mag took the note without answering a word; as she closed the door her face smiled again, but not her soul.

An hour after, Mrs. Wetherell's door opened, and Major Warren entered. Changed, too, sadly changed. The affable, pompous coxcomb was stooped and gray, and walked with heavier step. His eyes had become restless, as if in search of something they could not find — perpetually seeking.

The Major started in horror from the ghastly woman before him, but commanding himself, said, coldly: "I believe you sent for me, madam?"

"Yes," answered Mrs. Wetherell, quietly, with her wild, black eyes riveted upon the Major's face. "I wanted to beg of you again, what I have so often written in vain, to have mercy on me, and release me from this living tomb. You have kept me here already a year and a half. It seems like a century. I know I have sinned grievously; but, oh, has not my suffering been sufficient expiation?"

She leaned back in her chair pale and trembling. The Major

regarded her in silence a few seconds, with an expression of absolute loathing upon his once benign countenance, then said slowly and deliberately:

"You have had time to reflect and make atonement, I admit, and also to concoct several new villanies since you have had the exclusive pleasure of your own society."

"Oh, Major, can you never forgive me?" pleaded the wretched woman.

"No, never!" hissed the merciless Major, between his set teeth.

"Can I not once more see the light of day before I die?" she cried, wildly,

"Never, madam!" answered the Major, sternly. "You shall never cross that threshold until you are carried out."

In that living tomb forever, with that spectre at the window! The terror of the sentence overwhelmed the woman, whose nervous system was utterly shattered from nightly watching and horror. She sprang suddenly toward the Major, who was at the door, about to leave her, and fell prostrate at his feet.

A momentary feeling of mercy took possession of him. He raised her with difficulty, and placed her upon the bed, where she lay passive and lifeless. He bathed her face, and worked with her some time before he could discern the least indication of returning consciousness. Finally, after vigorous efforts to restore her, she opened her great wild eyes, glassy in death, and with great effort gasped:

"In the writing-desk is the history of my life. Read it, and send it to Mrs. Agnes Neal, Nevada. Learn what a fate mine has been — how I have been twice married, yet never a legal wife — mother of children who do not know me. Read with mercy in your heart, for my life has been what the fates decreed — inglorious and wretched. I am neither maiden, wife, widow, nor mother, yet all."

Her voice had almost died away, her breathing was labored and quick, when, with a sudden, almost superhuman effort, she raised herself upon her arm, and with all the venom of a devil, hissed, between her set teeth, with her dying breath: "Your fate will be like mine. There shall be no more peace for you. You are my murderer!"

She fell back upon the pillow, dead. The Angelus pealed out, "God have mercy on her soul!"

The Major took her writing-desk, and went in search of Mag to prepare her for burial. Still and white she lay upon the bed until after dark, when Mike brought a coffin, placed it on two chairs in front of the vine-covered window, and assisted Mag to lay the lifeless form in its narrow house, then closed the door and retired to sleep, for the next morning before daylight she was to be buried. The same heartless order she had given for the interment of Captain Wetherell by his servants had been given for her burial by Major Warren to his.

It was midnight; still Major Warren sat poring over the pages of Mrs. Wetherell's checkered life, written unsparingly by herself. Now and then he would give a sudden start and look searchingly about him, as if haunted by those last desperate words, uttered like a curse by the dying woman, "You are my murderer!"

It was the hour for Jack Hunter's visit. Day after day he had watched the sad havoc he was making of the once handsome woman. His life seemed to have merged into a relentless, hungry desire to see her fade day by day, and die inch by inch, as he was doing, that kept him at his fiendish work. He was growing so feeble it was with great effort he ascended the ladder to the fatal window. When he turned his light into the room, the bed was empty, and the frightened, terrified woman, who had glared at him so wildly, night after night, lay calm and still in an open coffin before him. He became suddenly dizzy — his lantern dropped to the ground—he lost his hold and fell among the rounds of the ladder. There, within a few feet of his victim, and almost as lifeless, hung the gaunt, dying man, until strength returned sufficiently, and he crawled down, and slowly tottered. away.

CHAPTER XLIII.

AFTER THE WEDDING.

"Nil desperandum" — Behind the clouds is the sun still shining,

THE afternoon following the wedding, Mr. Carlton and his young wife took the steamer for San Francisco, where they spent several days, accepting many hospitalities from George and Nellie Gray.

It was after dinner. The ladies had retired to the drawing-room, while the gentlemen lingered over their cigars. A friend called upon Mr. Gray relative to some urgent business; so he excused himself, leaving Mr. Carlton and Walter alone.

"This is your first visit to California, I presume, Mr. French," said Mr. Carlton, carelessly.

"Oh, no; I am a pioneer. Came here in '49, and have only been absent a year and a half since."

"Indeed!" answered Carlton, in surprise. "I thought this was your first visit."

"No; I passed several years in Grass Valley."

"Grass Valley!" exclaimed Carlton, "why, that used to be my stamping ground."

"Strange we never met there," and Walter gave him a searching look.

Carlton made no answer. As if to change the subject, he asked, abruptly:

"Perhaps you knew Miss Wetherell?"

Walter gave a start. It was the first time he had heard that name in a year and a half. He answered, coldly, "I had the pleasure."

Carlton had thrown back his head, and partly closed his eyes, as a great puff of smoke went wreathing over his head. He neither noted Walter's manner nor changed tone, but continued his interrogatories. "What became of her?"

"She married," answered Walter, laconically.

"Whom did she marry?" persisted Carlton.

"Major Warren, of Sacramento."

"Who?" thundered Carlton, in amazement.

"Major Warren, of Sacramento," again answered Walter, colder and harder than ever.

"She married Major Warren, of Sacramento?" repeated Carlton, as if he had not heard aright. "Where did you get that valuable information?"

"From the newspapers."

Walter moved restlessly in his chair, and puffed more vigorously at the inoffensive cigar.

"Don't you know that my wife is Major Warren's adopted daughter?" asked Carlton, with a sidelong glance at Walter, as he brushed the ashes off his cigar.

It was Walter's turn to be astonished.

"His adopted daughter! And you know his wife?"

"He has no wife."

"Then she is dead." Walter scarcely spoke above a whisper, and his head dropped upon his hand, as if in sudden pain.

"Of course she is dead. She died ten or fifteen years ago."

"But, Linda — I mean Miss Wetherell?" asked Walter, eagerly.

"He was never married to Miss Wetherell."

"Great God! can that be true?" Walter sprang to his feet and paced the floor. "Then that infamous thing that has been gnawing at my heart a year and a half was a lie. I doubted her fidelity, and went away like a coward, when I should have known she was true as a fixed star, and stayed to defend her. Carlton, she would have been my wife, but for that lying statement in the paper that told of her marriage with Major Warren."

"I do not understand how such an infamous lie could be published," answered Carlton, indignantly.

"Nor I; but I will find out," answered Walter, emphatically, and turning suddenly to Carlton, "where is she to be found?"

"I don't know. When I first returned, I went to Grass Valley to make some inquiries concerning her brother, who was in trouble when I left here on my return to New York. The answer was that he had been sent to State's prison for a term of seven years. The father was dead, and the family, consisting of mother and daughter, had moved away."

"Hold! I know how to find her. There was a widow residing in Nevada, who would know all about her. You are going home to-morrow?"

"Yes."

"Then I will accompany you, on my way to Nevada."

"All right; and if my wife would like to make a trip up into the mountains, we will go with you all the way."

"I would be glad to have your company; but it is a long and tiresome journey to undertake on an uncertainty. If you will excuse me to the ladies, I will go down street and telegraph to Nevada, and ascertain if Mrs. Neal is still residing there."

"All right; and send me word in the morning, will you?"

"Yes; as soon as the answer comes."

It was with a strange fluttering at the heart Walter went on his errand; that heart so cold and bitter seemed suddenly to have leaped into new life.   The words of the good Widow Neal, "Never doubt her, Mr. French, she has been wronged," came back with wonderful freshness.   She had been wronged, and he, the faithless coward, had decamped, and left her to bear her own burdens.

"Scoundrel that I was!" he muttered, in savage rage against himself.   "I don't deserve to find her.   Yet I feel such a strong conviction that I will, it seems already a reality.   I will find her the same faithful girl, whose great brown eyes — those soft, truthful eyes — will chide my faithlessness every time they are turned to mine.   A year and a half I have been wandering over the earth in search of happiness and pleasure.   A year and a half she has been closeted with sorrow.   I have grown restless and cynical; she patient and enduring.   I will not be worthy of her when I find her.   When I find her — if ever I do."

CHAPTER XLIV.

UNRAVELLING MYSTERIES.

"Non ignara mali miseris succurrere disco."

THE next morning Walter was pacing his room restlessly, when Nellie entered with a telegraphic despatch.   He tore it open hastily and ran his eyes over the contents, which simply read: "There is such a person living here."   Walter's face lighted up.   He grasped Nellie's hand, and, to her inquiring look, answered:

"Linda was never married to Major Warren, Nellie.   There

was something wrong about that. I got it all from Carlton. His wife is Major Warren's adopted daughter. The Major was not married at all."

Nellie regarded him with a strange, puzzled expression. "But that statement in the paper, what about that?"

"As you once answered me, with regard to that note, her mother was at the bottom of it. We will soon know all about it now, for I telegraphed to Nevada last evening, immediately after my conversation with Carlton, to ascertain if Mrs. Neal still lived there, and here is my answer. I will go to Sacramento this afternoon with Carlton and his wife, and they may accompany me on up to Nevada."

"Really, Walter, this is altogether strange. I can scarcely comprehend it at once. Poor Linda! What if we had judged her too harshly after all? To tell you the truth, Walter, although I never mentioned it before, for fear of fretting you, I have never been entirely comfortable with regard to that matter, especially the way we hurried off, without making any effort to ascertain the truth. We should have been prepared for anything, knowing the character of her mother as we did."

"You are right, Nellie; but it is rather late to be thinking of all that now. To-morrow night I will know and telegraph you at once."

"And bring her right down here, if you find her, Walter."

"If she will come, Nellie; but you forget we are the offenders, and she may not forgive us so easily."

"Never fear that. Circumstances strongly prompted our actions, and Linda has the good sense to understand it. But why did Mrs. Neal never answer the letter which I wrote her from New York?"

"You will have to ask Mrs. Neal that question," answered Walter, impatiently pacing the floor. "I will go down to the

hotel now, to give Carlton my answer.   There will scarcely be
time for me to come back again, so good-by, Nell.''

"Good-by, dear Walter.   I hope you will return a happier
man than you go away, and not alone.''

Walter found the young bride and groom in a happy state of
indifference.   It seemed perfectly immaterial to them whether
they took a trip down the bay, or over the mountains, so long
as they went together.

Everything was soon arranged, and the afternoon steamer
took them all to Sacramento.   The following morning they
drove to Mr. Carlton's home for breakfast, where the stage was
to call for them.   The roads were so muddy, it was utterly impossible to go in a private conveyance; besides, Alice had never
ridden in a stage-coach, and the whole trip was a novelty to
her, in which she entered with girlish delight.

Promptly the stage came dashing round the corner, and stopped with a suddenness almost incredible, considering its previous momentum.   "All aboard here for Nevada,'' rang out the
driver's voice in a high tenor.

The stage contained but one passenger.   On the back seat,
all muffled up in a great coat, sat Major Warren.   There were
exclamations of surprise from all excepting Walter, who did
not even know the gentleman by sight.

Carlton at once introduced him, and in his off-hand way explained the mistake he had so long been laboring under with
regard to his sweetheart.

" I think he will find her all right in Nevada,'' quietly remarked the Major; and, as if he was getting rid of a very un-
comfortable load, he related all the circumstances with regard
to the fraudulent marriage, slightly modifying his own rage
when he discovered what a dupe he had been.

"Where is the mother now?" asked Carlton.

"She is dead," answered the Major, laconically, with a nervous glance from one to the other, and for a long time there was perfect silence. A few passengers joined them for short distances, but most of the day they were alone.

Carlton was the very embodiment of sparkling fun — the life of the little party. The uncertainty of Walter's journey made him anxious and thoughtful.

The Major, although evidently relieved after unburdening himself, was so thoroughly possessed by the one subject, that he was continually reverting to it. He censured himself severely for his stubborn persistence in trying to marry a young girl, knowing she did not care for him, but he positively asserted he never suspected she loved any one else, or he would not have followed the course he did. To prove the duplicity of which he had been the victim, he read extracts from the dead woman's own story. They became so interested, that he began at the beginning and read everything excepting the last few pages, which related to Alice and Mrs. Wetherell's imprisonment by himself. Those he omitted, waiting to consult with Mrs. Neal.

It was a strange history to the bright young wife, who listened eagerly, as she sat with her husband's hand in hers, as one looks intently at a far-off storm from a place of security, never dreaming there could be any connecting link between her pure young life and the tempest-tossed creature who had written those pages, dark with crime, replete with suffering and wretchedness.

On their arrival in Nevada, the party stopped at the hotel, with the exception of Walter, who impatiently set out at once for the cottage of Mrs. Neal, where he had spent so many happy hours in the days gone by. As he ascended the steps, he heard the tones of a piano accompanying a soft, sweet voice that was strangely familiar. He stood and listened ; the song seemed a wail from a wounded heart, as the words came soft and distinct:

> You think, because you see me smile,
>   That I have never wept;
> That not a cloud of woe or guile
>   Across my life has swept;
> That mine has been a sunny way,
>   Bordered with thornless flowers;
> But, ah! my heart, though light and gay,
>   Has known its bitter hours.
>
> You think I have a happy heart,
>   Where grief has never been;
> But I have learned concealment's art,
>   And hide the tear-stains in.
> I fear the world's cold, mocking eye,
>   And shrink from piteous tones,
> And cleave to Him who reigns on high,
>   In silence and alone.

As the music ceased, the door opened, and a lady stepped out upon the porch. It was Lucy going for the physician, as Bill had suddenly grown worse. She was startled at Walter's presence, and he, in his confusion, scarcely knowing what he said, asked:

"Is Miss Wetherell at home?"

"Yes, sir; will you walk in?" answered Lucy, hurriedly, with her mind more on the doctor than the stranger.

Walter stepped hesitatingly into the dark room. Linda had finished her song, sung with a choking voice, for a dying man. It had come like an echo from her own sad heart, and when it was ended, she leaned her head upon her hands and wept bitterly. The room was quite dark, only lighted by the dim rays from the lamp in the adjoining sick chamber.

Walter stood silently wondering what to do or say. It was a strange way to enter a house, unannounced, perhaps an unwelcome guest. As he stood deliberating, Linda's suppressed sobs reached his ear and went to his heart like daggers. There was no more irresolution. With one bound he was kneeling by her side, with his arm about her, and with all the eloquent entreaty of his deep passionate nature, cried:

"Linda, my darling, do not weep so bitterly."

Linda gave a faint cry of joy.

"Walter! where did you come from? I thought I was never going to see you again."

"I assure you it is only forty-eight hours since I knew you were not another man's wife. I have lost no time in coming, my angel. But can you forgive me for deserting you in such a cowardly way?"

"There is nothing to forgive, Walter," answered Linda, in her old, frank way. "Mother told me all about it."

"Your mother told you before she died?"

"My mother is not dead."

"Yes, my dear, she is, and you have not heard. Major Warren came up with us in the stage, to-day, and told us her whole sad history."

"But, my dear Walter, it is you who are mistaken. You are talking of Mrs. Wetherell. Everything is changed since you were here, and all her unnatural conduct been explained. She was no relation of mine."

"Of course, I am confused. She told all about abducting you in the memoirs of her life, which Major Warren read us. I assure you, darling, it was a great relief to learn she was no relation to you, for a more dreadful woman never lived."

"Oh, I know it; but, Walter, I have found my own dear mother from whom she stole me. She unknowingly brought me back to her in this dear little cottage. She is our beloved Mother Neal."

21 *

"She is your mother, Linda! Is it possible?"

"Yes, Walter, and here she comes to confirm it. Come on, mother, in the dark." Linda took her hand and placed it in Walter's.

"Mother, this is Walter come back to us, just as you predicted."

"Let us hope never to part again," said Walter, earnestly, as he affectionately embraced the new mother.

Reunion and joy in one room, dissolution and sorrow in the next. There is always a thin partition between them.

Lucy returned with the doctor, and Linda was left alone with Walter.

There was a rap at the door. On opening it, Linda stood face to face with Major Warren, who was followed by Mr. Carlton. She involuntarily gave a start on seeing the Major, and went toward Walter.

"Do not run away from me, Linda; you have no more cause to fear me. I wronged you, child, innocently, but unpardonably. I should have known better than to think of winning your true young heart with gold. Forgive me, child, if you can. I am an older and a wiser man than I was when I persecuted you."

There were tears in the Major's eyes, and his voice trembled with emotion.

Older? Yes, twenty years might have passed, instead of one and a half, since Linda had seen him, he was so stooped and gray. She took the offered hand, and answered with deep feeling:

"Major Warren, I forgave you long ago; for I knew how you were wronged."

She raised her eyes for the first time to Mr. Carlton's face, and, with a cry of pleased surprise, sprang to his side.

"Bob Rivers! Where did you come from?"

Walter and the Major looked amazed.

Bob smiled at Linda as he took both her hands. "Little detective, I did not think you would recognize me."

That loudly spoken "Bob Rivers!" echoed in the next room, and Mrs. Neal came with a message from Bill. Walter introduced her to Major Warren, then regarded Carlton an instant with hesitation, when Bob promptly answered :

"Bob Rivers Carlton. I dropped the Carlton awhile, out of respect to my father. But, all things considered, I would like to drop the 'Rivers' now."

Mrs. Neal briefly explained that her son was in a dying condition. The name was familiar to him, and he had requested Mr. Carlton to come into the adjoining room. Bob followed Mrs. Neal to Bill's bedside. He did not immediately recognize the changed Bill Brown, but Bill had no time to lose, and he began his business at once.

"Bob, I am a dying man, and if the good mother will leave us alone a little while, I have something to tell you. I am afraid I am putting it off too long ; but, Bob, it is a hard thing to turn yourself into a villain the last hours of your life, and blacken your memory to all who love you."

"Yes, Bill ; but the truth blackens nothing. Make yourself just what you are, and love will be lenient."

"Bob, the good Lord brought you here. Of all men, none could do for me in my dying hours what you can. That good woman has led me so tenderly and confidently to the verge of my next life, I do not dread the final going. I have grown so light in mind and body, when I unload the one weight on my mind, I believe a breath would waft me over. Do not think I was going without telling her ; but I was waiting. If I had waited a little too long."

Bill laid still, with his eyes closed, a few seconds, and Bob thought he would not have long to wait, his going would be soon.   Bill opened his eyes, and continued, with difficulty :

"Bob, you remember young Wetherell, who was in jail with us, and sentenced to seven years in San Quentin for robbing a teamster?"

"Yes."

"I was the man who robbed that teamster, Bob."

"You!" exclaimed Bob, in a hoarse whisper.

"Yes, I did it," answered Bill, softly, with a pleading look at Bob.   Then, with a faint glimmer of the old fire, he added: "But the fellow lied.   I was out hunting, and he stopped me with a pistol, not seeing my gun, which I had set against a tree. It was more to punish the fellow than anything else, that I turned and made the same demand of him.   He was a coward, so he gave up his watch and five hundred dollars.   I cannot tell you how I felt the night young Wetherell's sister liberated me from jail — I, the guilty one, went out through her agency, while her innocent brother was left to his doom.   I went to his trial, and came very near confessing my crime, but I did n't. I was too weak in my selfishness."

Bill rested a few seconds again, then continued :

"I am Wetherell's half-brother, and we look wonderfully alike.   Mrs. Neal is his mother.   His wife and sister wait upon me like ministering angels, and I want to die that way — to pass off without their curses following me.   Can you fix it?"

"Yes," answered Bob, with choking voice.   "What has become of the teamster?"

"He was working ten miles from here a few weeks ago.   I never lost track of him.   There is pen and paper.   Would n't it be well to take my statement, Bob, and get a notary to fix it up? I have nothing to will anybody ; but that would bring them happiness — that is something. But, Bob, say nothing until I am laid away. Let them go with me to my resting-place with love and peace. Promise me, Bob."

Bob promised solemnly, then wrote the statement as Bill dictated; folded and placed it under his pillow. He hurriedly brought a notary, and the statement of Bill Neal was solemnly sworn to and sealed.

"Bill, if you will tell me where to find the teamster, I will go after him," said Bob, kindly, to the tired Bill, who seemed to think there was nothing more for him to do. "It might be best. Your statement might be doubted, as you are under the care of Wetherell's family, and beyond the reach of the law."

"That is so," answered the dying man, thoughtfully. Tired and exhausted by his previous efforts, he slowly explained where the teamster could be found.

Bob left him with Mrs. Neal and hastened to the hotel to explain his prolonged absence to Alice, while a horse was being brought for him to start in search of the teamster.

Ten miles in the mountains in December, with only the faint light of the stars to guide one, is not an easy task, even to one who has a thorough knowledge of the country. Bob neither heeded the loneliness nor the distance, but, intent upon his mission, hurried along, wondering what strange fatality had brought him at the eleventh hour to Bill Brown's death-bed to save Ben Wetherell.

His thoughts went back to the days of '49, when he crossed the plains in company with the West family, and Fannie, whom he had loved with all the fire of youth — sweet, gentle Fannie. Then her disappearance and his suspicions of Curly Smith. His thirst for vengeance. His reckless, desperate life with that villain and his pals, hoping to trace the crime and avenge the wrong. His meeting with Linda, and his oath to

her to let the dead past bury its dead. Soon after fate brought him to the man and woman in whose house Fannie had died; and, after all, the suspected villain was innocent.

"Why was I brought here? The answer is plain," he said to himself. " 'Cast thy bread upon the waters; for thou shalt find it after many days.' Linda saved me; for the reckless life I was leading was becoming fascinating. She put out her hand to me when I was sinking in the slough of moral degradation. Now I am to lift her brother from that slough. For the first time I fully realize there is a God. I understand the meaning of justice. Religion, so called, confuses and misleads more souls than it saves. It commands us to pray after prescribed rules, chant according to fashion, and believe as the minister dictates. His doctrines are according to the amount of brains with which he is gifted and the opportunities he has had in life, and they are in accordance with the amount the blessed pious can afford to pay. If we could renounce sects and factions, and all worship the one God in simplicity and faith; but that cannot be done, for the thousands who would be reduced to want would be fearful to contemplate. There are no fatter birds in the land to be plucked than these same fanatical sects, and no adroiter hands to pluck them than the pusillanimous, sycophantic proclaimers of religion, each with his new patent way to heaven at reduced rates. Plague take my cynical misanthropy! I will not constitute myself judge of others; for to-night, in this wilderness, under the cold stars, something has spoken to my heart. I bow reverently henceforth to the Almighty Power that governs me; in this age of progress I have gone back to the time when God walked with men. It is His hand that has led me."

Bob Rivers — Mr. Carlton — banker. It is the first time you have ridden alone at midnight in search of one who can bring freedom and happiness to those you love.   It is the first time the spirit of death has hovered over you; so near, it may have fled and left your efforts unrewarded.   You are doing a noble deed of humanity.   It fills your heart and soul with light and peace that transforms life.   Nothing is changed, only your eyes are looking inward instead of outward.   We can all find new worlds in ourselves, if we only explore for them.

CHAPTER XLV.

THE HARVESTER, DEATH.

> " The gay will laugh
> When thou art gone ; the solemn brood of care
> Plod on, and each one, as before, will chase
> His favorite phantom."— *William Cullen Bryant.*

SLOWLY the night was passing away, and with it the life of the young desperado in Widow Neal's cottage.   So quietly and peacefully was his soul going out, it did not seem possible it could belong to such a stormy life.   The widow, who had tenderly led him to this peaceful end, sat by his side wiping away the death-dews that gathered upon his brow, softly speaking of peace and rest — eternal, perfect.

In the adjoining room Walter and Linda talked softly of the past, the future, and the present, over which the spirit of death was hovering.

Apart sat Major Warren, where he could watch the sick man's bed.   His thoughts were of the mother who had cast her children upon the uncertain sea of fate, to perish or to live, as it might chance, and he said to himself, " It is well she is gone.

She would have no place here." Suddenly he sprang up, approached the dying man's bed, and whispered:

"Young man, when you were a little boy, you had a baby sister. You know how you were parted. Would it be any pleasure for you to see her once again?"

Bill turned his large dark eyes upon the Major's face with a yearning, longing appeal:

"Oh, yes. I have never known a human being who was any kin to me. Let me hold her hand in mine just once."

Day was breaking when Bob returned with the teamster. Again the door was closed, and the widow excluded. The teamster stood staring at the dying man.

"Do you recognize me?" asked Bill.

"I can't say I do, and yit you look like that there young man."

"I am that young man," said Bill, emphatically. "It was my half-brother you mistook for me, and sent to State's prison."

"So this here gentleman told me; but it don't seem I could make sich a mistake."

"Did it not seem a little strange to you that the young man made no charges against you?" asked Bill, with great effort.

"Charges agin me?" The man seemed greatly surprised.

"Yes; charges against you. That he did not tell how you pointed your pistol at him first, and demanded his 'coin.' How he answered, taking his gun and turning the tables, by making the same demand of you, to punish your rascality."

"By gal, young man, you speak the truth. That young man never said a word agin me; and it has worried me more than anything in my life ever done before."

"It was because he was innocent. He did not know what you had done."

"Well, young man, will you just tell me where we were when it happened?"

Slowly, with many resting spells, Bill recounted the whole scene. The teamster knelt by the bedside, took one of Bill's thin, wasted hands in his, and, with tears coursing down his sunburnt cheeks, sobbed aloud:

"Young man, it was the first time I ever done sich a thing, and the last, and you served me right. I will do anything in the world for you now. This here gentleman wants me to go to the Governor to git the innocent young man out o'jail, and I'll go; you can count on me."

Bill's mission in life was ended. He turned his head away and closed his eyes.

The teamster quietly left the sick chamber, as Major Warren entered, leading Alice by the hand, trembling and bewildered, called from sleep to her long-lost brother's deathbed. They were all surprised at her appearance, but no one uttered a word. The Major led her gently to the bed and placed her hand in Bill's, as he said, softly:

"It is the hand of your sister Alice, dear boy — parted from you in life, united in death."

Bill opened his great eyes, that had become dim and distant. A new fire burned in them. He slowly raised the hand to his lips and kissed it, murmuring, "Alice, my sister."

Alice stooped and kissed the damp forehead, as she whispered, "Is it possible, after all, we meet too late?"

"Yes, too late; but better so. Kiss me once again, sweet sister."

Alice leaned over the dying man and kissed him again.

The Widow Neal came softly to the bedside. He gave her a long look of love. A smile played upon his wasted, manly face, and the soul of Bill Brown, the outlaw, the discarded son, took its flight heavenward.

At Alice's request, the remains were sent to Sacramento, and

22

Major Warren had them interred by the side of his mother, from whom he had been parted in life, and perhaps in death. Yet they were mother and son.

After the sad event of Bill's death, Walter, whose claim upon Linda was no longer disputed, insisted upon taking her and her mother home with him at once. Then there were Lucy and the baby. Bob claimed them as his guests in the most peremptory manner.

The cottage was left in the hands of an agent for sale, and those whose lives had been parted in so many devious ways, to be reunited there, left it with a feeling of sadness, never to return to it any more as their home.

At Sacramento they lingered one day to bury their dead, which gave Bob and the teamster, who had accompanied them, much to the surprise of the rest of the party, time to fulfil the last request of the departed dead. The Governor's pardon was, without difficulty, obtained for Ben Wetherell. Bob bade the teamster good-by, and he religiously promised to keep the secret of the dying confession in his own heart.

The following day, as our friends were approaching the boat, on their way to San Francisco, their attention was attracted to a group of men standing near the gang-plank. In their midst, and evidently the object of their curiosity, stood a human skeleton. He was gesticulating wildly, trying to make his feeble voice heard amid the din.

"I tell you, I must go. I'm an escaped convict, and want to give myself up to the authorities."

"Get away, you crazy old loon. Hain't I told you a dozen times folks can't float on this 'ere boat without the tin to pay?" growled a burly porter, pushing Jack Hunter aside.

Poor Jack, too feeble to resist the slightest blow, fell prostrate across the plank, just as our friends were about going on board the boat.

Linda saw the emaciated face, and recognized it at once.

"Oh, mother, it is Jack Hunter. Walter, help him up, do."

Mrs. Neal bent over the prostrate form, took the bony hand in hers to assist him. He turned his wild eyes upon her, and gave one despairing cry, "Agnes!"

"Yes, Jack, it is I," answered the widow, kindly.

"Go on board; I will attend to him," said Walter.

Mrs. Neal started to obey, but the bony hand clutched hers, and, with a heart-rending wail, Jack begged, "For heaven's sake, do not leave me."

"Mrs. Neal will not leave you," answered Walter, kindly, raising him to his feet. "You wanted to go down the river, did you not?"

"Yes, sir; but I had no money, and they would not let me go."

"You shall go, and comfortably, too. Porter, assist this man to my state-room."

Jack turned his great eyes thankfully upon Walter, and asked, in a frightened way:

"Can she stay with me?" pointing toward Mrs. Neal.

"Yes, I will stay with you, Jack," answered the widow.

Again Mrs. Neal sat by the bedside of a departing spirit. The sands of Jack Hunter's life were fast running out. That last great effort to give himself up to justice, and return to prison, was too much for the dying man. The reaction, and the blow that had felled him, shattered the life that was held by a very slender tenure.

Walter and Linda watched with Mrs. Neal, but, before the boat reached San Francisco that night, the mortal Jack Hunter lay still and lifeless, and the spiritual Jack had gone to that rest and peace which he "could never find on earth any more."

CHAPTER XLVI.

FINALE.

" La patience est amère, mais son fruit est doux."
                                               Rousseau.

ALICE was inclined to be melancholy over the events of her brother's death, and the revelations of her own strange history, which Major Warren felt she and Bob had better know. So Bob insisted upon her attending the marriage of Walter and Linda, which was to take place the evening after their arrival in San Francisco.

Major Warren also accepted the invitation to accompany the party, and participate in the marriage festivities, which were to be entirely *en famille*, with George and Nellie. Notwithstanding the shadows of death that had hovered over them, they had been messengers of rest to the weary and afflicted, that could not leave deep traces of sorrow.

Poor Lucy, with her bright little girl, quietly followed the others, evidently with little interest in what was transpiring. The following morning, when all were busy over Linda's approaching marriage, she stood aside in a bow window, watching the passers-by, with an occasional unruly tear stealing its way down her cheek in spite of her efforts at self-control.

Linda approached her silently, put her arm about her, and said, in her sweet way:

"Cheer up, Lucy, on my wedding day. I know that happiness and mirth sink heavily into your sad heart, but Ben is with us in spirit, and to-morrow you shall see him. It is doubly sad to have him so near, and yet so entirely separated from us; but patience, dear sister, and no tears on my wedding day, remember."

"I have brought my wife to you early this morning," said Bob, entering in the most unceremonious way, leading Alice by the hand, "because the Major, Mr. French, and myself have to attend to the burial of that poor fellow down town, and I did not want to leave her alone." He turned to Lucy, and took her hand with a bright smile. "Cheer up, little woman; there are no clouds in the heavens: it is a perfect day." Then hurriedly joining the gentlemen who were waiting for him, they faithfully attended to the burial of Jack Hunter. Bob had confided to them the pardon of the unfortunate Ben Wetherell, who was suffering for the sins of his brother, and they took the first boat to San Quentin to free the captive and make that night one of festivity and happiness to all. They found him performing the last sad duties toward the heartbroken Walker. It seemed a harvest-time of wretched mortals weary of life.

The good tidings quite overcame Ben. He wept like a child. Soon mastering himself, he rose to his feet, straight, commanding as ever, and, with the same manly bearing, but an expression of sadness sorrow had stamped upon his handsome face, that made it handsomer than ever, he exclaimed:

"At last they know I am innocent!"

"No," answered Walter; "they know nothing. This is to be my wedding night, and we have kept the secret to fill them all with joy — to fill every heart with happiness."

"Can it be my wedding night, too?" asked Ben, dreamily.

Walter and Bob exchanged glances. Could there be anything wrong with him? Had the joyful tidings been too sudden?

"Your wedding night?" repeated Walter. "Why, man,

22 *   R

you were married long ago. Your wife and child await you now at my sister's house.''

"Yes,'' answered Ben, looking him straight in the face, "I was married long ago under the name of Wetherell. It is not legal. I want to begin life over again under my real name. I have suffered enough. The sins of my father have been visited heavily upon me. With these felon's clothes, I cast off the old life and name that gave it place. To-night let me be married to my wife, and give her legally the name which is justly ours.''

Walter took his hand and pressed it fervently. "It shall be as you wish.''

It was a festival of perfect happiness; all the more as the fruit of long-suffering. Mrs. Neal stood by her children as they were united to those they loved — the Widow Neal's children. The name of Wetherell was dead; the life of the Wetherells was dead, and the memory of it only known to that small circle of friends, who had all suffered from it in some way. It was a sad heritage, sacredly buried from the world. To see the happy Grandmother Neal of to-day, no one could dream of the tempest that had tossed her upon such a peaceful shore.

THE END.